THE TOMB OF THE HONEY BEE

A POSIE PARKER MYSTERY #2

L. B. HATHAWAY

WHITEHAVEN

WHITEHAVEN MAN PRESS

London

First published in Great Britain in 2014 by
Whitehaven Man Press, London

(http://www.lbhathaway.com, email: permissions@lbhathaway.com)

A CIP catalogue record for this book is available
from the British Library.

ISBN (e-book:) 978-0-9929254-3-7
ISBN (paperback:) 978-0-9929254-4-4

Jacket illustration by Red Gate Arts.
Formatting and design by J.D. Smith.

By rights, this book should be dedicated to the explorer, Alaric Boynton-Dale.

But in real life, it is for Eden (a true honey).

By L.B. Hathaway

The Posie Parker Mystery Series

1. *Murder Offstage: A Posie Parker Mystery*

2. *The Tomb of the Honey Bee: A Posie Parker Mystery*

3. *Murder at Maypole Manor: A Posie Parker Mystery*

4. *The Vanishing of Dr Winter: A Posie Parker Mystery*

PART ONE
London and Oxfordshire
(June, 1921)

One

The whole country was just a teeny-tiny bit in love with Alaric Boynton-Dale, the famous explorer.

Not a week went by without news of his latest daring exploits being splashed across the front pages of the London papers. His enigmatic character, rugged good looks and his refusal to give away any details about his private life kept the public hooked.

And interest in his notoriously eccentric family ran high too.

If pressed, Posie Parker, Private Detective and owner of the Grape Street Bureau in London would have admitted to knowing just as much gossip about the Boynton-Dale family as the next person, but no more than that. She certainly could not lay claim to actually having *met* any of them. It was therefore with a start of surprise that she greeted her secretary Prudence Smythe's announcement that the society beauty Lady Violet Boynton-Dale had arrived, totally unexpectedly, at the Grape Street office early one hot Tuesday morning in June.

'But *why* is she here?' Posie hissed under her breath, annoyed, refusing to be star-struck. She stared in exasperation at the mountain of paperwork in front of her. 'Why can't she make an appointment like anybody else?'

Prudence just had time to shrug helplessly before being bowled out of the way by Lady Violet herself, who breezed assuredly into Posie's neat office and brought with her the sharp tart smells of the London heatwave outside; soot and hot melting asphalt and the sweaty London Tube, all shot through with a hasty squirt of Penhaligon's rose cologne.

'I need you to work for me. But I can't pay you,' Lady Violet stated bluntly. 'I'm desperate. It's about a possible murder.'

She settled herself down in the visitors chair uninvited, removing her hat and crossing one long leg over the other.

'Oh?' Posie said, rather inadequately, sitting back down in her own desk chair and shifting her pile of papers out of the way. She tucked a curl of her dark brown bobbed hair behind her ear, as if the familiar gesture could bring a bit of normality to proceedings.

'Well, what makes you think I will work for you for free? How do you know about me anyway?'

'I know the Cardigeon family, of course,' the girl said simply, as if this explained everything. 'The Earl is my Godfather. He said you worked for him for a whole week risking life and limb and he didn't give you a red cent for your troubles! He said you were the gal I should come to.'

Inwardly Posie cursed. It was true: she *had* worked for the Earl of Cardigeon for a week straight that February, for free, solving a mystery involving an international ring of criminals and finding a priceless jewel which had been stolen from the Cardigeon family. What she *hadn't* counted on was the Earl going around the place advertising her services for free to all and sundry. Besides, much later on he had stumped up a hefty reward which had made Posie an independent woman in her own right, which would see her comfortably through the rest of her days, although it was fair to say that neither she nor the Earl had expected that that would be the case at the time of the mystery.

'Also, I've read about you in the papers. You're rather famous, in fact.'

There was a daredevil, easy grace about Lady Violet, and Posie saw immediately that she was not the famous Alaric's sister for nothing, although she looked nothing like him. Violet was a girl possessed of film star good looks, and her perfectly coiffed raven-dark features were familiar to every woman in the land – Violet was a favourite cover-star of the penny magazines – but Posie noted with surprise that today the girl looked unkempt, and her daring white linen trouser suit had definitely seen better days.

'What I mean is, I can't pay you in *money*. I don't have any. I even had to borrow the train fare to town from Jenks, our Butler. But I *can* start by giving you this.'

Lady Violet was rustling around inside a brown paper bag. From its depths she took out two jars of what Posie saw was a light, creamy-looking honey. Lady Violet pushed them across the desk.

'It's very good. It's from Alaric's bees. It costs ten shillings and sixpence a jar if you buy it at Fortnum's or Harrods. I'm down to the last two pots from last year's reserves. Take it, please. I saved a third pot to make my famous Oxfordshire honey cake. You can try some later if you like. *If* you're willing to help me…'

'Help you with what exactly?'

Posie was turning a jar of the honey politely in her hands, trying to keep the note of rising interest out of her voice. She liked a challenge, especially if it came from unexpected quarters, and her annoyance at the unconventional manner of Lady Violet was slowly ebbing away. Besides, she had never been paid in honey before. And this was honey which cost the same as a slap-up dinner for two and then a stay over in a top-class hotel afterwards.

'It's my brother, Alaric. He's disappeared. He's been missing since Saturday, for four days now. I fear something dreadful has happened to him.'

'Really?' Posie fought down the urge to laugh out loud. 'But he's an explorer! I thought he went away often on sudden expeditions? That's what he does! Maybe he's just headed off on another adventure. Why would something bad have happened to him? And have you reported this to the police?'

'Of course I've bally well been to the police!' Lady Violet cried out bitterly. 'Yesterday in fact, and a fat lot of good it did me too. I went to Scotland Yard and the fish-faced Inspector there basically laughed in my face. He thought the same as you; that Alaric had just taken off on another expedition. He said he couldn't do anything yet for lack of evidence.'

Posie nodded in sympathy. She imagined that the Inspector concerned had probably been the pedantic and insufferable Inspector Oats, whom she had had the misfortune of running into on more than one occasion, the experience of which was akin to hitting one's head against a brick wall.

Mr Minks, the office Siamese cat, was quietly taking forty winks in the direct path of the sunlight. Just then, he stretched himself out luxuriously, without a care in the world. Lady Violet reached down and stroked his cream-and-brown head, and was rewarded with a sharp hissing and a violent flash of claws which met in the fleshy part of her hand, drawing blood.

Posie sighed to herself: Mr Minks was only sociable on his own terms, and then usually only towards men. If *only* her clients would realise this and not persist in treating him like some cute teddy bear, several disasters could easily have been avoided.

'Oh dear, oh dear,' Posie mumbled apologetically. 'Shall I get you a bandage?'

But Lady Violet appeared not to have heard, or even to be bothered about the cut. She rubbed her bloodied hand on the side of her worn trousers.

'Please help me. Bad things have been happening lately

at our home, Boynton Hall. Very bad things. And now this disappearance. I fear Alaric may have been murdered. I'm frantic with worry! I suppose you know all about my family? Or do I need to tell you who we all are?'

Quick as a flash, Posie began to go over everything she knew about the Boynton-Dale family in her mind.

Both parents were dead, she was sure of it. In fact, hadn't there been some tragic accident many years ago in which they had died together? She remembered that they had left three children, all now grown up.

Alaric was the eldest of the children, and he *should* have been Lord Boynton. He had made a name for himself in the Royal Flying Corps in the Great War as a flying ace, but he was almost as famous for being an award-winning bee-keeper, and some said he made the finest honey in the British Isles. Posie remembered how, years before, at the age of twenty-one, Alaric had decided he would become a politician, and had caused a huge scandal by giving up his aristocratic title in order to do so. But Alaric was known for his itchy feet, and typically, he had only lasted as a politician for a couple of years before deciding to become a full-time explorer instead. He loved what he did, and he often spoke to packed-out audiences about his adventures. But the decision at twenty-one had had lasting repercussions, for when Alaric gave up his aristocratic title he was also obliged to give up Boynton Hall, and what was left of the family fortune. With fatal consequences.

These assets had passed instead to the second child, Roderick, who had become famous for squandering the fortune and running the house into the ground. A general bad egg, photos of Lord Roderick, half-cut, were often to be found gracing the celebrity pages of the British newspapers, stumbling out of shady London nightclubs in the foggy dawn hours. He was rumoured to live wildly beyond his means at Boynton Hall, his only source of ready cash being the deep pockets of his American father-in-law, who had made a killing selling ploughshares somewhere east of Texas.

Posie scrambled to remember gossip about a long-standing feud between the two brothers. Wasn't Alaric, when at home, obliged to live in a modest brick annexe at the back of the vegetable gardens, like a common gardener? And wasn't the only attraction for Alaric at Boynton Hall, apart from his precious honey bees, his treasured younger sister, Violet?

Her thoughts now turned to the third Boynton-Dale child, Lady Violet, the girl sitting before her. Not yet twenty-five, this was a girl who moved through life with the haunted manner of one who has been promised much, only to have had it taken away suddenly. And to a certain extent this was true: raised as an aristocrat, but with no fortune to call her own, it seemed that no suitable marriage could be arranged for Violet, and her future looked precarious. She scratched a living for herself by appearing in the press now and again, but Roderick was too tight, or too mean, or perhaps simply too broke to settle a fortune on her.

'Yes,' Posie said briskly. 'I know all about your family. So *why* would Alaric have been murdered?' She drew a notebook of lined paper automatically towards her and uncapped her pen.

Lady Violet spread her hands helplessly. 'I know it sounds ridiculous. Of course Al goes off on trips – Africa, India, sandy deserts, frozen snowy poles – you name it, he's done it. But he's never before just upped and left without a trace; he's not irresponsible. We're very close. He's *always* told me exactly where he was going before.'

'But not this time?'

Lady Violet shook her head and passed across a cream oblong of card. 'On Saturday morning he was gone. Then this telegram came in the afternoon for me. It's entirely out of character.'

Posie took the telegram and read:

HAD ENOUGH OF ALL OF THIS.
AL.

Posie looked sharply up at her visitor. She needed to make a difficult suggestion, and she didn't relish the reply.

'Forgive me, but you don't think it's possible, that perhaps – well, there's no easy way of saying this – we've got to consider the possibility that your brother has… perhaps…'

'Killed himself you mean?' snapped Lady Violet. 'That this is a suicide note?'

'The tone of the telegram, *if* it's genuine…'

'Rot! Utter rot!' the girl cried. 'Never in a million years. That wasn't his way. If it were my other brother, that worm Roderick, I would quite accept your suggestion, but Alaric? No. Not on your life! It doesn't add up.'

Posie turned the telegram over, frowning. It had been sent from the Post Office at Victoria Station, the departures side, where trains left for Dover and the continent. She drew this to the girl's attention.

Lady Violet nodded impatiently. 'Yes, I know. But I've already been to Victoria Station and asked the people in the Post Office there if they remember sending this telegram for Alaric. I got nowhere.'

'Never mind, let's leave it for now,' said Posie firmly. 'Do you have any other leads?'

Lady Violet shook her head.

Posie wrinkled her nose up in concentration, staring at the telegram again. 'Something bothers me about this telegram. If he was going abroad why would Alaric be using a train anyway? I thought he flew everywhere in his plane?'

'You're right,' said Lady Violet, nodding grimly. 'I was about to tell you. Alaric kept his Fokker in a private hanger at Croydon Aerodrome, and it would have made sense to use it if he was thinking of going anywhere abroad. But he can't fly anywhere now! The Fokker doesn't exist anymore! One month ago the plane was sabotaged and he was lucky enough to parachute to safety while flying somewhere over Kent. It was attempted murder. The sabotage was deliberate. A deliberate attempt on his life.'

Posie looked up from her notebook, shocked. 'Did he actually tell you that? It could have been an unlucky accident, perhaps?'

'No. My brother was a flying ace, he didn't have accidents. He didn't speak about the incident, but I could tell he was shaken up all right. A week or so later I came across some investigative reports about the crash which he had had commissioned. I didn't understand all the technical jargon, but the main thrust was that there had been deliberate cutting of fuel pipes to the engine and deliberate disabling of most of the plane's controls before he took off. This was the first of the bad things which have been happening lately.'

'Goodness! How dreadful. What happened next?'

'It got worse. Worse for Alaric, that is. You know he keeps honey bees? He has about one thousand and fifty hives at Boynton Hall. Two weeks ago he noticed that there were less bees than usual flying around the larkspur fields where he kept a quarter of his hives. When he investigated further he found that the bees in those fields were all dead, every last one of them, lying curled up and blackened on the ground. He was upset, but he was pragmatic too. He thought at first that perhaps they had died of some mysterious bee disease. He said that these things can just happen.'

Posie sat, pen poised mid-air, not liking the way the story was going.

'But when he dismantled those beehives he said he noticed a strange smell, and there were scorch marks on the ground where the hives had been. He asked the neighbouring farmer if he had been using some special fertiliser, or burning something toxic which could have filtered over the hedges, but he drew a blank. Then it all became horribly clear. Those hives had been used as a test run for a much larger, much more brutal piece of sabotage.'

Lady Violet stared straight ahead grimly as she told how exactly one week ago, in the early hours of the morning, Alaric had woken to the smell of burning fumes and had run frantically out of his annexe into the nearby wildflower meadows where he kept most of his beehives. The fields were a burning, seething mass of hives on fire, each hive having been injected with a deadly mix of petrol and cyanide and then expertly sealed up, trapping the colonies of bees inside. The fields had gone up like a dry powder-keg in the heatwave.

Lady Violet described how Alaric had run around like an idiot, ineffectually, dragging buckets of water from the swimming pool to stem the fires in the fields, but he had not managed to save even one beehive before the noxious and highly poisonous fumes had knocked him out and rendered him unconscious. He had woken up two days later in hospital, lucky to be alive but utterly bereft.

'So he then spent a glum couple of days at Boynton Hall trying to clear up the fields, and I did what I could to help him. But it was pitiful. Alaric refused to talk to any of the others in the house. He was simmering with hatred. He didn't come in to eat with us once in the Great Hall.'

'No question then? This was deliberate sabotage too? Was there a police report?'

'Oh yes!' Lady Violet laughed scornfully. 'But the police in the countryside are not much better than your lot here in town, it seems. Basically they decided it was carelessness, or an accident, or both.'

'So they don't suspect anyone for the crime?'

Lady Violet shook her head, but Posie noticed a keen light burning in Violet's beautiful grey eyes.

'But *you* suspect someone, don't you, Lady Violet? Who do you think committed these crimes against your brother?'

'Take your pick. There are several unsavoury characters I can tell you about, all staying at Boynton Hall at present. I wouldn't put these crimes past any of them. They certainly all have a motive for bumping Alaric off. As to *which* of them did these things, that's what you need to find out.'

Posie turned a new page and started a spider-diagram. Although, on closer inspection, she was surprised to see she had drawn a honey bee at the centre of the net.

Lady Violet started to tick suspects off on her long, beautiful fingers:

'First, my other brother, Lord Roderick – a first-class ape if ever you met one – always in the shadow of Alaric, always the black sheep of the family. About a month ago Alaric announced he was going to change his Will in favour of me, so that I would be able to support myself when he died. Roderick was to be entirely written out.'

'Does Alaric own much? Enough to kill for?'

'Not really. Not in his own right. But there *is* an old Family Trust which pays an income out to Alaric. He wasn't allowed to give it up when he gave up all his other rights when he was twenty-one. But the important point is this: the person Alaric names as the main beneficiary of his Will gets the final Trust money. Therefore, if Alaric decides that Roderick is cut out of his Will, Roderick can't get the money from the Trust either. It's worth a great deal, almost Two Hundred Thousand Pounds, I believe.'

Posie gasped and scribbled this down. 'Good grief! What a lot of money! Certainly enough to make a difference to Roderick, anyhow. I have heard he lives… how shall I say, extravagantly?'

Lady Violet nodded. 'That's true enough. Perhaps Roderick thought he would try and kill Alaric before he had a chance to change the Will?'

'And *has* Alaric actually got around to changing his Will in your favour yet, do you know?'

'I don't know. I called his solicitors, but they won't speak to me. They say it's "confidential".'

'I might be able to help you there,' Posie said, noting down the name and address of the firm of lawyers concerned, an ancient firm just ten minutes' walk away, near the Grey's Inn Road. 'I can try and obtain that information. Any other suspects?'

The girl nodded quickly and continued:

'Lady Boynton, Roderick's American wife. Plain old Eve Burns, as she *was*, before her marriage. A dreadful creature: has all the looks and personality of a cuttlefish.'

'And her motive?'

Lady Violet smiled ruefully.

'To help Roderick, I guess. She'd do anything for Roderick, she adores him. And she hates Alaric, she's jealous of his fame. Why, do you know, I've even seen her cutting up newspaper articles about Alaric before? She was scoring through his face with a razor blade when I entered the Library one day and crept up behind her! She pretended it was a coincidence and that she was just sharpening the blade on whatever was to hand, but I wasn't fooled for a minute! She was cutting his face to shards! Also, it would be very much in her interest if this Trust money comes their way, and quickly, too. It's no secret that Roderick only married Eve for her money…and there's going to be no more of that!'

'Oh? Why?'

'Papa Burns is over from Texas right now. He said he wanted to pay a visit for the "English summer", but what he really wanted to do was check on how Roderick has been spending Eve's money. He's none too pleased – I heard him shouting with Eve in the Library last week – he was telling her he'd be shelling out no more cash for their "indolent lifestyle" and that he didn't want his money to go on maintaining an old dump like Boynton Hall!'

Posie noted this down, nibbling the top of her pen.

'Anyone else you suspect?'

'Yes. The third person is Codlington, my brother Roderick's Valet. He's a nasty piece of work. Four weeks ago Alaric told me he had found out something suspicious about Codlington, but he didn't elaborate on it. I *think* Codlington was stealing things from Roderick, but I'm not entirely sure. Alaric hinted that he wanted to fetch the police and make sure Codlington left Boynton Hall without a good character reference. That would have spelled the end for a man like Codlington. He'd never get a job as good as this one again.'

'So what happened?'

'I don't know. I'm not sure how it was resolved. Maybe you can find out?'

Lady Violet continued: 'The fourth person is a guest at the house. In fact, she's our second cousin. Dame Ianthe Flowers. Do you know of her?'

Posie nodded. Ianthe Flowers was a prolific and popular women's fiction writer. She usually wrote crime mysteries set in impossibly dreamy settings. She was known to have made a great deal of money from her novels.

'Ianthe has been staying with us for the last few months. She writes most days, keeps herself to herself up in her room. She said she wanted some inspiration for a new book, a murder mystery set in a vast country house. She was going to use Boynton Hall as the inspiration for the book.'

Posie frowned. She had seen newspaper photos of Dame Ianthe, a cheerful-looking blonde woman in her mid-forties who looked as if she wouldn't hurt a fly, let alone plan a series of horrible destructive events against her own cousin.

'I know what you're thinking!' trilled Lady Violet excitedly. 'Ianthe is the *last* person to do this! Butter wouldn't melt and all that! But you're wrong! For weeks she'd been trailing around after Alaric like a little lost dog, mooning around the place. She even professed a passion for bees. Imagine! How embarrassing! She's madly, crazily in love with him. And then Alaric dashed all her hopes: he told her he was still in love with someone else, a previous lover whom he couldn't forget in a hurry. Ianthe went to pieces. She shut herself off in her room for days. That was about a month ago now. But you know what they say…'

'"Hell hath no fury like a woman scorned?" Is that what you mean?'

'Exactly.'

Posie pursed her lips, unconvinced. 'And the final suspect? Is this by any chance the "lover he couldn't forget in a hurry"?'

Posie noted with interest that Violet almost squirmed beneath her gaze, and flushed a dark unbecoming beetroot colour.

'No. Not exactly. It's the *husband* of the lover Alaric couldn't forget. Not a pretty situation, I'm afraid.'

'Ah! I see! A case of the husband's classic revenge? The "husband scorned". Who is it?'

'I know you'll be discreet, of course you will. But maybe don't write this down? The lover was Lady Cosima Catchpole. Her husband is Hugo Marchpane.'

Posie caught her breath, trying not to look surprised or impressed. 'You mean the war hero, Major Hugo Marchpane?'

Hugo Marchpane was very famous, perhaps even more so than Alaric Boynton-Dale. A flying ace, he had been badly injured in the Great War, but had since gone on to become a senior government advisor. There was even talk of him being knighted in his own right.

'The very same,' Lady Violet nodded. 'In fact, he was Alaric's best friend. They flew together in the war. Cosima and Hugo live across the meadows from us on the estate. Cosima broke poor Al's heart last summer. He was crazy for her, but last year she decided it would be best to end their affair and save her marriage with Hugo. The trouble is, Hugo has only just found out, and he's gone ballistic. There have been loads of ugly scenes, broken windows and such like. Hugo can't believe it's all over. He thinks Alaric and Cosima are still pulling the wool over his eyes, even now.'

'Golly! How on earth did Major Marchpane find out about the affair, after all that time?'

'He was tipped off. Got an anonymous telegram. I'm guessing Ianthe sent it. Major Marchpane asked Cosima straight up if it were true and she answered him honestly and admitted the whole affair. He went stark raving mad.'

'*When* did he find out exactly?'

'Just over a month ago, perhaps?'

Posie chewed her pen top. The timing for each suspect worked. In each case, just over a month ago, some event had triggered a reaction which had necessitated action or actions against Alaric Boynton-Dale. Bad, dangerous actions. But *how* dangerous, exactly? And had someone managed to murder Alaric for real, or had he managed to escape the danger and flee? And if so, where was he now?

'So now what?' Posie said, closing her notebook. 'What do you want me to do about it all? It sounds like a mare's nest.'

'I need you to find out what's happened to Alaric. I need to know the truth,' Lady Violet said simply. 'I think you should come back with me to Boynton Hall in the Cotswolds. You can investigate further there. Say you'll do it, please? I want somebody discreet to look into this.'

'But surely this is a police matter, given the severity of what you are saying. Surely you can see that?'

'I told you, the police are only interested when there's a body lying dead in the gutter. Can't you come with me now?'

Posie laughed and shook her head. She had an enormous stack of clients on her books since the case of the Maharajah diamond earlier in the spring, and even now she could hear the rustle and polite scraping of chairs from the waiting room. She had a full day ahead, with appointments booked back-to-back throughout the afternoon.

'Frightfully sorry, but I can't come today, Lady Violet. But I *can* come tomorrow. As luck would have it I have booked the next two weeks off for a holiday. So I am happy to be at your disposal.'

She winked at Lady Violet. 'And yes, I will work for you for free. It just so happens that my holiday plans have been…er, cancelled. But please, don't mention that this is a freebie to anyone, I do have a business to run. Shall I come to Boynton Hall in disguise? As an old school friend of yours, perhaps? Where did you go to school, just so I know? Roedean? Wycombe Abbey?'

'The latter,' Lady Violet said. 'But don't worry about a disguise. Come as yourself, as my guest. That will put the wind up the blighters! That's what I want!'

Posie shrugged. 'If that is your instruction, so be it.'

Lady Violet left after making arrangements to collect Posie the following day at the train station of Stowe-on-the-Middle-Wold. Just before her next client came into the room, Posie couldn't resist unscrewing the top of one of the jars of Alaric's honey. Hunting in her desk drawer for a clean spoon, she gave up and dug out a good spoonful with her scarlet-painted fingertip.

And when she tasted it, she realised just why Alaric Boynton-Dale's honey had won all those awards, why it was famed as the best in the land, why one jar alone was worth paying eighty-four pence for.

The honey was perfect.

****

17

Later that evening, having called Alaric's solicitors and been sent away with a flea in her ear, Posie was clearing her desk ready for her holidays when Prudence Smythe popped her head around the door on her way home, eyes bulging with anticipation behind her thick tortoiseshell glasses.

'So, what was Lady Violet like then? Do tell me! Was she like she is in all the magazines? Wasn't she tall? And she didn't look as sleek as I would expect, somehow…'

Posie remembered the grease marks on Lady Violet's linen-covered knees, the lack of any lipstick or hair pomade. And then instantly she felt ashamed of herself. Who cared about the glamour factor, really? This was a slice of real life, a real girl in real distress, going out of her mind with worry.

'She was intriguing,' Posie said carefully, telling the truth. 'The whole case sounds intriguing.'

Posie looked quickly around her familiar office, grateful for her own lot in life. She noted the purple evening shadows creeping slowly up the wall, Mr Minks licking himself all over in his snug basket, the string shopping bag in Prudence's hand with its couple of unexciting items inside it for her tea.

There was nothing at all precarious here.

* * * *

Two

The 11.48 from Paddington the next day took an hour and a half to reach Oxford, where Posie had to pick up a connecting train to Stowe-on-the-Middle-Wold, and she spent most of that first journey lost in a none-too-rosy world of her own.

It would be fair to say that this mystery had come along at a good time for Posie. While she had heaps of business on at the Grape Street Bureau, she needed a distraction, a pick-me-up. She needed to be shaken out of the wreckage of her car crash of a personal life. Not exactly a heartbreak, but an upsetting and gut-wrenching heart*ache* had befallen her. And even now, she was not quite sure what to make of the whole thing.

Only one month previously she had been eagerly looking forwards to the return of Len Irving, her unofficial business partner and almost-boyfriend.

Len had dutifully rushed off to the South of France in February, summoned by his dying father, interrupting both the start of their love affair and his prosperous and lucrative business as an undercover 'shadower' at the Grape Street Bureau. Since then Posie had heard from him only in sporadic dribs and drabs. In early May he had sent flowers, yellow mimosa, and he had written, promising to return to London very shortly. In fact, Len's father seemed to have made a miraculous recovery and Posie had begun to expect Len's imminent arrival with mixed feelings of relief and excitement.

But then, nothing.

The letters and the postcards from France had just stopped, had dried up entirely. Anxiously Posie had continued to write to the private boarding-house address which Len had given her. But she had heard nothing in return. At first she had feared something catastrophic or deadly had befallen Len, and in a panic she had booked herself two weeks of holiday so that she might travel down by train to the Cap d'Antibes, where Len's father lived, and see for herself what the problem might be. She had tried to tamp down her feelings of rising panic.

And then the niggling doubts had set in. Had something terrible *really* happened to Len or had Posie just been replaced in his affections by some new woman, a French *femme fatale*, perhaps? In which case the last thing she wanted to do was turn up, unannounced. Len was very good-looking, and the South of France was famously a romantic, glamorous, easy-going kind of place, and it was easy to imagine swarms of beautiful tanned women roaming like packs of hungry wolves up and down the seafront, looking for new, tasty prey.

Or had Mr Irving Senior's health simply taken another turn for the worse, and Len just didn't have the time to answer her letters? And if that was the case she didn't want to travel down to France and get in the way of a delicate situation.

Or perhaps Len had simply changed his mind about their budding relationship? If so, he probably didn't want to upset Posie with his change of heart, but he also wouldn't want to upset the lucrative working arrangement they had come to at the Grape Street Bureau, which saw them take a 50/50 split of all profits.

Whatever the case, Posie had decided to stop writing altogether, to refrain from booking herself a train ticket and to take effective, closer-to-home action of a sensible, definite sort. She decided that all she wanted to know was if Len was still residing at the same boarding-house. At least then she would know he was well, and that he had received her letters.

Posie had turned to the ever-dependable Inspector Richard Lovelace of New Scotland Yard, who, without asking any questions, had got in touch with a colleague of his, Inspector Leferb in Cannes, the nearest big town to the Cap d'Antibes, asking for his help.

The telegram, when it had arrived for Posie the week previously, had brought a feeling of relief, but also a stinging sadness which refused to go away. It had read:

INSPECTOR LEFERB HAS CONFIRMED LEN IRVING IS STILL RESIDING AT THE SAME BOARDING HOUSE ADDRESS IN CAP D'ANTIBES. NO PROBLEMS. HAPPY AS LARRY.

LEN'S FATHER NICELY RECOVERED FROM ILLESS AND LOOKING SPRIGHTLY TOO. HOPE THAT HELPS?
YOURS,
R. LOVELACE.

But Posie couldn't help feeling that there was something Inspector Lovelace or Inspector Leferb was holding back.

Now, as Posie waited on the sweltering tarmac of the Oxford Station platform, clutching a copy of *The Lady* and a greasy, paper-wrapped sandwich under her arm, she repeated to herself her current mantra: she would *not* humiliate herself by writing letters to a man who did not want to receive them, and if it ever came to it and Len returned to London with a perfectly good reason for his silence, she would listen to him and judge as she always did, on the strength of the case and the evidence of the facts.

But she was well aware that she was deluding herself. Affairs of the heart were so much more difficult to manage than the mysteries which had become her bread-and-butter trade. For who really likes to be jilted in love? Posie was aware that her heart was as ripe for bruising as the next person's, and that even prominent, famous people could apparently suffer heartache. Take for example the wealthy Dame Ianthe Flowers, whom Lady Violet had described so disparagingly the previous day, a woman hopelessly and uselessly in love with Alaric Boynton-Dale. Or even Alaric Boynton-Dale himself, hurt by the delectable Cosima Catchpole in her own giddy pursuit of happiness. Posie was grateful for the purpose this new case had given her, and she felt a sense of relief that she had not had to face a lonely two weeks of empty nothingness in dusty, sweltering London, in her small and airless South Kensington bedsit. After all, she had made no alternative plans for the holiday and most of her friends were either away from town for the summer or else already booked up.

The onward train journey to Stowe-on-the-Middle-Wold took forty-five minutes and Posie was pleased to find she had a whole first-class carriage to herself. It was very hot on the train and she rolled down a window and pulled down the canvas blind for some shade. She slung her leather overnight bag in the holder overhead, forced herself not to think about Len, and instead curled up cosily to read her magazine. And then, with a rush of pleasant surprise, she recognised the woman looking up at her from the front cover!

Lady Violet was staring out, her sharply-cropped hair immaculately arranged and her lovely face primped and powdered almost out of all recognition. She looked very different to the *au naturel* vision of yesterday in the worn trouser suit.

Turning in some excitement to read the article within, about 'Lady Violet – the Thinking Woman's Very Own Crumpet', Posie was unsurprised to read about Violet's family and her difficulties in life generally, but she *was* surprised to discover that not only did Lady Violet profess a love of baking almost unheard of in one of her class, but that she revealed herself to be a cool and level-headed businesswoman in the making: declaring a desire to open a chain of tea-shops in London to rival the success of the famous Lyons Corner Houses. Lady Violet also spoke at length about her plans for her very own cookbook to be published just before Christmas.

Mildly shocking pictures of Lady Violet posing in the kitchen at Boynton Hall followed, as did her recipe for her apparently famous Oxfordshire honey cake. The recipe was beautifully illustrated and sounded so tempting that Posie found she was almost drooling.

Unsurprisingly, the limp lettuce and tomato salad sandwich which she had bought from the station shop at Oxford for her lunch seemed particularly unappetising in comparison, and tasted like sawdust in the mouth.

* * * *

Later, tearing along very fast in Lady Violet's risky little two-seater, they negotiated wild country lanes and shady hedges at great speed, and Posie caught flashes of the scorched yellow country fields ripping past, rolling endlessly on under the ceaseless and surprising English heatwave.

All of a sudden, around a bend and past huge iron gates, Posie caught her first glimpse of Boynton Hall at the end of a very long drive.

She gaped. The house itself was breath-taking, a real country manor house made of glorious yellow Oxfordshire stone. Boynton Hall was English to the core. It was Tudor-built and turrety, with small mullioned leaded windows flashing in the sun like a thousand eyes. Pink roses scrambled up all over the front.

As they drew up, the sun dappled the broad sweep of lawn running alongside the drive, and although the grass was badly in need of a manicure and the cedars of Lebanon and beeches which framed the house looked like they needed a good pruning, the overall effect was dream-like and romantic.

'Here we are then,' said Lady Violet, bringing the car to a sudden stop on the shingle outside the huge oak front door. A tall, sullen-looking young man in uniform was standing waiting on the broad stone steps, staring fixedly at Lady Violet. Posie disliked him on sight, and the unwelcoming brief look he threw at her. He took Posie's overnight bag from the luggage rack at the back of the car without saying a word, disappearing into the house. Lady Violet tutted disapprovingly:

'That was Codlington, the Valet. I told you about him yesterday, remember? Charming manner he has, doesn't he? Jenks the Butler is very old, and is probably having a nap, so I'll show you up to your room myself. I'm afraid you'll find that Roderick is operating a skeleton staff here at Boynton to keep costs down, so at times it can feel rather unsatisfactory.'

Lady Violet ripped off her leather driving helmet and goggles and leapt out over the driver's door.

'You can freshen up first, and then please do feel free

to wander about the house and grounds as you wish. I've already told everyone you're coming, so no-one will be surprised to see you. But you'll find the house quiet; people tend to take to their rooms and sleep after lunch. You'll meet everyone formally at afternoon tea. It will be served on the lawn behind the house at four o'clock.'

Inside, the house was dark but refreshingly cool. Lady Violet took Posie up a twisting dark wooden staircase hung with coats of arms and tapestries, and then along a heavily carpeted landing on which intimidating portraits of long-dead Boynton-Dales looked down in a none-too-friendly fashion. Posie felt like she was being watched: she almost imagined their eyes swivelling and following her along the dim corridor, and she checked herself sharply. She normally had such a cool, clear head, and was never one for melodrama, but it seemed somehow that Boynton Hall was the sort of place to give one strange flights of fancy.

Fortunately the guest room which she was ushered into was very pleasant and welcoming, full of light and with a small four-poster bed and a writing desk tucked into a corner. A large bow-window overlooked the enormous back gardens, with a charming view of the church beyond. Lady Violet turned to go.

'If you need me for anything please do come and grab me. I'm down in the kitchen, trying out a recipe for my new cookbook. Baking in the kitchen keeps my mind from wandering, stops me thinking about Alaric. And thank you, thank you for coming here. I know you'll be a great help.'

Left alone, Posie changed out of her dusty black town clothes and replaced them with the only other outfit she had brought with her, a broad straw hat and a loose-fitting cream day dress cut in the new style. She splashed her face with the cold water she found in a patterned Delft china pitcher on the dresser and flicked her lips with the new bright-pink lipstick which she had bought as a holiday present to herself in the Army & Navy Stores a couple of weeks back; the name of the lipstick alone, 'Coral Dream', had been enough to convince her that this was the *very* thing for the Cap d'Antibes and for her big reunion with Len. Posie laughed now at her own foolishness and quickly grabbed her carpet bag, setting off for an exploration of Boynton Hall.

Lady Violet had been right: it was deathly quiet in the house, and Posie supposed that the other residents were either sleeping off a heavy lunch, or were taking advantage of the wonderful weather and were all outside sunbathing or swimming. There was no sign of the aged Butler, or the skeleton staff, or even of Codlington, the surly Valet.

But as Posie walked through the vast entrance hall she had again that strange feeling of being watched, regardless of the apparent slumbering emptiness around her. That tell-tale prickling feeling at her back which she knew of old made her swing around several times, but there was never anyone there.

Feeling like a first-class fool for getting so easily spooked, Posie decided that the heat was affecting her judgement, and that she would leave the oppressive house behind her and make a start outside, in the grounds. She let herself out the way she had come in, through the ancient front door, and wandering around the side of the house, she found herself in the back gardens, as empty and full of heavy silence as the house.

If anything, the aspect of the house and grounds from the back was even lovelier than from the front. At the bottom of the undulating formal lawns flashed a gleam of the wide river, famous for its trout fishing. On the far right was the village church and you could just make out the village on the horizon, as if it were a smudge in the hazy distance. On the left, wide rolling fields tumbled away as far as the eye could see. There was a surprisingly large quantity of land. Posie remembered that in some of these fields fairly close to the house Alaric had kept his beehives.

She decided to start by exploring the nearby fields and she walked briskly away from the formal back gardens in that direction, through cedar-hedges and past a silent swimming pool and an empty tennis court. She came to a small stile and climbed over, finding herself in a large overgrown vegetable garden, now running wild, with rabbits hopping around the place. There was a tumbledown red brick wall surrounding the garden, featuring an archway through which she could just see a field of blackened, stubbly earth on the other side. Posie strode through the archway and found herself in an enormous, flat, fire-scorched field. She supposed this was where Alaric had kept the majority of his bees, but there was absolutely no trace now of any hives. No sign of any life at all, in fact.

The fire had burnt away everything in its violent wake, even the trees and hedges which had grown on the sides of the field were burnt and shrivelled to blackened husks. A nasty chemical smell seemed to seep up from the earth itself, tar-like and suffocating. In a horrible flashback, it reminded Posie of the devastated fields of the Great War; the fields of Passchendale and Ypres after the end of the bloody battles, when Posie and her colleagues in the ambulance brigade had had to take advantage of ten minutes of ceasefire here and there to run in with stretchers and pick up the dead and dying. She shivered at the memory of those horrors, despite the hot sun.

Suddenly the vivid blue of the sky on the horizon was broken by the silhouette of a huge black hunting horse. A blur of scarlet from atop the horse made Posie wonder if this was someone who was taking part in a hunt. But surely it was too hot for such activities today. And was she imagining things, or was the rider staring at her, observing her with a great deal of interest?

Posie squinted, trying to stare back. She shielded her

eyes under her hat, but she couldn't make out whether the horse was being ridden by a man or a woman. Then, as quickly as the horse and rider had appeared, they vanished over a ridge. Posie sighed and turned back, kicking the burnt clods of earth at her feet as she walked. There seemed little to gain from standing out here, frying in the sun, breathing in the fumes. It all seemed exactly as Lady Violet had described it – a horrible, sad, twisted mess of a place – the ruin of so much hard work and passion.

Turning back towards the overgrown vegetable garden, she wandered through the long grass, making sure not to step on any of the broken glass which was lying around, the detritus of long-disused, smashed-up glasshouses from a bygone age; from before the Great War when the house had probably supported a full crew of gardeners to tend the vegetables and lawns, as well as a huge staff of household servants for its domestic affairs.

Looking up, she suddenly saw a long, low, red-bricked, single-storey building ahead of her, half-hidden by the boughs of an ancient apple tree. At first she thought it was an old storage shed, perhaps for those long-gone ghostly gardeners, but closer inspection revealed that this small place was well-cared for. The windows were intact, the roof tiles were immaculate, the wooden window-frames and the front door were all painted neatly in a carefully applied duck-egg blue. Realisation dawned: this was the annexe which presumably Alaric lived in when he was here at Boynton Hall.

Stepping ahead with a feeling of great excitement, Posie reached the front door. Here at last she felt she might find some evidence of the man himself. The door swung ajar on its hinges, as if beckoning her in. Posie knocked anyway, feeling slightly ridiculous, remembering Lady Violet's words to '…*feel free to wander about the house and grounds as you wish…*'

Posie stepped across the stone threshold of the annexe.

Inside it was pleasantly cool, a welcome relief from the heat outside. The heavy linen curtains were drawn at the windows and Posie went over to them, opening them, allowing light to flood the small space. She gulped in surprise: the place was in total chaos. Papers, maps and expensive-looking books were tipped haphazardly all over the flagstone floor and strewn carelessly across the small pine trestle table which obviously served as a desk. At first sight it looked as if the room had been subjected to a burglary.

Or perhaps Alaric Boynton-Dale was just very messy in his daily life? But somehow, Posie felt, that wasn't very likely. Something was amiss here. She observed the space carefully, looking for clues as to its owner's personality lurking beneath the disorder.

The room, about the same size as her own bedsit in London, was obviously usually tended to by a scrupulous person who liked minimal fuss and detail. She noticed how across the longest wall of the annexe a series of six elaborately-carved African masks were placed with exactly the right amount of space between each to show them off to their best advantage. An ancient-looking map of the world hung neatly above a small clean sink in the corner and a gorgeously-coloured oriental rug had been hung with great care on the wall above a single bed.

Padding over to the far corner, and feeling like a terrible sneak, Posie opened the single chest of drawers. Here, she found her suspicions were correct. Alaric was obviously a man who was near obsessional in ordering his own belongings. Linen drawer-boxes contained the carefully-folded clothes and possessions of a seasoned explorer: silk travelling scarves; travel-sized boxes of unopened Pears soap; a tiny travelling shaving kit and a new Swiss army knife. A canvas holdall was propped against the chest and revealed what looked like a tent inside, together with a travelling sleeping-bag, a small first-aid kit, a blanket and a flask for storing water in. There was also a stash of dry biscuits and even some Fry's peppermint cream chocolate wrapped in silver foil.

If Alaric had left the annexe of his own accord then he had left all of his usual travelling kit behind, which seemed a bit fishy. It was beginning to look horribly like Lady Violet's suspicions might be well-founded: that Alaric had somehow been *forced* away, perhaps against his will.

Bemused, Posie turned back to look at Alaric's mess of a desk. She cleared the chair of its heap of paperwork and sat down. She flicked on the desk lamp and it illuminated a cork-board carefully pinned with Alaric's bee-keeping information: a neat map of the surrounding fields and the exact location of the many beehives. The only personal touch was a photograph pinned at the very bottom of the cork-board. It showed two men standing together next to a bi-plane. Posie recognised at once the angular, familiar features of a laughing Alaric Boynton-Dale, his lanky form propped up companionably against a much bigger man. But just *who* exactly the second man was in the snapshot was unclear: his face had been carefully destroyed, burnt away with what looked like a cigarette. Posie took the photo from the board and stared at it.

Lost in the world of the photo, Posie suddenly realised that all the light in the room had been obliterated in an instant. Turning, she saw a flash of a scarlet red jacket. A huge man was blocking the doorway, his face in total shadow. He was holding a liver-coloured pointer dog which was straining tightly on a lead. The dog had its sharp-looking teeth bared and was emitting a rather frightening growling sound. The whole attitude emanating from the doorway was one of total hostility.

'Who the very devil are you?' snarled an angry, aristocratic voice from the depths of the red jacket. 'And what on earth are you doing in *here*, might I ask? This is private property. You're trespassing.'

Posie stood up as calmly as possible. She rummaged in her bag and found one of her business cards, and advanced with it outstretched on the palm of her hand, like a talisman. She avoided the dog carefully, pressing the card into the one free hand of the big man. She explained in as few words as possible what she was doing, who had invited her and why.

She watched the man visibly deflate, and step inside the annexe.

'Forgive me, my dear,' he muttered politely.

'I live across the meadows, and I thought I saw a stranger hanging around the place. Turns out it was *you*. I've made it my business to watch over this place these last few days, ever since Alaric disappeared. I dress up like I'm out with the hunt and then it makes it seem more believable somehow, that I'm roaming around these quarters with a real purpose. Strange things have been happening here. Well, you can see for yourself, can't you? Alaric kept this place like a clean new pin. Now look what's happened! Someone, or *some people* have been all over it, grubbing around looking for something in the paperwork. Goodness only knows what they thought they'd find!'

The man sat down on the single bed, which wheezed uncomfortably beneath his weight. At ease, the pointer sat companionably at his feet, tongue drooling with thirst. The sunlight shone briefly on the man, illuminating him for the first time. He was around forty, a heavily built, slow-moving man with what must have once been a handsome, cherubic round face. But the skin across half of his face was now puckered and raw, burnt badly away, and he was wearing a black eye-patch where the fire in his aeroplane at the end of the war had seared away his eye. His breathing was shallow and asthmatic, the result of burnt, irreparably-damaged lungs. No question about it, despite the lack of introduction, this was undoubtedly Major Hugo Marchpane. The man who had been friends with Alaric Boynton-Dale and was now his bitter enemy.

Posie crossed the room to the sink and fetched a bowl of water for the dog. She placed it gingerly at his feet, trying not to think about the huge teeth which had previously been on display. She filled two glasses of water for herself and Major Marchpane, and he drank thirstily. She settled herself down again at the desk chair in the ensuing silence. How best to approach this rather delicate situation? A man like Major Marchpane would probably appreciate directness.

'So, Major Marchpane, I take it you have no idea where Alaric could be?'

Major Marchpane shook his head, draining the last of his glass. He wiped his lips brusquely. 'No. Wish I did though. It doesn't feel right, any of this. Alaric wouldn't just take off with no warning. Someone or something must have got at him.'

Posie nodded thoughtfully. 'I'm beginning to think Lady Violet is right in having suspicions. Forgive me for asking, but why do you care so much anyway? Why do you bother keeping an eye on this annexe? I understood you and Alaric Boynton-Dale were sworn enemies, arch-rivals, in fact. All because of…er, because of…'

She found she couldn't bring herself to mention Lady Cosima. It seemed wrong somehow to mention such unsavoury gossip, particularly when it could only serve to cause hurt.

'Because of my wayward wife, you mean?' the Major replied, utterly deadpan, a glint of humour filling his one good eye.

Posie flushed and nodded. 'I've heard you hate him, after what happened. That there have been lots of rows, physical attacks. How do I know you weren't behind sabotaging his plane? You'd have the relevant knowledge to do it. And you live nearby. Perhaps you set fire to the fields out here too?'

The Major spluttered in what sounded like a

combination of indignation and incredulous laughter. When he realised Posie was entirely serious he rubbed his burnt skin tetchily:

'So I'm a suspect, am I? I must say, you're remarkably well informed. Violet tell you all this, did she?'

Posie nodded but stayed silent.

'Hmmm. Poor little Violet. I'm not surprised she's got you down here, nosing around. Poor kid seems to be going out of her mind with worry about Al. I don't know what she'll do without him. Saying that, she's always been a fragile creature. Alaric made it his business to look out for Cuckoo. She's been brittle for years, ever since the accident.'

'Accident?'

'The one in which her parents were killed outright. Happened about fifteen years ago, when she was only a little nipper of ten or so. Poor little Cuckoo was in the car when it swerved off the road, careering down a sharp bend. She was the only one in the car to survive. Took it badly, poor little kid…'

Posie nodded, a vague memory about the motor accident reconfirming itself in her mind.

'But your feud with Alaric, Major Marchpane?'

'*What* feud? You're barking up the wrong tree there, Miss Parker. Sure, I was pretty mad at Alaric for a few days when I got that anonymous tip-off last month. I might have said some terrible things, raged around the place, but it was all just hot air; I was letting off steam. It was all bluff. They both swore to me that the affair was over, and I believed them.'

He sighed and crossed his badly burnt hands in his lap.

'Have you ever met my wife? No? She's the most beautiful woman in these parts. Like a racehorse, she has a delicate temperament. And an Earl's daughter to boot, which is how she comes to have a title and I don't. Not that I mind, of course, but it's led to a certain degree of her thinking she is entitled to whatever she wants. She loves to act, for example, but the sad truth is that she's not very good at it – she threw a real strop last year when the local Amateur Dramatic group refused to cast her in the lead role. Well, in the same way, she obviously felt she was entitled to Alaric, too.'

The Major smiled sadly. 'I can't say I blame Alaric really. I was away such a lot in London working for the government. I realise now that was a mistake: Cosima was left all alone out here and she's not a woman to leave unattended, she gets bored easily. The irony is that I almost forced the two of them together! Can you believe it was *me* who asked Alaric to look out for her when I started to go away for great patches of time? I hardly go anywhere now. It's safer that way.'

Posie sat silently, trying to decide if she believed the Major's contrite manner. It was certainly surprising.

'Besides, Alaric is one of my oldest friends. I jolly well owe him my life. It was Alaric who pulled me out of the burning wreck of my Sopwith Pup when it came down in France in 1917. I took a hit and came down blazing. He was flying beside me and followed me down, risking a ruddy dangerous landing, getting shot at all over the place on the way down by those new Spandau guns the Germans had just installed. He risked his life for me. He pulled me out of the burning cockpit. Sure, I'm not a work of art anymore, but I lived. You couldn't understand of course, Miss Parker, what it was like in the war, not being there. Binds men together, you know?'

Posie tilted her head to one side but refrained from speaking: *Oh, but I was there. And I can understand.*

'What's a woman, even one's own *wife*, between friends after something like that? As I said, I forgave them both. Besides, it's old news.'

Posie reached onto the desk, ignoring the other paperwork and took the single photograph. She handed it to the Major.

'This is you two together, is it? You're the one missing the head?'

The Major squinted at the photo. He nodded slowly. 'Yep, that's us. That was us standing next to Alaric's first Sopwith Camel. But hang it all, something here is very strange…'

He scratched his head in puzzlement.

'What is it?'

'I was here on Saturday when Al first went missing, and again over the next couple of days, checking up on the place. I noticed the mess of papers of course, but I thought I'd better leave everything as it was, in case the police were called in. I haven't touched a thing. But I swear on my life that this photograph was not damaged when I saw it last. I'd have remembered if Alaric had burned a hole right through my face! Flipping cheek! I'd have given him merry hell for doing that! Perhaps it's a clue? But really, I'm the last person to be trusting with *clues*. Things like that go right over my head.'

Posie had the feeling he was about to tell her something important. She often had that effect on people; they chose to tell her things entirely of their own accord, with very little prompting. *Go on*, she willed him. *Go on*.

He was stroking the head of the dog carefully, and staring at Posie rather disconcertingly from his one eye.

'I say, I have this strange feeling I can trust you, Miss Parker. Talking of things going straight over my head…'

'Go on, please.'

'You'll need to keep this a secret. It might be important. I haven't told a soul up until now. Not even Violet. Didn't want to worry her. And I certainly haven't told Cosima about it either.'

Posie nodded.

'This dog here, Bikram. He isn't mine. He belongs to Alaric. He's his faithful pal, goes everywhere with him, even up in the Fokker when he had room. In fact, it was this dog who saved Alaric. When Alaric collapsed out there in that burning field due to the chemical inhalation from the beehives this dog created merry hell. He barked himself into a frenzy on the doorstep of Boynton Hall, waking the entire household up, insisting people came and found Alaric. Alaric would have been a gonner otherwise.'

The Major took something from his pocket and stared at it.

'The first inkling I had that something was very wrong came on Saturday, very early in the morning. Bikram here appeared all alone at our house. He came up to me, barking and whining. Around his neck he had a piece of leather cord, and attached to it were two things. He seemed to know he needed to deliver them to me, somehow. Clever bally dog!'

Posie almost held her breath. She could feel her heart racing.

'The first thing was a note from Al. It said "Take care of Bikram" or something like that. And it also said "You know what *this* means." I can't remember the exact wording, and I burnt it immediately in case Alaric meant me to destroy it. The second thing attached to the cord was this…'

The Major was looking at a small dull bronze-coloured pendant. He polished it up on his sleeve, and passed it to Posie.

'This must be what he refers to in his note. But he was wrong! I have no idea what it means! Do you think it's a clue?'

Posie took the thing and studied it. Close inspection revealed it to be a coin of some sort featuring a honey bee, its wings splayed across the width of the coin.

Even to her inexpert eye, she could tell it was a simply stunning artefact of a very high quality. A tiny hole, just big enough for a cord or chain to fit through punctured the top part of the coin. When Posie turned the coin over she saw a strange pair of words etched into the back of it:

Serafina / Hyblaea

'Have you seen Alaric wear this before, Major Marchpane? Was it a lucky charm of his, perhaps? Did it mean something special to him?'

The Major shook his head sadly. Posie wasn't surprised: she had realised that the Major was not really a 'details' man. Even if Alaric had worn this coin as a necklace day-in day-out, she thought the Major probably would not have noticed.

'No. I don't recognise it. But it doesn't surprise me, either. We were great pals, Alaric and I, but a lot of what he talked about went straight over my head. He was very interested in old things and fusty old history, like his father before him, who practically lived in the British Museum coin department apparently. I think his father gave quite a collection of coins to the museum, you know, and Alaric inherited a few of the less valuable ones when his father died. Me, I prefer new things.'

The Major stood up and headed over to a space by the side of the desk. Posie now saw a small grey metal filing cabinet, with several tiny drawers pulled out willy-nilly, adding to the general chaos. The Major started to rifle through them:

'These are his father's old coins in these cabinet drawers here. Perhaps there's something similar here to that bee coin which can give us a clue as to what he meant by sending it to me? It must mean *something*. Unless the coin collection has been raided by the intruders? Although Alaric always told me the coins here had little value. So heaven only knows what it was that the intruders were after! I simply can't imagine…'

Posie *could* well imagine, and the thought of Alaric's newly-executed Will now flashed up before her eyes as clearly as if she were holding the document in her own hand. Surely that must have been what the intruder was looking for when they ransacked the place? For what else was there of any real value here? She nearly blabbed her thoughts aloud, but at the last second she held her tongue: best to keep some things to herself, for now, at any rate.

Together they checked on the contents of the coin drawers, but nothing appeared to be missing. And nothing looked remotely similar to the bee coin. There was one typewritten sheet too, listing and describing the coins in the cabinet, the work of Alaric's tidy mind. Posie scanned quickly through the descriptions, but it was as she had thought; all the coins were of a fairly low quality, and there was no mention anywhere of a bee as a motif, or even of those strange, exotic-sounding names.

'What of the names, Major Marchpane. Do you recognise "Serafina" and "Hyblaea"? Who are they? Do you know?'

He shrugged. 'I've no idea. You'll have to find out by yourself, I'm afraid. You can keep that bee pendant if you like. If it helps you find Alaric, or find out what's happened to him, I'd be glad if you had it.'

Posie was pleased. Of course, it could turn out to be a mare's nest and mean nothing at all. Perhaps Alaric had simply given the coin to Major Marchpane as a memento of himself, or to ensure its safekeeping.

But she felt instinctively that the coin might lead her somewhere. Perhaps she could ask Lady Violet later. Perhaps those strange names on the back would mean something to her.

The Major was edging for the door. On a peg on the back of the door hung Alaric's now-redundant bee-keeper's outfit, its strange and alien-looking rubber mask propped uselessly on top of the white padded suit. The Major seemed to come to a standstill and he stood wordlessly, staring at it. For a horrible moment Posie thought he might be about to cry. He turned to her sadly.

'Know anything about bees, Miss Parker?'

'Only that they have a nasty bite.'

The Major laughed.

'I have a feeling Alaric would like you, Miss Parker. He'd approve of Lady Violet's choice in hiring you. And I approve too. We need someone with a clear head to sort through this mess, even if you are just a slip of a girl. No offence meant.'

'None taken.'

'If there's anything you need you can find me in the house over yonder, The Gatehouse. We were invited for dinner at Boynton Hall today, but I said no: it doesn't feel right somehow. What is there to celebrate with Alaric gone? Besides,' and here he looked at Posie full on, 'there's danger in that house. I can feel it. Here too. All around us. You seem a sensible enough lassie but you'd do well to watch yourself. Bad things are happening here at the moment.'

Bad things. That was a phrase she was hearing over and over again. Posie watched the Major's retreating back, watched him untie the black horse from a post near the vegetable garden and ride away. Bikram was lolloping along at the big horse's feet.

She sighed heavily. Major Marchpane had seemed utterly sincere, a loyal, trusted friend. And he had seemed anxious enough to help, too. Posie mentally struck him off her list of key suspects. But then she reconsidered. For was *anyone* ever really excluded from being a suspect until the final hurdle had been reached?

Her wristwatch told her it was almost four o'clock. She slipped the bee pendant carefully into her bag, and on second thoughts she quickly added Alaric's typewritten list describing the worthless coin collection for good measure.

Then she headed off over the gardens in time for tea.

* * * *

Three

What a difference an hour or so could make! As she approached, Posie saw that Boynton Hall had sprung to life while she had been over in the annexe, and people were gathering on the lawn.

Steps led down from the French windows of the Library and onto a paved terrace where cakes and wafer-thin sandwiches were being placed upon small white cast iron tables. White chairs were scattered around the place. It was a beautiful late afternoon and the sky was heavy with a hot golden-pinky glow. The amber light filtered through the foliage of the oak trees, throwing long shadows onto the lawn.

Surely in this sublime setting Posie could throw off the feeling of unease which had been her constant companion since her arrival? She looked around her with genuine interest, ready to begin her task of interviewing or at least trying to understand the handful of suspects Lady Violet had sketched out for her.

A few people were drifting towards the carefully laid out tables. Posie recognised Lord Roderick Boynton-Dale from his newspaper photographs, and she assumed that the dark woman who stuck limpet-like to his side, giving him adoring looks, must be Lady Eve, his American wife.

As yet, there was no sign of the famous crime writer, Dame Ianthe Flowers, or of Lady Violet herself. There were extras here, too: Posie noticed a beaky-looking man in a dog-collar who must be the local Vicar, together with a young church Curate, both wolfing down cucumber sandwiches as if their very lives depended on it. The black-and-white livery of professional servants was on display too and Posie recognised Codlington's scowling face in a row made up of two serving maids and an ancient-looking Butler.

'There you are, Posie!'

Posie caught sight of Lady Violet as she came striding down the steps from the French windows, bearing aloft a golden-coloured frosted cake on an elaborate ceramic cake-stand. Everyone turned and stared at Violet, transfixed. A maid bobbed behind her uselessly.

'Just in time for some of my honey cake, still warm from the oven. Have you met anyone else here yet? No? Let me make the introductions. Everyone, listen! This is Miss Posie Parker. Remember? I told you all about her – she's simply the hottest private investigator in London right now and she's going to find out what's happened to Alaric. So be on your best behaviour and help her with anything she asks for. Now, who wants the first slice?'

Posie was still standing a little way off from the main body of the group and was conscious of everyone staring at her. She gave a fixed smile while inwardly cursing under her breath: she wished wholeheartedly that Lady Violet had been a little more subtle in her introductions. Posie glanced over at the girl now, still in her rumpled trousers, busily cutting cake and giving orders to the servants as if for all the world she were the mistress of the house. The household servants seemed to move around Violet like poor little planets to a brightly burning sun.

But surely the orchestration of any event involving outside visitors should be undertaken by the *real* mistress of the house? And that would be Roderick's wife, Lady Eve. What did she feel about all of this?

Turning, Posie found herself face-to-face with that very person. Lady Eve Boynton was uncomfortably close by at Posie's elbow, a pink Sobranie cocktail cigarette dangling in a long ebony holder from her lips. She had evidently managed to peel herself away from her husband's side for a few moments. Eve was a clumpy-looking woman in her late thirties, with that American thing of being exquisitely groomed. The blood-red of her fingernails matched the slash of her lipstick and the obviously expensive rubies that glittered at her ears. She flashed Posie a look of real dislike, ignoring Posie's outstretched hand.

'Enchanted, I'm sure,' she drawled sarcastically in what Posie could only suppose was an accent from the Deep South.

'Thank you so much for your hospitality in having me here to stay, Lady Boynton,' Posie said graciously, almost bowing her head and dropping her eyes subserviently, mainly to cover her lack of conviction. She had never been made to feel *less* welcome in a place before.

Eve snapped to life. 'It wasn't as if *I* had any choice in the matter! That little minx over there just informed us you would be arriving and we had to like it or lump it. Little madam!'

Just then a hugely fat man dressed in a loud yellow tartan suit approached, cramming fistfuls of cake into his mouth and smiling broadly. He shared the same dark heavy features and small brown eyes as his daughter. There was no doubt that this was Eve's father, the Texan millionaire, Mr Burns.

'That's one thing y'all make better this side of the pond,' Mr Burns said between bites. 'CAKE! An' that little girl Violet sure can cook like an angel! I don't hold with many traditions, but afternoon tea on an English lawn has got to take some beating, don't you agree, Miss Parker?'

He was as warm as his daughter was icy cool and Posie laughed alongside him while his daughter looked on at both of them with contempt. But Posie remembered there had been 'words' between the pair of them recently about money, and she swore to tread carefully. It wouldn't do to suck up to the father and exclude the daughter.

'So you're here to spy on us all, are you, Miss Parker?' drawled Mr Burns good-humouredly.

'It looks like it, doesn't it?' said Posie with a short laugh. 'But really I'm just here on a fact-finding mission. To try and find out where Alaric may have got to. It seems that his disappearing like this is entirely out of character. Would you agree, Lady Boynton?'

Eve Boynton took a deep drag on her Sobranie.

'Good riddance, that's what I say,' she spat vehemently.

Hadn't Lady Violet said that Eve hated Alaric with a passion? But what lengths could such a passion really run to? Posie studied the flushed, burning face of the plain woman, almost lit up out of all recognition by an inner fire, her quick peering eyes sparkling with intensity, her small mouth set in a grim line. What on earth had Alaric done to Eve to make her hate him so?

'Dratted man,' Eve Boynton continued. 'What we really need around here are people pulling their weight, pumping money into this wretched sink-hole of a house. What we *don't* need are flaky family members, swanning off to goodness knows where on a mere whim, garnering attention, attracting all manner of newspaper coverage…'

'Forgive me, Lady Boynton, but I think the whole point of my being here is so that the newspapers *don't* get involved just yet, or the police. I'm the discreet option. As far as I am aware, no-one but the immediate family and the people staying at the house are aware that Alaric has gone missing. You seem to object to my being here, to my asking you questions. Can I ask why?'

'Oh, ask me what you want to,' snapped Eve. 'It's no secret I disliked Alaric. I suppose you'll get it out of someone eventually, so I might as well tell you myself. All he did was cause us trouble. I suppose you know he announced to my poor darlin' husband that he was changing his Will? The money which was rightfully to stay in the family was going to pass instead to that little horror, Violet. A disgrace, I call it! We need the money *here*. Now, if you will excuse me, I will no doubt see you later at dinner.'

Eve stalked off to another small table where she started to take a maid to task over something trivial.

Posie sipped her tea and re-ran the conversation which had just passed. Curiously, Eve had referred to Alaric in the *past tense* throughout, but was that just a careless manner of speech or indicative of something more sinister?

And there it was again. That recurring motif which kept cropping up and which seemed to be at the very centre of this puzzle; that wretched newly-changed Will! Well, there was nothing new there: money was the oldest of motives for murder in the book. But it was the Will itself, *or what it represented*, which was somehow central to this case, Posie was sure of it.

Mr Burns was swatting at his face with a highly starched handkerchief, wiping away the continuous beads of sweat which were forming there. He had obviously mistaken Posie's silence for shyness, or else discomfort. He took another piece of cake from a maid's passing tray and patted Posie's arm in comfort. He winked over at his daughter:

'Take no notice of *her*, ma'am,' he said reassuringly. 'A case of the pot calling the kettle black, indirectly. She doesn't despise Alaric. It's Roderick who causes her the real heartache, much as she swears blind she loves him. *He's* the flaky one who attracts the bad press. In and out of the rags every week. Gee, you ever met Alaric? No? A nicer fella you couldn't hope to come across. I hope to goodness he's all right. If you ask me my girl Eve has taken his disappearance mighty badly. I think she may actually be jealous that he's managed to get away from this crumbling ol' wreck of a pile and she's still stuck here… Do you know they don't even have air conditioning here? What sort of a dive doesn't have air conditioning, or at least a few fans? Especially in this darn heat! They promised me England would be cool…It's the very opposite!'

Posie mumbled something by way of reply, not liking to admit that she had no clue what 'air conditioning' might be. She gulped at her tea and took a bite of perhaps the most delicious cake she had ever eaten; she made a note to congratulate Lady Violet on it later. But for now she wanted to be rid of Mr Burns, nice though he was, and focus on the real suspects. Where the blazes was Dame Ianthe? Was she still writing here at Boynton Hall?

Posie had been aware for some time now of Roderick Boynton-Dale flitting around the tables, throwing her dark looks, but he seemed less than keen to introduce himself. His voice was high and reedy, and it carried across the lawn unpleasantly. He was a tall, lanky man, twitchy and restless. At one point she had seen him cloistered together with the Vicar and Curate, who had both now peeled off and set off across the lawns in the direction of the church with looks of some relief. Now Roderick was bunched together with Codlington and the two of them were furtively swapping what looked like small pieces of newspaper. Roderick was tapping at his wristwatch impatiently.

'Dratted fellow,' growled Mr Burns under his breath, following Posie's gaze. 'I'll call him over for ya, shall I? The man has no manners. Damned rudeness! He still dances to my say-so, you know. Thinks I'm still ready and waiting with my cheque-book open at every turn. But those days are long gone, let me tell you! Now that I've found out where my money has been going!'

'*Where* has your money been going, Mr Burns?'

'Dogs and horses, my dear. Betting! This week it's Ascot. That's what he's doing there with that good-for-nothing servant,' snarled Mr Burns.

'It's an addiction. Just one of many, I'm sorry to say.

Every day it's the same old story. That leech of a Valet takes Roderick's betting instructions and trots into the village with them. Codlington's a real bad lot: he's on a hot-line to some dodgy bookmaker in London, probably taking nice big cuts for himself. Codlington calls through to London from the Post Office in the village: it would never do of course for Roderick to place the bets himself, or for the calls to be traced *here*, him being Lord of the Manor an' all, but the whole village realises what's happening. Roderick's a local laughing-stock.'

'And does Roderick win much?'

'What do you think? Of course not! It's a case of good money being thrown after bad! It's the usual story! He's a worm, he's got no backbone. He's weak-willed and in thrall to that wretched young Valet. No wonder this place is falling apart around our ears! I'll get him over for you.'

Mr Burns whistled across the grass at Roderick, as one might call a favourite dog. Roderick scowled, then smiled, then patted Codlington on the back before ambling over ungraciously. Codlington skulked off inside the house.

Mr Burns did a mock half-bow and disappeared. Eve too obviously felt she had done more than enough for one afternoon and had gone. The servants were clearing away the tea-things and Lady Violet seemed yet again to be in charge of the whole process. Only Posie and Roderick remained on the lawn. He came up to her reluctantly.

Suddenly Posie felt exasperated, her patience worn thin. She felt no obligation to be nice to this man, for all his aristocratic status. She decided on the spur of the moment not to bother. She found Roderick and his wife abominably rude, and whatever the circumstances of her visit, she was first and foremost a guest and therefore entitled to some courtesy. She stood silently regarding the gardens. Across the lawn the church clock was chiming five o'clock. She sensed Roderick lighting up a Turkish cigarette, but he didn't offer her one. He smoked in silence, then said:

'I'm sorry but I can't help you. Alaric never told me anything.'

'Anything about *what*, Lord Boynton?'

'Anything at all, really. We're not on the best of terms.'

'So I have heard.'

Roderick kicked his cigarette butt onto the gravel after a minute or so and ground it under his heel. Posie watched as he took out a silver hip-flask of whisky and drank steadily, as if it were water. The sour-sweet reek reached her nostrils. She noticed now that his hands were shaking violently, trembling continuously as if in the grip of a palsy. So, the newspapers were right about one thing: Roderick was an alcoholic. Posie was the last person to pass judgement on a man for such an addiction – she had seen too many men take to drink with good reason as a way of forgetting the horrors of the trenches of the Great War, including her good friend Rufus Cardigeon – but she happened to know that Roderick had never served in the Great War, he had been excused on account of a weak heart. This man was a professional drunk, a man who escaped the horrors of his own daily life by resorting to alcohol at any given hour.

Posie searched his face in profile for a second: a weaker, less distinguished version of Alaric's face. She felt a tiny stab of pity for Roderick. What could it be like, rising every morning and looking into the mirror at such a face? It would serve as a reminder of a brother whose life and achievements were gilded by success, a brother who was as much loved as Roderick himself was ridiculed; a brother who had been born to rightfully inherit a title and a house which Roderick was now spectacularly ruining. Did Roderick actively resent Alaric enough to try and get rid of him?

'Where do *you* think Alaric has got to, Lord Boynton?' asked Posie in an innocently bland way.

Roderick shrugged, tucking his hip-flask back inside his navy blazer. 'I wouldn't like to guess.'

Posie changed tack:

'And what about his Will? *If* he's changed it you're going to be Two Hundred Thousand Pounds poorer as a result! I've known men kill for much less. In my line of work that makes you a suspect. A prime suspect, even. Heaven help you if Alaric turns up dead now.'

At that, she noticed, Roderick stiffened: a rabbit caught in an open field, nose twitching, alert, sensing danger. He turned to face her full-on, and she saw real disbelief in his eyes.

'Don't be absurd! I don't know what my sister has been telling you, but Cuckoo is way off the mark. There's a world of difference between not getting along with someone and doing away with them! Sure, I can't say I was overjoyed when he told me he was going to change his Will, but I can't say I was counting on that money coming to me, either. Even if he *hadn't* changed it I'd have had a long wait for the money! Alaric's not yet forty! He might live to be a hundred! You can't rely on money promised in a Will! That money would only be paid over on his death…not for ages!'

'Exactly!' said Posie sweetly. 'Can't you see? That's the best motive in the world! Murder him before he got the chance to change the Will and the problem is sorted! No need to wait around for years, and the certainty of all that money coming to *you*. *Now*. Rather than to your sister.'

Roderick looked at Posie, daunted in the face of her argument. He shook his head miserably, his hands quivering at his sides. Posie was puzzled at his weakness, his lack of self-defence.

She fished in her carpet bag and held on tightly to the bee coin. She would not give away *how* exactly she had come by it, but Roderick might know something useful. She passed him the coin and he held it for a minute in a shaking hand. He gulped, and looked at it as if it were a real bee or wasp, itching to take a bite out of his sweaty palm. Was it her imagination or had his hand started to shake even more so than before?

'Does this mean anything to you, Lord Boynton? I think it does. What is it?'

He passed it back to Posie gingerly. 'Alaric wore it. As a sort of necklace thing. Damned effeminate if you ask me! Where did you find it?'

Posie ignored the question. She felt a smidgen of rising excitement and congratulated herself: she had *known* the Major would never have noticed such a little trinket, important enough though it was.

'You mean he wore it every day, or just sometimes?'

Roderick tutted and shrugged. 'I wasn't with my brother every day, thank goodness. But when I saw him he usually had this on.'

'What does it mean? Was it special? Was it one of your father's coins, do you think? I gather your father was a coin-collector, a numismatist?'

Roderick looked at Posie and narrowed his eyes. 'Sharp, aren't you? Be careful you don't cut yourself, Miss Parker.'

Roderick was suddenly spiked into anger. 'I don't know anything about coins, so don't bother asking me. You're wasting your breath. And I'm not into bees, so don't ask me anything about them either. But that doesn't mean I'd go around killing fields of them; that took a very sick mind. Mine might be addled by drink, but I'm not a psychopath. And you've got a cheek, coming here and pointing the finger at all of us. I can't ask you to leave, but don't think I'm not counting every second until you go.'

He stalked off, leaving Posie alone on the lawn in the falling shadows. She didn't care a jot that she had annoyed him: that was what she was paid, or in this case *not* paid, to do in her line of work.

She tucked the bee coin away again safely. It was

important, she knew. She needed to find out more about it, but the answer did not lie here at Boynton Hall. And the Will too: *that* was important.

She decided on the spur of the moment that she was going to cut short her stay at Boynton Hall. Posie was itching already to be back in London, where answers could be found, and where people treated each other with a good deal more respect. She would stay on one more day and leave first thing on Friday morning.

But she needed to make a few things happen first.

****

Four

The Post Office queue stretched out ahead of her, with one inconsiderate person creating a hold-up at the counter.

Posie shifted her weight from foot to foot. It was boiling hot and stuffy in the crowded shop. A long queue of restless, impatient villagers snaked behind, everyone eager to be served just before closing time.

There was a flurry of movement up ahead as the woman who had been holding everything up at the counter had obviously finished. As the queue shunted forwards the villager behind Posie muttered, half under her breath:

'Wretched Lady Cosima!'

Suddenly interested, Posie craned her neck for a better view as Lady Cosima Catchpole swished past. Like Lady Violet, Cosima was obviously someone who garnered attention, and every eye in the place followed her retreating back. Posie had a fleeting impression of a very tall, slender woman shoving a wad of letters carelessly into a string bag. Her skin was translucent as porcelain, her eyes like huge blazing emeralds. But her most striking feature was her hair – Lady Cosima had obviously never had it cut short, as almost everyone else Posie knew had – and its fiery redness was swirled up into a large knot at the back of her head, straining for freedom. Cosima was dressed in a long jade satin dress, rather as if she were about to step onto a stage and act, not simply visit the local shop. She left an impression of exotic inappropriateness trailing in her wake.

Posie could quite see why Cosima had held Alaric in her thrall, and she wondered if she might have time to go and speak to her during her brief stay. What a pity she and the Major would not be at the dinner tonight.

Posie was absentmindedly running her eye over a stand of gaudily-coloured picture postcards and wondering if she should buy a couple when her focus sharpened and came to rest on a basket stacked high with different coloured blocks of wax.

A sign tacked underneath read:

HEELBALL/ BRASS-RUBBING WAX
(5p per block)
*Come and see the famous Stowe Church
Brasses and create your own souvenir!
Special paper available to buy separately!*

What a good idea! Posie grabbed a stick of the plain black wax. She hunted around in her bag and located a slightly dog-eared envelope and a piece of not-too-crumpled thin paper from its depths.

She whiled away the wait leaning against a shelf, taking an impression of Alaric's bee coin as carefully as she could, slowly rubbing the black wax against the thin paper with careful strokes until the image of the insect was revealed, much like a church brass, in all its fine-winged detail.

When she was satisfied with her copy, she folded the paper in half and tucked it into her envelope, throwing in one of her business cards before sealing it up. She scribbled an address on the envelope:

Mr Binkie Dodds, (FIRST CLASS POST)

The Royal Numismatic Society,
The British Museum, Bloomsbury, London WC1

She finally reached the counter. 'I need to use the telephone please. Two calls to London, and I'll be quick.'

She pushed across some money for the first-class stamp to the British Museum and also to pay for the black wax. 'How much will the calls cost?'

'No can do,' said the tiny dried-up looking Postmistress with a small cackle of laughter. 'If you want to use the telephone you'll have to come back tomorrow. I hope it isn't anything urgent, Miss? His nibs Lord Boynton has sent his Valet down here. He's on the telephone to his bookmaker, same as every day. He'll be here until I shut up shop at six o'clock. Isn't that right, folks?'

The rest of the queue erupted into derisive laughter and for some reason Posie felt strangely embarrassed for Roderick and more so for Lady Violet. Did *she* realise the whole village were laughing daily at this silly charade? And now Posie observed Codlington, hunched up tightly into a wooden cubicle tucked far behind the counter. He was turned away from the prying eyes of the villagers, a marked-up newspaper and a stubby pencil clutched in his hand. He was whispering furtively into the receiver and striking off newspaper columns as he spoke.

'Okay. Two telegrams instead,' Posie declared. Aware of the interest in her as a non-villager she whispered the addresses and the contents of the telegrams as quietly as she could to the Postmistress, and checked them before paying.

The first read:

To: THE GRAPE STREET BUREAU, WC1
DEAREST PRUDENCE,
I NEED YOU TO STEP AROUND THE CORNER
TO THE BRITISH MUSEUM AND FIX ME UP
A MEETING WITH BINKIE DODDS. TELL HIM
TO EXPECT ME THIS FRIDAY MORNING. YES
– THAT'S RIGHT – I'M CUTTING THIS TRIP
SHORT AND COMING HOME.
TELL BINKIE HE WILL RECEIVE SOMETHING
IMPORTANT IN THE POST TOMORROW AND HE
HAD JOLLY WELL BETTER KNOW WHAT IT IS
BY THE TIME I MEET HIM.
HOPE EVERYTHING ELSE IS FINE.
ANY PROBLEMS TELEGRAM ME HERE
(POST OFFICE, STOWE-ON-THE-MIDDLE-WOLD),
OTHERWISE, SEE YOU FRIDAY.
BEST,
POSIE
P.S. I HOPE MR MINKS IS BEHAVING
HIMSELF. DON'T FORGET HIS CHICKEN NEEDS
TO BE **LIGHTLY** FRIED. NOT TOO MUCH BUTTER.

The second read:

To: NEW SCOTLAND YARD, THAMES
EMBANKMENT
DEAR INSPECTOR LOVELACE,
I NEED YOUR URGENT HELP! CAN YOU
CALL ON A FIRM OF SOLICITORS FOR ME?
(PRING & PROUDFOOT ON BEDFORD ROW.)
CAN YOU FORCE THEM (WITH A WARRANT
IF NECESSARY) TO TELL YOU IF THE WILL OF
ALARIC BOYNTON-DALE HAS BEEN CHANGED

RECENTLY? AND WHERE IS IT?

I HAVE TRIED ASKING THESE QUESTIONS MYSELF (AND SO HAS HIS SISTER) BUT THEY WILL NOT SQUEAL ON ACCOUNT OF 'CLIENT CONFIDENTIALITY' OR SOME SUCH PIFFLE.

TELEGRAM ME HERE (POST OFFICE, STOWE-ON-THE-MIDDLE-WOLD), TOMORROW IF POSS. V. IMPORTANT!

THANKS. I OWE YOU BIG TIME.

BEST,

POSIE.

Having paid up, she made a zipping motion across her lips and pushed a seriously hefty tip across to the Postmistress, who was eyeing her with barely disguised wide-eyed wonder, no doubt at the use of the New Scotland Yard address. Satisfied that she had bought the woman's silence, Posie left.

The early evening heat continued undaunted outside and Posie walked along the main street of Stowe-on-the-Middle-Wold unhurriedly, digesting all that she saw. It was one of those villages with a tendency to length rather than breadth, its houses and shops straddling the fast-flowing river which was its main and most glorious feature.

Posie walked in the opposite direction from Stowe church, whose clock was just chiming six, and she wandered on past a full quota of village shops, all now closing up for the day. She was in no hurry to return to the poisonous atmosphere at Boynton Hall and she dawdled on a small wooden bridge, lazily watching a family of ducks crossing the river, feeling the still-boisterous sun on her face. The village was tranquil and typically English, and Posie was horribly aware that she should have been savouring every minute of the change of air, the contrast to London. And yet she found herself longing unaccountably for the dry grey grit of the busy London pavements, the sticky pollen of the plane trees which covered your skin on damp summer days and most of all for the way you could lose yourself in the crowds, throwing on a cloak of anonymity at any given second. The very opposite of here, in fact.

She was suddenly aware of that familiar prickling feeling at her back. Someone was watching her.

Turning sharply she saw Codlington standing some distance away on the river bank, observing her keenly. He stood in in his shirt-sleeves, his servants livery of black tie and jacket now conspicuous by their very absence. Something glittered brightly at his wrists.

He approached the little bridge. Close up, he was a fair, narrow-faced young man with a mouthful of awful teeth, and Posie had to stop herself visibly shuddering in his presence, for there was something sinister about him. He had airs well above his status as a servant.

'You wiv' the police?' he blurted out bluntly in a thick east London accent. There were no social niceties employed and Posie was almost speechless at his rudeness.

'Why on earth would you think that?'

'You're not the only one who can give that Postmistress a fat tip. I asked her who you was telegramming and she showed me where they was bein' sent. I saw one was for Scotland Yard. She wouldn't show me any more though. I reckon she thought you was from the police yourself. Put the wind up her nicely, you did.'

Ah, Posie thought, *so this was it; he was scared.* But of what exactly? She stared at him with real interest now. He looked slightly uncomfortable and wiped his brow. There it was again – that glitter at his wrists – cufflinks! Fancy ones, too.

Posie could see even from this distance that the cufflinks were something a servant could only aspire to in his wildest dreams. But if they were stolen goods why on earth was Codlington being so brazen and wearing the wretched things out in public for all the world to see?

'They're very smart cufflinks,' Posie said carefully. '*Real* by the look of things, too. Here, let me see.'

Codlington's face darkened in a cloud of anger but

he stretched out a wrist for a closer inspection, like an obedient child. Sure enough the cufflinks were gold, with a tiny twinkling ruby set in a star-shaped mount. The initials 'B-D' were carefully inscribed on the cufflinks.

'Where are these from? Have you stolen them from Lord Roderick? Is that why you're worried I'm from the police?'

Codlington said nothing in response. But Posie persisted. 'Did Alaric notice you were taking things from his brother and threaten to report you and dismiss you? Did you think you'd get your own back and get your London pals to smash up his plane and then burn his beehives when the first plan failed? Because that's not just criminal damage, you know. It's an attempt at endangering life. Manslaughter, I'd say.'

Codlington's surly face turned from blackest anger to palest white in a second. He seemed to stagger under the weight of Posie's words. All the bluster had gone out of him. But he knew *something*, Posie was sure of it.

'Do you know what's happened to Alaric?' Posie snapped, taking advantage of his silence.

'I ain't got a bleedin' clue wot you're on about,' the man said at last. 'I've no idea where Alaric Boynton-Dale has got to. Why should I? It's his bruvver, Master Roderick, that I look after, not Alaric.'

'I'm not from the police, but I'm just a phone call away from one of the best Inspectors at Scotland Yard. So be careful how you reply to my next question. Do you deny stealing the cufflinks?'

'Yes,' he scowled, but there was still fear etched across his face.

'I do deny stealin' them, and Alaric's never accused me of stealin' anything! What you on about, lady? I'm not some petty thief! If you *must* know, he discovered I was placin' bets for Master Roderick on the nags and hounds, and he asked me to stop it right away. Maybe in his book that was the same thing as stealin' but it ain't in mine: I was simply takin' instructions from my Master. Plain and simple.'

'So there was no mention of Alaric dismissing you without a reference?'

Codlington shook his head, a look of smug satisfaction creeping over his face.

'Not on your life! Besides, there ain't no-one else who can handle Master Roderick like I can when he's had a skinful up in London,' he boasted. 'I've covered his back more than a hundred times, kept him out of trouble. For every newspaper photo you see, there are twenty I've managed to prevent from being published. I'm his wingman. Why would Alaric get rid of me? Anyway, it ain't in his power to do so! He ain't the Lord of the Manor here anymore. He gave that up! Master Roderick is!'

She had to admit that Codlington's explanation seemed to make sense, surprisingly.

'So what about those?' Posie said, pointing at the cufflinks, trying not to let her confusion show. 'Where are *they* from then?'

Codlington drew himself up to his full height, and looked for all the world as if he were looking down his nose at Posie. The dratted cheek of the fellow!

'I can't tell you,' he replied infuriatingly. 'But I'll tell you somethin' for nuffin'. I ain't never stolen nuffin' in my life! Now good-day to you, lady.'

Posie watched the strange Valet in disbelief as he swung proudly away along the river in the direction of Boynton Hall. Posie could quite believe he made a very good servant, *if* he was telling the truth about not stealing. He was exceedingly loyal and seemed to live by some sort of warped code of honour.

But something was not quite right in his story, and Posie couldn't put her finger on it.

****

58

Five

Dinner was served in the Great Hall at eight o'clock. There had been no mention of any drinks beforehand, as was the usual custom in English country houses, and Posie could only assume that this was a further show of rudeness which Roderick and Eve Boynton-Dale seemed determined to present her with.

Well, she wouldn't be hanging around any longer than was strictly necessary, Posie thought to herself grimly, but it wouldn't do to let the family know that just yet. Let them stew in their own inhospitable juices and squirm in discomfort at the presence of a 'spy' in their midst for as long as possible.

She entered the Great Hall on the stroke of eight, and saw that she was the last to arrive.

'Good evening!' she trilled cheerfully. There were six of them for dinner in all: Roderick, Eve, Mr Burns, Lady Violet and Dame Ianthe Flowers.

The room was large and high-ceilinged, decorated in a faded flowery crimson style from the turn of the century, but despite the huge open windows, the heat inside was cloying. The room felt inappropriate for the hot summer's night, and the candles and shabby silk draperies which were reflected a thousand times over in the huge crystal chandeliers were like something from a Christmas scene. Lady Violet, wearing the same clothes as earlier, flashed Posie a weak welcoming smile, but lowered her eyes immediately as if she could not engage in small-talk. Posie was puzzled: dinner was obviously going to be a strained affair.

Mr Burns nodded pleasantly, but Roderick and Eve did not so much as raise an eyebrow or a glass in Posie's direction, their aim was obviously to simply pretend she wasn't there. The only really nice surprise of the evening was Dame Ianthe, the famous author, who Posie found herself sitting next to.

'Can you forgive me?' Ianthe smiled, extending a hand glittering with rings. 'I couldn't meet you at tea earlier. I had one of my "heads" and I took to my bed. It must be this infernal heat. But I'm much better now, thank goodness!'

Ianthe started to eat her soup lustily. A button-nosed, fair-haired woman in her early forties, Ianthe was naturally bubbly and vivacious in manner. Her eyes, not unattractive, were the colour of cornflowers. She grinned impishly:

'I'm so very pleased to meet you! You might provide me with some inspiration for a little run of books I'm planning! I'm also told you are here to track down Alaric? How thrilling! He is our very own spectre at the feast! The ghost whose presence can be felt everywhere!'

At the mention of Alaric's name used in such a casual, carefree manner everyone around the table seemed to visibly freeze, and five pairs of eyes, Posie's included, looked at Ianthe aghast.

Five spoons of lobster bisque remained frozen mid-air somewhere between mouth and bowl. Posie smiled and tried not to look shocked; she had expected to meet a woman in the throes of an unrequited passion, a woman whose bitterness at having been passed over by Alaric had caused her to inflict real hurt by sending that fateful telegram to Major Marchpane. But perhaps Ianthe was a good actress as well as a good writer?

Ianthe was keen to speak about the possible series of novels which she was planning: these would apparently feature a female sleuth as the lead character, with the love interest being a glamourous young Police Inspector at Scotland Yard. Posie laughed uncontrollably at this, for apart from dear Inspector Lovelace, who Posie thought of as a brother really, she couldn't think of anything *less* likely. She described in detail some of the least romantic specimens she had come across in her dealings at the Yard, although in truth she was mainly thinking of Inspector Oats, whose resemblance to a trout was most striking.

Ianthe Flowers proved both a good listener and a good talker, which was just as well, as the other four at the table said not one word during the three further courses which followed the soup. Posie noticed how Lady Violet pushed the food around her plate in a lacklustre way, like a scolded child. Perhaps she had been told off by Roderick for her bossy conduct at the tea-party and had been told to take more of a back-seat this evening? But if that was the case why on earth wasn't Eve stepping up and 'running' the dinner instead? It was perhaps the strangest dinner Posie had ever attended.

The climax to the horrible evening came very quickly after dinner, at coffee. It was served in the Library. Perhaps because of the small size of the dinner party, or the fact that there were only two men present and neither of them liked each other very much, conventional form which saw men and women peeling off to separate rooms did not apply here. Instead, the group stood awkwardly together, smoking and sipping coffee by the French windows. It was still very hot, and the light breeze blowing in from outside was very welcome. The lights blazed out from the house, casting a cosy glow a few feet over the terrace and gardens below.

'What's the matter?' said Mr Burns loudly and impatiently to Roderick and Eve, who were smoking together in silence. 'Cat got your tongues?'

Posie purposely withdrew a little and busied herself in studying a studio portrait of Alaric in a silver picture frame which was propped up on the fireplace. Ianthe had been right: Alaric was present somehow by his very absence. She wanted desperately to get out into the fresh air and she looked out at the terrace longingly.

Mr Burns suddenly shouted at Eve, goaded into fury, his anger filling the room:

'I sure didn't bring you up to show such a level of discourtesy to your dinner guests, little lady, and that includes *me*, by the way. What a darned uncomfortable evening! And all this talk of Alaric's Will earlier, it's got me thinking. Based on this evening's little performance, I've decided that I've given you two quite enough of my time and money. I'm not giving you another penny. Not just now, *ever*. I'm cutting you out of my Will, Eve. And before you think of murdering me, like you may have done to Alaric, don't bother. First thing tomorrow morning I'm leaving. I'm out of here. I never want to see you again.'

In a split-second Roderick and Eve had almost thrown themselves at Mr Burns, their coffees and cigarettes abandoned. Their attempts to waylay him and plead with him were almost comical to watch. The three were arguing frantically together, swarming over each other in a mixture of anger and disbelief.

Lady Violet, Posie and Ianthe Flowers stood uncomfortably together at the fireplace. 'You'll see, there'll be a body in the Library tomorrow!' joked Ianthe comically. 'Shall we place bets on which of them will finish Mr Burns off first, and with what? I say Lady Eve, with a poker!'

'It's not funny, Ianthe!' snapped Lady Violet.

'Don't joke about murder. My God, you've got murder on the brain! For all we know Alaric may be dead and buried and yet we're standing here talking about murder as if it were a game! Even Mr Burns thinks Alaric's dead… You heard him just now!'

'I'm so sorry, my dear,' mumbled Ianthe. 'It's an occupational hazard of being a crime writer. Of course I'm worried sick about dear Alaric.'

Violet turned sharply. 'Have *you* made any progress yet, Posie? Has anything occurred to you at all since you've been here?'

Posie took an intake of breath at this surprisingly blunt question: she felt like a child being examined on her times-tables in front of a class of fellow pupils. What a very strange girl Lady Violet was! She seemed very out of sorts.

'Early days yet, but I've one or two ideas, Lady Violet. I'd like to show you something later, if I may? It might be a clue. It's up in my room. I didn't want to bring it down with me.'

'Of course.'

Lady Violet crossed the room to the sideboard, splashing a generous measure of whisky from a decanter there into the dregs of her coffee, which she downed in one go. She began what looked like a heated conversation with Jenks the Butler.

To her surprise, Ianthe grabbed at Posie's sleeve, her blue eyes suddenly wide and insistent. Her manner was completely changed. Posie had a horrible feeling she was about to be warned that *bad things* were happening, yet again.

'I say,' Ianthe whispered. 'Now that I've got you alone and no-one else can hear us I need to tell you something. I think it's important. I trust you.'

'Is it about Alaric?' Posie whispered encouragingly.

'In a way, yes. But not entirely.' Ianthe sounded impatient.

'You loved him, didn't you?' Posie said quietly, trying to sound sympathetic. 'Romantically, I mean?'

She was rewarded by seeing a flush of red rise up into Ianthe's face, spreading across her freckles and the snub nose.

'Funny you should say that! I didn't realise anybody knew! How embarrassing! Especially as he's my second cousin! What must you think of me? I can't deny I was attracted to him when I first came to stay here some months ago. Who wouldn't be?' She was staring at the photo in its silver frame on the mantel. She tore her gaze away firmly.

'But I realised very quickly it was just a silly infatuation, a crush. It lasted all of a couple of days. Can you believe it? At my age! An old crock like me! No fool like an old fool, eh? It was clear that he was still in love with Cosima Catchpole, although by all accounts it was over. On her side, anyhow. But he still carried a torch for her. I'm not silly enough to chase a man who doesn't want me!'

'What? But I thought…'

Posie's words were drowned out by the ruckus of Mr Burns storming out of the French windows, leaving Roderick and Eve standing speechless on the threshold, staring out after him as if struck dumb. Lady Violet was doubling back towards the fireplace, the cut-glass decanter of whisky clutched tight in her hand, three tumblers balanced precariously in the crook of her arm. Lady Eve came over to the fireplace too, with Roderick hot on her heels.

'Look,' whispered Ianthe urgently, casting a nervous look around at the others. 'Walls have ears. Can you meet me tomorrow, early, before breakfast? In my room at around six-thirty? I'm next to you, along the corridor.'

Posie nodded, frowning. 'Of course. But why so wretchedly early?'

'Because *I'm* leaving here too tomorrow. I must get away as quickly as possible. I finished up my novel today and my agent, Bernie Sharp, is coming tomorrow morning at eight to collect both me and the manuscript. He's a funny fish but he's the best in town: always got a nose for what sells. He's always early too, bless him. He doesn't like to be kept waiting. He's taking me back to London. I must speak to you before then.'

'Did I hear you say you were leaving tomorrow, Ianthe?' asked Lady Eve, lighting up another pink cigarette. Violet was busy pouring generous measures of drink into the tumblers. She was slightly calmer now, the alcohol having taken the edge off her previous mood. She smiled over at Ianthe:

'So you've finished your novel at last? How exciting for you. What's it called?'

Ianthe laughed breezily, her cares of a minute ago seemingly set to one side. 'It's called *The Tomb of the Honey Bee*,' she said casually.

'It's a murder mystery, set in a stately home in the Cotswolds. Very much like here, in fact.' Ianthe threw Roderick and Eve a watchful look. Their faces drained of all colour.

'What a strange name for a book!' said Eve, recovering her poise. 'It sounds positively macabre. *I* for one won't be buying it, I'm afraid. I never liked murder mysteries. And certainly not one based on all of us!'

'Well, never mind, Lady Boynton. I'd like to thank you anyway for having me here to stay these last few months. It was absolutely invaluable to my research. I'd have loved to have thanked Alaric too, in person. Especially given what he taught me about bees and bee-keeping in such a short space of time. The main character in the book is based on him actually. Alaric was such a sport: letting me trail around after him for days on end to source my material.'

Ianthe took a glass of whisky and swilled it around carelessly. She seemed lost in another world. 'I hope Alaric gets to read the book,' Ianthe said, very softly.

'I dedicated it to him, incidentally.'

* * * *

Later, up in her room, Posie took a few moments of blessed peace and quiet to sit on her bed and reflect on the day. In truth, she felt stumped. Stumped and overwhelmed. Her famous gut instinct seemed to be distinctly off-radar and she had no sense as to which way she should be turning next. It was all so very difficult: she was looking for a murderer without knowing if there had been a murder, and the suspects so far had all come to nothing.

Everything was topsy-turvy.

Posie held Alaric's bee coin in her hands, turning it over and over. She was putting a great deal of faith in it, she knew. Would Binkie Dodds, fellow of the Royal Numismatic Society and old school friend of her dead brother, Richard, *really* be able to shed any light on what the bee coin might mean?

'Come in,' Posie said, coming out of her cloud of worry at the sound of a soft knock at her door.

Lady Violet entered and came across the room, a worried smile playing on her lips. She threw herself into a wicker chair near the writing desk.

'I say,' said Posie carefully, 'are you quite all right, Lady Violet? You seem preoccupied, if you don't mind my saying so. I hope I'm not stepping out of turn but there was a definite atmosphere at dinner. I know that Alaric going missing isn't easy for anybody, but I have the definite feeling that my presence here is resented.'

Lady Violet shook her head and exhaled deeply. 'Take no notice. There's always an atmosphere in this house. Eve wants to act as if she were born to run the Manor, but she hasn't a clue how to run the place, or even how to manage the servants. I've known the house and staff all my life, so I do it: they respect me. But sometimes I guess I step over the line, then Eve sulks and Roderick feels as if he has to pull rank and shout at me. We argued before dinner about it. I'd leave if I could but where would I go? I don't even have a tiny flat for myself in London!'

Posie remembered the glamourous magazine article about Lady Violet from earlier, her hopes of setting up a chain of tea-shops, her supreme talent for baking. Those dreams seemed very remote now somehow. She found herself feeling distinctly sorry for the girl. What sort of aristocrat couldn't even dress up in nice clothes for dinner?

Posie passed the bee coin across to Lady Violet. 'Know anything about this?'

'This was Al's,' the girl said, a panicky note creeping into her voice. 'Where did you find it?'

'It was in the annexe,' Posie said quickly. She felt a need to protect Major Marchpane's confidence.

'Do you know anything about it, Lady Violet? What it means? What those words mean on the back, for instance?'

Violet turned the coin, then shook her head miserably. She passed it back, looking worried. 'I've no idea,' she said, looking like she was on the verge of tears. 'I never was much good at clever things. Alaric was the boffin of the family. Are they Latin words? Do you think they're important?'

Posie patted the girl on the arm. 'Don't worry, I'll find out. I have a friend in London, a coin expert in fact, who can help me. I'm going to meet him on Friday. I think this coin might be important.'

'So you're going? You're leaving? I would have thought you needed more time *here*?' Lady Violet sounded almost desperate, a note of rising panic in her voice.

'Yes, of course I'm leaving,' Posie said kindly. 'But I'll still be here for the whole day tomorrow.'

'Do you want me to come back to London with you? To meet the coin expert?'

Posie smiled. 'I don't think that's necessary, but I'll let you know what I find out. I'll update you all the way along.'

Just before getting into bed, still clutching the bee coin, Posie was staring absent-mindedly out of the window at the dark lawn under its cover of a patchy moon, when she was startled to see a loping black shadow crossing the grass, ringing around the formal gardens and then moving away again in the direction of the burnt flower fields and towards Alaric's annexe.

Then she heard a lonely, heart-rending noise. A plaintive howling, over and over again. It was Bikram the dog, mourning his missing master.

Ironic, Posie knew, but in that moment she realised that the one soul who could probably tell her just what had *really* happened to Alaric Boynton-Dale was not a human. *If only Bikram could talk*, she thought to herself grimly before turning out the light.

That would make her job a whole lot easier.

****

Six

It was strange, Posie thought later, the odd things you noticed at a time of real crisis. She said as much to Inspector Lovelace, when he was taking her formal statement in Lord Roderick's study the very next day.

Shortly before six-thirty in the morning, bleary-eyed and hardly at her best, she had knocked on Ianthe's bedroom door. The dawn had been spectacular, and it was almost as bright as day outside. On the corridor and in the very depths of the house all was still. The heavy oak door to Ianthe's room was slightly ajar, and Posie pushed it wider, calling softly so as not to wake anyone else who might still be sleeping nearby.

'Ianthe? Are you here?'

She had stepped tentatively inside. The curtains were flung wide open and the room was filled with golden morning light. The room was a mirror-image to her own, and seemed strangely familiar as a result.

But the details were all different, and they would remain etched in her mind for hours, if not for days afterwards: a glass bowl of sweet peas, just past their best, placed on the wash-stand, filling the room with scent; a pile of monogrammed Louis Vuitton suitcases stacked ready to be collected; a sleek black Underwood Number 5 typewriter sitting in its case on the desk, next to a neatly stacked typewritten manuscript.

It was the room of a guest at the very end of her stay.

And then Posie had caught sight of Ianthe, still in bed, tucked neatly under the red silk coverlet, a hand placed under her tousled fair head. She had known immediately something was wrong.

Pulse racing, she darted across the room and shook Ianthe vigorously by the shoulders. But Posie was aware that her every movement was futile. Ianthe was dead, her face grey and pallid, a faint black flush spreading underneath the freckles.

Posie shuddered in the rising heat.

Although not a doctor, Posie's old medical knowledge kicked in from her time on the ambulances, and she estimated that Ianthe had been dead already for several hours, judging by the state of rigor mortis. Heart hammering, Posie sunk down on a chair next to the bed, trying to think clearly while holding back a wave of panic and fear. Her gut feeling was that this was murder, pure and simple, and that Ianthe had been silenced deliberately. What was it that Ianthe had wanted to tell Posie which was so important that it had cost her her life?

Or could this just be a terrible coincidence? Ianthe's grey face was calm; she looked like she was sleeping. There was certainly no sign of a struggle, or of a shot or a stab-wound. Posie's eyes scanned the details nearby: an alarm clock, its alarm set efficiently for six-fifteen; a glass tumbler with an inch or so of water left in it; a small golden tin filled with white powder – a sleeping draught perhaps? Nothing out of the ordinary.

But the niggling doubt wouldn't go away. She felt out of her depth. In fact, what was needed here was the calm authority of Inspector Lovelace.

Fleeing the room, Posie threw herself down the dark wooden staircase as fast as she could and down into the carpeted empty entrance hall downstairs. She rang the golden dinner gong which hung near the door to the Great Hall. Within moments Jenks the Butler emerged. He looked supremely unruffled.

'Where is the telephone here?' said Posie as calmly as possible. 'This is an emergency!'

'An emergency? What, this early in the morning, Miss? Are you sure?'

'Of course I'm sure. Now WHERE is the telephone? And for goodness' sake send someone for the local doctor, even if it is too late. There's a dead body lying upstairs, and I'm quite willing to bet it's murder!'

* * * *

What followed was chaos. Posie would remember it later as a series of disjointed snapshots.

On being led to the telephone in Lord Roderick's dark, wood-panelled study, Posie had found it to be dead, its wires cut. Posie took matters into her own hands and started off for the village instead at a brisk half-run, intending to wake the Postmistress so she could use the telephone at the Post Office.

As she rounded the bend in the drive she was suddenly overtaken by Codlington, hurling himself flat out down the drive on a rickety black bike in a state of high excitement, calling out to her importantly that he had been tasked with fetching the local doctor and the local police.

And then she was overtaken again by a nervy Lady Violet at the wheel of her little two-seater, insisting on picking Posie up and giving her a lift to the village to save on time; an acceptance which Posie regretted almost immediately as Violet's driving was both shaky and erratic and the short journey was punctuated twice by Violet's urgent need to stop the car to vomit at the roadside, detaining Posie from reaching the Post Office as quickly as if she had gone on foot.

Posie only had one objective in mind – getting a message to Inspector Lovelace at Scotland Yard – he would come, she knew it. He wouldn't fail her. And he would be able to suss out if there was something fishy going on. She wished wholeheartedly that she had involved the Inspector from the start, that she had told him about the disappearance of Alaric Boynton-Dale. She should never have floated around conducting such a dangerous investigation on her own.

At last she managed to speak to the ever trusty Sergeant Rainbird, who could always be relied upon to be at his desk at Scotland Yard well before seven o'clock in the morning, and he assured her the Inspector would indeed help. Relieved, Posie and Lady Violet set off home again.

But on the way back to Boynton Hall the little two-seater had run into difficulties and Lady Violet had had to park up at a kerb, cursing shakily under her breath as black smoke poured in streams from the engine.

'Oh, dear!' Posie had murmured ineffectually, all the while wishing Lady Violet had never been good enough to offer her a lift in the first place. 'Can I help at all? I could run for someone from the village to tow the car to a garage?'

She had watched Lady Violet, still looking green about the gills and shocked, shake her head ruefully and climb out, hoisting the bonnet up and grabbing at a spanner.

'It's just the gasket,' Violet had muttered from beneath the sleek chrome of the hood. 'I'll get it fixed in two little winks… Just let it cool down first.'

And sure enough, after five minutes of prodding they were on their way again.

Back at Boynton Hall Posie found herself ushered into

the Library, together with Lady Violet. Jenks the Butler, unruffled as ever, pressed iced coffees into their hands and indicated towards the shabby sofas and the small coffee table where plates of sweet biscuits had been set out. Posie picked up a plate and began munching through the biscuits methodically.

The Library was quite full of people, but horribly silent. Someone had obviously woken the entire household and informed them of Ianthe's sudden death, and the same cast of characters as were at dinner the previous evening were now gathered together again, gawping on in a baffled silence, uniformly looking as if they had just shoved their clothes on in any old fashion. In fact, Lady Eve Boynton was still wearing her satin dressing gown, its bright ruby red colour draining any natural colour from her unmade face, making her appear positively ghost-like.

The small team of servants were ranged nervously along a far wall, darting guarded looks of fear at each other. Codlington was there too, but, as ever, he was on the periphery of both groups, lurking in a corner, muttering with Lord Roderick.

A nervy young police Constable was standing guard near the French windows, sipping an iced coffee through a paper straw, obviously waiting for a higher-ranking replacement to arrive. He kept checking his wristwatch. It was now a quarter to eight.

'Say, are you keeping us here indefinitely?' drawled Lady Eve nastily to the Constable. 'Are we all under arrest?'

'Eve!' shouted her father, making the whole room jump. 'Have some darned manners. A woman is lying dead upstairs! It's the least we can do in the circumstances to sit and wait awhile.'

Fortunately any further argument was stopped in its tracks by the arrival of two middle-aged men, both of whom obviously fancied themselves as important in their own ways. One introduced himself as Sergeant Plummer, dismissing his lowly coffee-drinking Constable and taking his place over at the French windows, and the other introduced himself as Dr Greaves, the local doctor.

Dr Greaves helped himself to some biscuits, fanned himself with the salmon-coloured death certificate he was clutching and then addressed the room:

'Natural death, I'm pleased to report.'

Posie stared at the doctor in amazement. Could it be that Ianthe had really just died of natural causes? And if so, what wretchedly unlucky timing! And now she had insisted on dragging Inspector Lovelace and his team up here from London on a fool's errand, for nothing. Posie groaned softly, imagining the Inspector's displeasure.

'Sad thing. Seems Dame Ianthe must have had a very weak heart. She died in her sleep, probably from a heart attack. Untimely. I'll be submitting this to the Coroner of course, but there should be no need for a Public Inquiry.'

'So,' said Sergeant Plummer, clearing his throat importantly. 'I can't see as keeping you good people here tethered together will help anyone. No need to detain you. No funny business at all. Apologies for the wait. I'll be sending the Funeral Director around shortly to sort things out upstairs, and that will be an end to it.'

Just then an unfamiliar, very small bald little man with a marked and unfortunate resemblance to a rat swung through the Library door with a force which quite belied his tiny stature.

'NO! That will *not* be an end to it! We have a problem on our hands here! A big problem!'

The man stared accusingly around the room, taking everyone in. He was immaculately dressed in an extremely loud purple striped suit which even Mr Burns would have thought twice before wearing. In his hands he was clutching a thick wad of cream papers. His eyes bulged with rage. Everyone stared at him in a kind of fascinated horror.

'Who the very devil are *you*?' Lord Roderick asked petulantly, rising to his feet. 'This isn't a ruddy hotel, you know. This is a private residence! You can't just come wandering in here.'

Posie got to her feet and smiled at the ratty little man as best she could in welcome, as obviously no-one else was up to the job.

'You're Mr Bernie Sharp, aren't you? Dame Ianthe's literary agent? She told me all about you. I'm Miss Parker, a guest in this house. I'm guessing the police and the doctor have kept you up to date with the sad news? I'm so very, very sorry about Ianthe. What a shock for you, and what a tragedy.'

Mr Sharp looked at Posie with a quick look of barely-concealed distrust before turning to the doctor:

'I heard you, just now, doctor, telling everyone that this was a natural death. But I'm telling you Ianthe was as strong as an ox; no weak heart about *her*! Tough as old boots, she was. And yes, Miss Parker, I'll admit this is a HUGE shock to me! I turned up ten minutes ago and went upstairs and found Ianthe lying in bed as dead as a doornail and all manner of people flying around her room filling in paperwork!'

He gave the doctor and the policeman a scathing look.

'But I'll tell you what's upsetting me more than her death. I came down here to pick up her new bestseller – the book which was going to make both of us rich – and what do I find?'

The whole room gaped, incredulous.

'THE FINAL PAGE OF THE MANUSCRIPT HAS BEEN REMOVED! It's gone missing!'

'Gee, was it important?' said Mr Burns, genuinely interested.

'I'll say!' shouted Bernie Sharp at the top of his voice. 'It revealed who the murderer was! The whole book and my career are worthless without it! Pointless! I'd go as far as saying Ianthe was killed for it!'

There was silence. Puzzle pieces were coming together in her mind, but Posie kept her cool. Ianthe had said that the book was a murder mystery set in a Cotswold country house such as Boynton Hall, and that the main character had been based on Alaric. But what if she had known a great deal more?

Had she in fact known who it was who wanted to hurt Alaric? And was that real-life person revealed as the murderer on the final page of the 'fictional' novel?

Suddenly Bernie Sharp's protestations didn't seem quite so ridiculous or outlandish. Posie turned and addressed the room:

'I think there may well be something in what Mr Sharp says. It's just as well that I have called in one of the best Inspectors from Scotland Yard. He's on his way here now, together with his team.'

She watched with some pleasure as Sergeant Plummer turned puce.

'In fact, they should be here in about two hours' time, roads and traffic permitting. Hopefully they'll be able to make some sense out of all of this. Sergeant Plummer, if you'd be so good as to refrain from calling the Funeral Director. And Dr Greaves, perhaps you could hold fire on submitting that death certificate to the Coroner for a while. Inspector Lovelace will be bringing his own Home Office Pathologist with him, and he'll need access to the body in order to conduct his own investigation. And in the meantime, until they get here, I suggest that no-one should leave the house. No-one. Not even you, Mr Burns. I'm sorry, I know you were planning on leaving today. Could you delay?'

Mr Burns nodded instantly, puzzled shock showing clearly on his face. 'Of course, Miss Parker. Only too willing to help.'

Lord Roderick was looking at Posie with real hatred and Lady Eve had started shouting uncontrollably at the top of her voice, a stream of bile all seemingly directed at Lady Violet, as if the whole sorry mess were somehow her fault.

'See what you've gone and done, you little minx? Bringing interfering busybodies into the house! Now it seems we've got a proper murder on our hands! As if we don't have enough on our plate!'

But Lady Violet gave no indication of having heard her sister-in-law. Posie sat down again on the sofa and tried to put her arm around the girl, who was rocking to and fro, shaken by uncontrollable sobbing, jolted out of any show of decorum. Posie had been surprised earlier by Violet's attacks of nausea in the car, but she was more surprised by this: Violet was a mess. A far, far cry from the cool, collected girl who had walked into the Grape Street Bureau only a couple of days before. Had Ianthe's death tipped her over the edge?

Posie looked around at the people in the room, feeling uncomfortable. Well, now there *had* been a murder, in all probability. At least now there was a body and evidence to investigate, even though Alaric Boynton-Dale, her main focus, was still missing.

She remembered with a sharp shivery chill Ianthe's light-hearted joke of the previous evening about the possible murdering of Mr Burns for his money. But it had turned out that it was Ianthe herself who had possessed something far more precious than a million Texan dollars.

What had been on that final page of the novel? And *what* was it that she had wanted to tell Posie?

The answer was locked somewhere here in the Library amongst these people. But where?

* * * *

Seven

Tea and a sandwich brunch had been served in the Library, another dismal affair, and no-one apart from the policemen had had any appetite. The family and servants had taken to their rooms, having all now been formally questioned.

The strange languid silence which Posie had felt in the house yesterday was back again, punctured only by the heavy footsteps of policemen's hobnailed boots tracking up and down the ancient wooden staircase, the occasional ringing of the now-repaired telephone and the opening and closing of the door to Lord Roderick's study, where Inspector Richard Lovelace, maverick detective of Scotland Yard, had set up an impromptu headquarters, together with his trusty crack-team of Sergeants Binny and Rainbird.

The interviews and inspection of Ianthe's room and body had all now been concluded and Inspector Lovelace was finalising details with typical efficiency.

Posie sat on a hard chair next to the sash-window in the study. She had given her formal statement about finding Ianthe's body much earlier and filled Inspector Lovelace in on the background as to why she was staying at Boynton Hall. She had given him all the details as to the catastrophic events leading up to the disappearance of Alaric Boynton-Dale and the Inspector had simply nodded, making his usual careful list of action-points. He hadn't asked any questions about Alaric at all. Indeed, the explorer seemed a very distant and unimportant concern right now, even in Posie's own mind.

Posie had been asked to come in for an update. So far she had not been asked for her opinion on anything. So she sat quietly, as unobtrusively as possible, which was hard, as she was dying to know what was going on.

It was airless in the room and Posie would dearly have loved to open the sash-window, but she had been ordered not to do any such thing. She gazed out as a black police van drew up next to the two gleaming police cars already stationed outside, and men in dark suits emerged. Minutes later they were seen traipsing back, carrying a black-shrouded stretcher between them, accompanied by a jittery Bernie Sharp and a resigned-looking Sergeant Plummer.

'She's off then,' Posie announced to no-one in particular. 'Ianthe, I mean. Poor love.'

But no-one heard her. Inspector Lovelace and his Sergeants were locked in a hushed conversation with the Police Pathologist, Dr Poots, whom Posie had met once before.

Mr Maguire, the senior Forensics Officer from Scotland Yard, was sitting just along from Posie on another hard wooden seat, filling in slips of paper with obvious enjoyment and placing several different objects into clear cellophane bags marked 'EXHIBIT'. She watched now as he wrapped up a lipstick and an old powder compact, and then he made a big show of wrapping up Ianthe's sleek black Underwood typewriter in tissue and protective layers before putting it into a cellophane bag. Maguire was a man who relished the small and varied minutiae of his job and he was obviously savouring the celebrity connection in this case.

He handed over one of the cellophane bags to Dr Poots at his request, giving his colleague a knowing nod, and

Posie saw something golden shining within it, glinting in a ray of reflected sunlight. It was the small tin of sleeping powder that she had first observed this morning on Ianthe's bedside cabinet.

Dr Poots shook it with a meaningful raise of the eyebrow towards Inspector Lovelace and put it into his own heavy metal suitcase which seemed to be filled with glass jars of strange-coloured liquids and various chemical paraphernalia.

Dr Poots and Mr Maguire had obviously got 'enough' of whatever it was they were after, and they smiled all around before leaving the room, bowing out unobtrusively and taking the precious cellophane EXHIBIT bags and the heavy metal suitcase with them. From the window Posie craned her neck and watched them get into the back of one of the police cars, their heads bent together in earnest discussion.

When she turned back into the room she saw that the Inspector and his Sergeants had packed their papers together, and were also now ready to leave. They were regarding her with a look she interpreted as a mixture somewhere between 'serious concern' and a mild amusement that she was up to her old tricks again.

'You were right to call us in, Posie,' said Inspector Lovelace appreciatively but seriously.

'So you *do* suspect foul play?'

The Inspector nodded. 'Poots can't be one hundred per cent sure until he's got the body back to the lab in London and done an autopsy, but he's ninety-nine per cent sure she was given a huge overdose of a sleeping draught. Veronal, to be precise. That gold tin was full of it, and the glass by the bed contained some dried up grains at the bottom. It has a particular smell apparently, like very bitter almonds. Very similar to powdered cyanide. Acts like cyanide, too.'

'But some would say that the presence of veronal could indicate this was a suicide, or an accidental overdose?' Posie said provocatively.

Sergeant Rainbird flicked through his police report. 'No. No way. There is evidence, which needs to be confirmed of course, that *in addition* to having given her the sleeping draught, which she wouldn't have noticed by the way, as veronal is flavourless and colourless, Dame Flower's killer made double sure she was dead by using a pillow to suffocate her when she was already drowsy.'

'That accounts for the black flush on the face,' cut in Sergeant Binny.

'And we think the killer placed the gold tin of sleeping powder next to the bed as a nice little finishing touch, just for show. Bernie Sharp insists that Ianthe Flowers never took sleeping powders in her life; slept like a baby apparently. And he swore he'd never seen that gold tin before, either. We'll fingerprint it, of course, but if the killer is as clever as he seems to be, chances are it's clean as a whistle. So, even before the autopsy, the hard evidence and the fact that this crucial page from her new book has gone missing leads us to think that this is murder.'

Inspector Lovelace rubbed his stubbly ginger chin distractedly. 'The killer was obviously hoping that the local country doctor and the equally dim-witted local policeman would come to exactly the conclusion they reached: that this was a natural death, with no reason to investigate further. What a pair of noddles! The killer obviously hadn't reckoned with you, Posie, and your bloodhound's nose for sniffing out trouble.'

'What I don't understand,' interjected Sergeant Rainbird, 'is *why* if the killer thought everyone would assume it was a natural death, he did such a stupid thing as to remove the final page of the manuscript? It's damning – it makes the death look instantly suspicious – it makes it look as if the manuscript contained a secret which couldn't be allowed to leak out.'

'That's exactly what it probably *did* contain,' said Posie, nodding.

'Well, why didn't the killer just leave the final page where it was, or else remove the *whole* manuscript?' said Sergeant Rainbird in exasperation. 'Surely the killer should have realised that the literary agent, Bernie Sharp, would have checked the manuscript within an inch of its life! Mr Sharp told us that was the first thing he did here following finding out that Dame Flowers was dead.'

Posie wrinkled her nose, thinking hard.

'What you say is absolutely right, Sergeant, but only if the killer *knew* that Bernie Sharp was coming here today. If Mr Sharp hadn't turned up, no-one would have thought to check the manuscript for any missing pages. Why would they? It would have been the last thing on people's minds. Everyone would have assumed the book was intact, and in a few weeks' time when the dust had settled it would have been posted back to Ianthe's solicitor or agent, and if any pages were *then* noticed to be missing it would have been easy enough to blame the post, or the servants who had packed up the bags. As far as I know, Bernie Sharp's appearance here this morning was a shock to everyone in the house. In fact, I think Dame Ianthe only told *me* that Bernie Sharp was coming to pick her up today. She told me last night in the Library, at the same time as she told me she had something important to tell me. I think she knew something about Alaric's disappearance.'

'And you're sure no-one else overheard her talking about Bernie Sharp coming down here?'

'No. But Ianthe did tell the whole room she was leaving today and she thanked people for their 'hospitality'. So everyone in the house knew she was going.'

'And one of those people realised that she had to be silenced,' said Sergeant Binny with a smidgen of ghoulish relish.

'Looks like it,' said the Inspector, fiddling with his tight starched collar which was growing limp with sweat and damp. The oppressive heat, nearly as bad as in London, was making him uncomfortable and he was longing to be away; a town boy at heart, his house with its sliver of shady garden in Clapham was as close as he came to country living.

'Let's go,' he said, standing up and picking up his brown attaché case. 'I think we've enough evidence gathered and statements taken to get somewhere with this. No point lurking around here any longer. Let's be getting on. Posie, go and grab your bags. There's room in our car if Binny rides up front with the driver.'

'Sorry?' said Posie, flummoxed for a second. 'Ah! Thank you, but no. I'm coming back tomorrow on the first train to Paddington. I'd like to stay here and lend my support. Lady Violet seems to have taken this badly. And she seems to have few enough friends in this place as it is. Also, I'd like to interview one more person about Alaric's disappearance.'

She watched as all three policemen gave each other incredulous looks and Inspector Lovelace's rugged, handsome face took on even more of a red tone than could be strictly attributed to the heat.

'You must be joking!' he roared. 'There's no way I'm leaving you here! I'll arrest you if I have to, Posie, in order to keep you safe! Don't you realise that we're dealing with a killer who is capable of playing the long game? This murder isn't a single one-off event, you know. It's part and parcel of this whole other business you're up here investigating. If the killer has already disposed of one person to keep things quiet, he'll do so again. Only this time it will be you, Posie. You're not safe here.'

'So you *do* think Alaric's disappearance and the string of events leading up to it are suspicious?' she said, relieved. She had begun to think herself slightly paranoid of late.

Lovelace nodded.

'Of course! Just because Oats dismissed this out of hand when Lady Violet reported the disappearance doesn't mean it's not important. I'll apologise to Lady Violet myself in a minute personally, reassure her we'll look into it. I understand the family don't want policemen and the press creeping around the place, but frankly it's too late for that now. Dame Flower's death will be all over the papers before we've had time to blink! She was very famous in her own right. The hacks will be clamouring at the gates here. I'm giving an order that no-one is to come in, and no-one is to go out: the whole household are under house arrest from now on. I'm instructing Sergeant Plummer to stay here with his men for the next few days, too. He might not be any good at detective work, but let's hope he can keep an eye on the house, ensure no-one leaves the place at least. Now, let's get a shuffle on.'

Just then there was a rap at the study door. Lady Violet poked her head around the door.

'Hullo,' she said nervously, looking around at the policemen. 'I just wondered if I could assist you in any way? Poor dear Ianthe. You know she was quite alone in the world? No real family to speak of…'

'Ah, Lady Violet, I was just saying I was coming to see you before we go,' said the Inspector with a bashful look on his face. Could it be that the Inspector was ever so slightly star-struck? Looking around, Posie almost chortled to herself as she saw how all three Scotland Yard policemen were gazing at the girl as if hypnotised. Having spent a good deal of time in her company of late, Posie realised that she had forgotten quite how beautiful Lady Violet really was, and how famous.

Posie listened with only half an ear as the Inspector laid out his plans for the next few days to keep the Boynton-Dale family and household safe. But how safe could they really be with a killer in their midst? And anyhow, the Inspector's plans for their 'safety' were as much about imprisoning them all here in the house as anything else.

When the Inspector had finished his speech he opened his attaché case and Posie was startled to see him bring out the same magazine which Posie had bought yesterday at Oxford train station. Almost shyly, the Inspector passed *The Lady* across to Lady Violet.

'My wife Molly is a big fan of your cookery articles, my Lady,' he said with a faint flush of embarrassment. 'Your honey cake has really made her the talk of our street! She won't forgive me if you don't sign this for me. I wonder – would you oblige?'

Almost laughing, Lady Violet inked her name across the glossy front page. She turned to Posie with a look of real regret.

'So you're off too?'

Posie nodded. 'But I won't stop searching for the truth, Lady Violet. I promise you. The first news I have of Alaric, or of anything at all in fact, I'll telegram you.'

* * * *

Posie was silent all the way down the drive, her carpet bag clutched precariously on her knees, her sweaty back pressed uncomfortably up against the hard leather seat. She felt relief to be leaving Boynton Hall but it was going to be a long and sticky three hours' drive back to London.

The police car passed a red-bricked and honeysuckle-covered Victorian house which Posie had not noticed properly before. It nestled in the shadow of an oak tree by the big iron gates. Posie read the sign, half-hidden in overgrowth: 'The Gatehouse'.

'Stop the car!' she shouted through the glass divide at the police driver. 'I've *got* to get out here. I promise I'll be quick, Inspector! I promise! This is the house of the person I wanted to interview. PLEASE! Please indulge me on this.'

Inspector Lovelace sighed and rolled his eyes. He

nodded at the driver who drew up on the grassy kerb.

'Ten minutes!' he said, patting his wristwatch and giving her a wry half-smile. 'No more.'

Posie hopped out and banged on the front door.

She heard a wretched howling coming from inside and then the door was opened by a housemaid in full uniform. On being ushered into a Drawing Room, she found Lady Cosima Catchpole reclining luxuriously on a floral sofa, a glass of white wine in one hand, a book in the other. Cosima was dressed in a Japanese silk kimono and Posie had no idea if it was a nightdress or perhaps some theatrical costume she had put on for the sheer fancy of it.

Bikram was sitting over in a corner, looking mournful and excluded. He let out another howl and made an odd chewing noise. Posie introduced herself hurriedly.

'Don't mind that bally dog,' Lady Cosima said with a glance of irritation over to the far corner, putting her book down and cracking its spine carelessly.

'He was Alaric's. I suppose you know? The dog doesn't seem to like me much, never did really. He tolerates Hugo, but hates me. He likes to annoy me by being sick on my nice Persian carpet. Wretched animal! But I've never really got on with dogs, especially not this one. I think they sense my fear. He's missing Alaric awfully, and Hugo has had to go out and leave him behind today, so he's feeling doubly deserted. But won't you sit down?'

Her manner was vague and off-hand, slightly annoyed at being disturbed. Posie came straight to the point:

'I appreciate we don't know each other, Lady Cosima. But I need your help. I have something here which belonged to Alaric, and whilst I know this must be a sensitive subject for you, I hope you may be able to shed some light on how I might be able to find him.'

She passed across the bee coin.

'Does this mean anything to you at all? I think it's important.'

Cosima held onto it and swigged her white wine down in one go, her flame-red hair swinging wildly into her face like uncoiled serpents.

Posie waited with bated breath. Cosima then told her the same thing Lord Roderick and Lady Violet had done: that it was a necklace which Alaric wore almost always, that it was almost unthinkable he would go anywhere without it.

'But do you know where it's from?' persisted Posie. 'Did *you* give it to Alaric, perhaps? Is the clue in its origins? A love-token, maybe? I know you were lovers…'

Cosima shook her head firmly, coldly. 'I can't help you, I'm afraid. Alaric and I *were* in love briefly, but I decided we had to part, and I don't regret that decision one jot: it was for the best. He loved me far more than I loved him. My love for Alaric was not strong enough to make it work in the long-term. I need my marriage with Hugo to work. Both Hugo and Alaric know the score on that point, and we are all fine with it. What is past is past. Over. *Fini*. I can't help you I'm afraid.'

Posie cursed silently: she felt like she was at a dead end. From outside came the BEEP! BEEP! of the police car horn. Her ten minutes was up.

'Thank you anyway,' she said politely, reaching out for the coin again.

'Wait! Just wait!' said Lady Cosima, her pupils dilated suddenly with more than just the effect of too much wine.

'Did you see the words on the back?'

Posie nodded, biting her lip. 'I don't understand them though. I thought they might be names?'

Cosima turned her enchanting green gaze on Posie for a minute, a flicker of recognition illuminating her eyes.

'I have no idea what "Serafina" is,' she said quickly. 'But I *do* know what "Hyblaea" is!'

'What? *What?*'

'Alaric spoke of it. I think he used to compare his honey

to it, said he was striving to make his better year upon year, like Hyblaean honey! It was a type of honey! A true honey! A mythical honey! It was known to be the best honey in the world.'

Posie stared, open-mouthed and uncomprehending. '*Where* was it?' she asked, trembling.

Cosima passed the coin back and sighed. Her whole body seemed to sag with the effort her revelation had cost her.

'Oh, good grief! I have no idea,' she said wearily, bored now. She flung an arm out theatrically, indicating the conversation was at an end.

'I don't know if it really exists. I don't even know if it was a *real* honey. Maybe Alaric told me, but in truth, I probably wasn't listening. Sometimes I just drifted off when he was talking. You know, you can only hear so much about ruddy honey. It's boring. Honey is honey. It's all the same to me.'

* * * *

Inspector Lovelace was slightly interested but not overly encouraging when Posie reported Lady Cosima's words back to him in the car. She showed him the bee coin but he didn't think it was much of a lead, and not worth pursuing.

'This however, *is*,' he declared. He brought out Posie's telegram to him from the previous day and Posie could see that he had filled the reverse side almost completely with his tiny neat handwriting.

'I was going to cable you this morning about the information I got from the solicitors' office about Alaric's Will,' he said, by way of explanation. 'But then I found circumstances had overtaken me and I was meeting you here in the Cotswolds anyway.'

'What did you find out? That was quick! I expected you to go to their office today.'

Inspector Lovelace shook his head. 'I popped around last night after work to Pring & Proudfoot. They work late, these lawyer fellows. I had a warrant with me, just in case, but old man Proudfoot was obliging enough without it.'

'And?'

'Curiouser and curiouser. Alaric *did* change his Will. In a mad hurry, apparently. About a month ago. Everything, including the end proceeds of a nice fat Trust, passes to his sister Violet on his death. He signed it in the office in front of the lawyers as his witnesses. But then he did something strange. He told old man Proudfoot that he was taking the new Will with him, to keep it safe.'

'Is that unusual?' Posie asked.

The Inspector nodded. 'Unusual and dangerous. Normally Wills are locked in the client strongrooms at the offices of Pring & Proudfoot. Old Proudfoot said he pleaded with Alaric to leave it behind with him; he knew Alaric led an "adventurous" life and he feared for the safety of the new paperwork.'

'Hmmm. What happens if Alaric dies and this new Will is found to be missing?'

'There's the rub!' said Inspector Lovelace, unhappily. 'And that's what has been causing poor old Proudfoot sleepless nights! If the new Will can't be found, the old Will steps in and replaces it. And that old Will is the exact *opposite* of what Alaric wanted to happen.'

'You mean everything, including the Trust money, goes to Roderick?'

'Yep,' said Lovelace, a glint in his eye. 'And therefore, if Lord Roderick knew that Alaric had changed his Will it would be worth him making sure that this new Will favouring Violet never came to light. That the old Will was used.'

Posie remembered the chaos in the annexe, the papers

thrown willy-nilly all over the place as if someone had frantically been rummaging there for a particular purpose.

'So at the moment Lord Roderick is the main suspect?'

Lovelace winked at Posie. 'I didn't say that,' he said. 'Good detective work is all about keeping an open mind.'

* * * *

Back in London, they dropped Posie off in Victoria. It was Thursday night, which was late-night shopping night in central London, and she was dangerously close to the Army & Navy Store. She felt in dire need of some retail therapy.

Somehow, by seven o'clock, Posie had emerged from the depths of the store, and she found herself tripping gaily along Victoria Street armed not just with her carpet bag and her overnighter, but weighed down by two carrier bags containing a smart cream linen trouser suit, a new pair of sunglasses, a new crimson lipstick and a bottle of expensive sun-tanning oil. As if she were going on holiday!

She also found herself (somewhat surprisingly) the proud new owner of a number of things she had no idea when she would ever use: a clever and expensive little sleeping-bag which packed down to the size of a small rucksack, a glossy Swiss army knife and some silk travelling scarves. It seemed to Posie that she had floated through the store in a subconscious daze, thinking more about the Boynton-Dales and their exciting lifestyles than about the realities of her own daily London life. But she clutched her new purchases with some degree of pride.

Standing at Victoria Station on the dirty hot tarmac, in two minds about whether or not to head home to her bedsit in Nightingale Mews, Posie found herself inexplicably turning on her heel and heading back towards the city, towards Bloomsbury and the Grape Street Bureau. The thought of her bedsit, so unhomely and unwelcoming, with Mrs Rapier, her old dragon of a landlady making her presence felt at every step, filled her with gloom; she longed to be back in the busy hustle of the city, and to see Mr Minks again after what seemed like an age. Uncuddly though he was, the cat would at least be pleased to see her in his own haughty way, which was more than could be said for Mrs Rapier. Besides, Posie now had her expensive little sleeping-bag to try out, and there *might* be news awaiting her at the office from Len, a letter or a telegram from France perhaps?

She hadn't spoken to Inspector Lovelace about Len at all in the car, despite the kind telegram he had sent her about Len's location the previous week. There had been too much going on with the Boynton-Dale case, of course. That, and she hadn't wanted to put the poor Inspector on the spot, especially if he knew more than he was letting on from his colleague Leferb.

As she passed a news-stand in Covent Garden Posie saw a few cheap paperback copies of Dame Ianthe Flowers' most recent novels for sale. She chose one at random and added it to her hoard of new purchases. It would occupy the evening ahead at any rate, and would help turn her mind from thoughts of Len if there was still no news from him. And it would remind her of Ianthe, of course.

As she let herself into the office on Grape Street and heard Mr Minks' familiar yowl of welcome, Posie chided herself: it really was high time she sorted out her living arrangements; she couldn't continue to pay rent on a bedsit she hated living in, and likewise it looked unprofessional to keep staying over at the office, even if dear Prudence never raised an eyebrow about her boss' somewhat unconventional style.

She really needed to buy herself a nice little flat in a

convenient spot. After all, she had the money now, given to her by the Earl of Cardigeon, a cool Ten Thousand Pounds, which had set her up for life. A nice little flat somewhere nearby would probably cost a couple of hundred pounds at most, leaving most of her nest egg untouched. She vowed that if this case sorted itself out quickly over her 'holiday', she would start searching for a flat seriously upon her return.

But even with these misgivings playing in the back of her mind, Posie looked around her spick-and-span modern little office with a sigh of relief: everything here was exactly as she had left it, and as she liked it. She felt better already, and almost impossibly at home.

* * * *

Eight

Posie took the telephone receiver from Prudence with a still-sleepy nod of thanks.

'Posie? That you? You sound a bit muffled.'

She had overslept and was still in her pyjamas. It was eight o'clock on the dot, and if Prudence, who was an early bird, had thought anything strange about Posie already being in the office before her and the sight of a hastily rolled-up sleeping-bag on the floor in her boss' room, she was too polite to say so.

'It's Lovelace here. Old Poots has come up trumps with his autopsy results. And guess what? Sure enough it's murder!'

Inspector Lovelace sounded business-like and brisk, the opposite of how Posie felt, in fact. Prudence busied herself at her desk, trying not to listen, sorting the early mail into four wire baskets: Posie's mail, Len's mail, one marked 'BILLS TO PAY' and the other marked rather more hopefully 'INVOICES OUT'.

'It's as he thought. Dame Flowers had been given a big enough dose of the sleeping draught to kill a horse. A normal amount of veronal for sleeping purposes is just under one gram, whereas Dame Flowers had more than four times as much in her bloodstream – 4.4 grams to be precise. And the killer wasn't taking any chances, either. The black flush on the face *is* evidence of suffocation, a pillow most likely. Although let's be grateful for small mercies: fortunately Dame Flowers wouldn't have known a thing about it, poor soul.'

'Mnnn, hmnn.' Posie made frantic '*I need a cup of tea*' gestures at Prudence, who was only too willing to scurry off.

'So I'm going to steam ahead as suggested yesterday, Posie. The local bobbies are watching Boynton Hall. But this story will need some degree of management bearing in mind the personalities involved. I'm going to put statements out to the press now so we can at least be on the front foot. I'll use your contact at the *Associated Press*, and a few other journalists too. For now I'm going to leave Alaric's disappearance out of it. Then I'm going back to Boynton Hall later today to re-interview the whole bally lot of them again and hunt for incriminating evidence. I'm taking a big team up with me.'

'Do you need me to do anything for you at all, Inspector Lovelace? And if not, do you mind if I keep on the trail of Alaric Boynton-Dale?'

Posie kept the note of keenness out of her voice: she needed the Inspector not to curtail any of her activities and not to feel he needed to worry about her, but they both knew that the missing explorer had *something* to do with Ianthe's murder and she expected the Inspector to warn her to tread cautiously.

'No, I don't need you for anything. The lot of them are under lock and key so I'm confident you're not going to run into problems from *that* end. Do as you like. But be sensible, eh? No leaking of any news stories of your own to the press, either…'

Half an hour later, cup of tea in hand and wearing her new cream linen trouser suit, Posie was standing at her window munching on a Danish pastry when Prudence knocked at her door.

'Telephone message,' she said, removing her thick spectacles and consulting her efficient secretary's notepad with a slight squint.

'It was that funny Mr Dodds on the telephone. The coin expert you told me to contact at the British Museum? He sounded terribly excited about something. Asked if you were in already – I said yes, I'm afraid – and he asked if you could go around there as soon as possible. "Now, this minute!" were his exact words…oh! Oh my goodness!'

Prudence had replaced her glasses hurriedly and was staring at Posie – or rather, at the new cream trouser suit – in disbelief.

'Oh, dear! I say!' Prudence goggled at Posie, on and on.

'Is that all?' asked Posie, rather tetchily.

Her aim had been to be modern, bright and summery, *not* to be the object of incredulous stares. She worried for a second – could she *really* carry this off? – but then she thought of Lady Violet and her effortless film star chic and she grabbed her carpet bag and headed for the door.

* * * *

The Royal Numismatic Society had no headquarters of its own, and had been at the British Museum in a few dark rooms in the basement for as long as anyone could remember.

Binkie Dodds, or rather Professor William Dodds (to give him his full, correct title), was a Cambridge-trained coin and medal specialist and moonlighted between his official day job as one of the keepers of coins at the British Museum and working as a secretary for the President of the Numismatic Society, Sir Harry Omman, who kept Binkie busy as his right-hand man.

It was into one of the dim brown-painted rooms in the basement that Posie now found herself being ushered, and she took in the sparse details with interest: books and papers everywhere, paper charts depicting various coins tacked to the surface of every wall, the strip of bubbled, frosted glass in the ceiling which was the underside of a pavement somewhere outside in the real world, over which women's sharp high-heeled shoes could be heard clicking.

Binkie was sitting at his desk in a state of high excitement. In fact, Posie had never seen him look so alive. He was young to hold such an eminent position, around thirty-two (the same age her brother Richard would have been right now if he had survived the trenches of the Great War) and he had a shiny round face with small peering eyes behind the thickest spectacles Posie had ever known a person to wear. Binkie had been at school with Posie's brother, and for many years Binkie had spent parts of the Eton summer holidays at the Norfolk Vicarage which had been Posie's home, his own parents being far away in Delhi.

But with his bookish ways, his general lack of fitness, his highly-strung manner and his terrible eyesight he had always been rather more of a favourite of Posie's father, the Reverend Parker, than of the outdoorsy, adventure-seeking Richard, who seemed to have spent most of his childhood sitting in the tops of trees.

'So? Have you got it?' Binkie said, wasting no time on niceties or introductions. Posie saw another, younger man hanging back behind Binkie, an embarrassed smile playing about his lips.

'Nice to see you too, Binkie,' Posie said, hunting around inside the depths of her bag.

She presented him with Alaric's bee coin without further ado and watched as Binkie sat silently at his desk, a magnifying glass and a small strange tubular light fixed firmly over the coin. Next to him a thick book on the desk lay open at what looked like a blown-up picture of the very same coin. Posie looked on with interest. Binkie motioned to his as-yet-unnamed colleague, who came over and stared at the coin too. The second man let out a low, appreciative whistle.

'I can't believe it's come *home*,' Binkie said reverently. 'At last.'

He was turning the bee coin over and over in his long pale hands. 'I can't believe he's drilled this wretched hole into the top of it, for a necklace to go through by the look of things. But it's essentially undamaged, which is a relief. And it's come home! Where it belongs!'

'What on earth do you mean?' Posie countered, confused.

'Well, it belongs here! At the British Museum, of course! Surely you saw the inscription on the back of it? That was our cataloguing system for coins more than a hundred years ago. The inscription shows *where it came from*. I hoped beyond hope when you sent me that shabby little wax rubbing that this was the real deal! And I was right! Do you realise quite how special this piece is, Posie? Or how old it is? There will be a huge celebration here when everyone hears about this. Perhaps even a whole new exhibition will be constructed around it!'

Binkie's words were coming faster and faster and he was getting more and more flushed in the face. Posie stared at him in mild disbelief and then smartly reached across the desk, taking back the bee coin in one quick move and placing it into her bag again.

'Now just you wait a minute,' she said sharply. 'I happen to know that this coin is *personal property*. I came here today to ask for information about it, not to return it here as if this were a London Underground Lost & Found Bureau!'

'I take it you mean that this coin is Alaric Boynton-Dale's property?' Binkie said sourly, almost sneering at the explorer's name. Binkie looked like a child who had had his favourite toy taken away unexpectedly. He crossed his arms and glared across the desk at her.

Posie nodded, sticking to her guns. 'Yes. It belongs to Alaric, as you say. I am acting as his…er, his *agent* in this matter.'

Posie tried to look as convincing as possible. What was a small white lie between old acquaintances anyway? No matter that Alaric hadn't really instructed her to act for him as his agent. How could he when he had never met her before, had never even heard of her?

She wasn't yet at liberty to tell anyone that Alaric had gone missing so she would just have to bluff this out with Binkie. She hoped against hope that the coin wouldn't turn out to be stolen property, in which case she could find herself in a very tricky situation.

'If you *are* acting as his agent, I'm very surprised that Alaric should be asking for any information about it at all,' snapped Binkie. 'I would have thought he knew everything there was to know about this coin, possibly more than we do here at the museum. Although how he acquired it was obviously highly *irregular*.'

'What do you mean?'

Posie's heart was beating wildly. What on earth had she got herself into? Or was this just Binkie being difficult? Before she could ask him anymore however, Binkie was getting to his feet and pocketing his magnifying glass. You didn't need to know him of old to know he was in a first-rate strop.

'So are you going to leave that coin with me or not?' he demanded petulantly.

'No, of course not! Don't be such a noddle, Binkie! Sit down!'

But before she could say any more, Binkie had flounced from the room, slamming the door shut behind him. Posie stared at the space where he had vanished in wonder. This visit was supposed to have been easy, and it had proved anything but! She gathered herself together as the young man in the room started up with a flurry of apologies. He introduced himself quickly as Harry Redmayne, an Egyptologist at the museum.

'You'll just have to forgive Professor Dodds,' he smiled kindly, sitting down at Binkie's vacated desk chair. 'He gets awfully excited about coins. He could even kill for one! This one in particular, it seems.'

'Can *you* help me?' Posie asked, sensing a more approachable soul.

'Of course. What is it you want to know?'

'Start with how Alaric owns this coin. What is "irregular" about it?'

Mr Redmayne smiled. 'Actually, I should tell you that I am an old, old friend of Alaric's, we go back a long way. In fact, I was stepping out with his sister Violet for a while there…such a stunning girl. Unfortunately, I was deemed not wealthy enough for her,' he trailed off, staring at the wall, miles away.

He jolted himself back to the present sharply:

'Anyway, what was I saying about Alaric? Golly, ah, yes! We are both bee-keepers in our spare time. And that's why Professor Dodds called me in here today: he thought I might be interested in seeing this coin. It's very famous, you know. I'm leaving today, so the timing was good. I'm off to conduct an archaeological excavation for the museum in the Valley of the Kings in Egypt. It seems that paintings and hieroglyphs about bee-keeping have been found in one of the tombs there. They think that the tomb may be a monument to a Bee Goddess or a Bee God, and hence they want me to have a look. Anyway, sorry… you were asking me about the coin…'

Mr Redmayne flicked through the fat catalogue on the

desk. He jabbed at a place on the page with his index finger and nodded:

'It seems that Alaric's father was perhaps the most important coin-collector in the country at the turn of the century. In 1893 he is recorded as donating his best, most specialist pieces to the museum, keeping only a few worthless pieces for himself. His original collection was priceless – mainly Roman, it says here – and he exchanged a collection of more than two thousand precious Roman coins for that single bee coin you now have in your bag.'

Posie gasped. '*Why?*'

Mr Redmayne smiled. 'All because his eleven-year-old son Alaric wanted it: he fell in love with that coin. You see, he had a fascination for bees, and the legend behind that coin from an early age. The bee coin belonged to the British Museum, and they agreed to the swap. At the time it must have seemed a very good deal to them.'

Mr Redmayne continued:

'That wouldn't happen anymore, of course. In the last few years ancient coin specialists like Professor Dodds have been getting very hot under the collar about it. The story of this bee coin has assumed an almost mythical reputation, which is appropriate really. People see it as a disgrace that the exchange was allowed to happen: people such as Professor Dodds think that the coin still belongs here.'

Harry Redmayne splayed his hands apologetically. 'Although strictly speaking, the coin is an *Italian* national treasure. It's from Sicily. It belongs there.'

'Sicily?' breathed Posie eagerly, on the edge of her seat. Mr Redmayne flicked the pages of the fat journal again.

'Yes, the coin is from the seventh century B.C. It's truly ancient.'

Posie almost fell off her chair in disbelief. Mr Redmayne smiled:

'Little is known about the coin really, although it's the only one of its sort to survive. The ancient Greeks, Romans and Egyptians have long worshipped the bee: certain types of honey were believed in ancient times to be more precious than gold. It was believed that some types of honey could cure people of illnesses, even bring about eternal life…'

'And what about the inscription on the back?' Posie whispered. 'Do you know what that means?'

Harry Redmayne frowned. 'I can't help you with the first word, "Serafina". But I *can* help you with "Hyblaea". It means several things. Hyblaea was the Bee Goddess, worshipped by the ancient Sicilians, and it's possible that this coin is a reference to her. It also refers to a string of volcanic mountains in eastern Sicily, called the Hyblaean mountain range. But I think the reason Alaric was interested in the coin from such a young age was because it alluded to a *honey*. A truly legendary honey from Sicily.'

Posie nodded eagerly. This seemed to fit with what Cosima Catchpole had been mentioning the day before. Encouraged, Harry Redmayne pressed on:

'You remember what I said about mythical honey being more precious than gold? The Hyblaean honey is one of those: it has medicinal qualities, but it's also understood to be perhaps the finest honey in the world. It is legendary, the Latin writer Vergilius even mentioned how fine it was in the first century B.C! Imagine!'

Posie had never heard of Vergilius, but she did her best to give what she hoped was a knowing nod. 'So what was so special about it?' asked Posie, wrinkling her nose up in concentration, tucking her hair behind her ear.

'What *is* so special about it,' grinned Mr Redmayne. 'It's still being produced! And to answer your question, it's special because of a number of things. The bees on the island harvest on unique flowers which grow near the salty sea and which grow in the earth of the ashy Hyblaean volcanoes. The taste is truly original, but *why* it is so special remains a closely-guarded secret.'

'So it definitely exists?'

'Yes. But it's very rare. It's known to be produced in only one place in Sicily, by one set of bee-keepers. The existence of this place is top-secret, the secret passed down from generation to generation. You *can* buy the honey in a shop in a town on the island, but one spoonful alone will cost you the earth! If I had time I would try and track it down. I might just learn a thing or two from those bee-keepers: *if* they let me observe them at work, that is. Just as that coin you are holding onto is seen as a sort of Holy Grail by coin-collectors, so the Hyblaean honey is seen as a kind of Holy Grail by bee-keepers. I strongly believe that the coin in your bag is from the place where Hyblaean honey is made. *That* is what would have interested Alaric.'

He cocked his head and smiled. He had kind eyes.

'Is that where Alaric has gone to?' he asked quietly. Posie looked at him, shocked. She hadn't said anything about Alaric's disappearance.

'I tried calling him earlier this week, that's all. I wondered if he might like to come with me to Egypt, to see the tomb paintings. But I think he must be busy. He never returned my calls.'

Posie knew her face had turned blush-red and she tried to avoid the sincere gaze. She had been found out, of sorts.

'Don't worry,' said Harry, standing up and closing the journal. 'If he's engaged on something secret, I know he can't be disturbed. Now, if you'll excuse me, I have to check on my travelling bags. I think I may have forgotten my sleeping-bag in my rush today. Is there anything else I can help you with?'

In an instant Posie had made up her mind. She had heard enough and she was losing precious time. If this was a fool's errand she'd beat herself up about it later. But she felt that everything pointed towards this island, the island of Sicily, off the coast of Italy. It seemed possible now that Alaric had gone there deliberately.

'If you were to go to Sicily, to look for the place where this honey is made…where would you start?'

Harry Redmayne nodded as if he had expected such a question.

'Ortigia,' he said certainly. 'It's a tiny island off the city of Siracusa, in the south-east of Sicily.'

'Why would you go there?'

'Ortigia is very near the Hyblaean mountains. But more importantly, it's where the only shop which sells the honey is located. Chances are that's because it's the nearest place to the bee-keepers who make it.'

The obliging Mr Redmayne wrote down an address on the back of his business card. He passed it across to Posie:

'Go there.'

* * * *

Posie sat quite undisturbed, Mr Minks asleep on her lap, a cup of fresh tea and a plate of uneaten chocolate biscuits in front of her for her lunch.

She was enjoying the calm of the quiet office, the window open over the dirty London rooftops, the smell of gently melting tarmac wafting in. She was leaving tonight.

She had been lucky. She had managed to ring through and book the last available first-class sleeper carriage on the *Train Bleu* down to the South of France. From Nice she would take a connecting train on to Genoa in Italy, and then she would embark on a long ferry ride of twenty hours over to the island of Sicily. The whole journey would take around three days.

Posie loved travelling and it was with a feeling of rising excitement that she contemplated the adventure before her. Posie had already thrown her new Army & Navy purchases into her overnight bag from Boynton Hall, and she had decided that her trip abroad did not necessitate a trip back to her bedsit in Nightingale Mews; she had almost everything she needed with her, and she liked to travel light. Much to Prudence's horror.

'You don't need anything else, Miss?' Prudence had almost pleaded, staring at the one small leather bag in disbelief. Prudence had stared in panicky horror too at the neat sleeping-bag which sat alongside the overnighter.

'Oh, yes! There *is* something I've forgotten, now you mention it.'

'Go on, Miss. You want me to step over to Liberty on Regent Street and buy you a nice sensible cotton dress, suitable for travelling alone in?' Prudence had cast a look over at Posie's trouser suit with distaste.

'No, no. Nothing of that sort, Prudence dear,' she smiled, not taking the bait. 'Can you go to Stanford's Map Shop on Long Acre and get me a really good detailed map of Sicily – especially of Ortigia – if they have one? And then, on your way back, stop off at Mr Bernie Sharp's offices in Covent Garden. He has a parcel for me.'

Posie kept being revisited by the full horror of Ianthe Flower's death, and the thought of the missing end page of Ianthe's novel had kept playing over and over again in her mind.

She had called Bernie Sharp on her return from the British Museum. All of Harry Redmayne's talk of bees and honey and Egyptian tombs had made something twitch in her mind about Ianthe's incomplete book, *The Tomb of the Honey Bee*. Posie had found herself wondering about the novel in general.

Would reading it help her understand what it was that Ianthe had been wanting to tell her on that last fateful morning at Boynton Hall? It couldn't hurt to read it, anyway, provided Bernie Sharp was willing to let her have a copy, *if* he had a copy to spare. Besides, there was a very long journey ahead in which to while away the time.

She had been surprised by the uncharacteristically friendly tones of the ratty little man on the other end of the receiver. She had been expecting obstructiveness, or at least hostility.

'You're in luck, Miss Parker,' Bernie Sharp had said almost amiably.

'Of course, the police have now got the original; "evidence", they call it. But I've had three of my best typists working day and night all through yesterday and I've now got three copies of *The Tomb of the Honey Bee*. One will be sent to the printer next week ready for typesetting, I will keep one copy here and therefore there is one spare, so you can take it. Promise me that you won't lose it though, or show it to anyone, or leave it anywhere? This is my livelihood we are talking about, after all.'

Posie promised solemnly. 'Golly! So you're going ahead? Printing it without its final page?' she had asked, somewhat incredulously.

'That's right. I've taken instructions from Ianthe's only surviving heir, well, the only heir who can be *found* right now. She now controls the literary estate, too. She thinks we should just publish and let the reader decide who did the dastardly deed for themselves. No point hanging around to see if the missing page turns up.'

'Oh? I thought Lady Violet said Ianthe had no family? Who is the heir you are talking about?'

There was a shrill of laughter from the receiver. 'It *is* Lady Violet. They were second cousins. Ianthe has left Violet and her brother Alaric everything, half each. Of course it seems Alaric can't be found just now, so I'm taking my instructions from Violet alone. It was a huge surprise apparently! Of course, it will be months until

Violet and Alaric can get their hands on any money; it's all tied up, but the end result is the same. And *The Tomb of the Honey Bee* will prove to be a nice little money-spinner for us all! In the meantime, I've agreed to get Lady Violet's cookbook published. That too will be quite a sensation. She always pumps up sales when she appears in magazines and newspapers! I'm actually expecting her to drop by my offices shortly to sign the necessary paperwork.'

So *that* was why Bernie Sharp was feeling so happy, Posie realised. No obstacles in his way to publish Ianthe's last (and likely to be most successful) book, and a new client who seemed to have the potential to make him yet more money. Posie felt pleased for Violet. At least *something* good might come out of poor Ianthe Flowers' terrible death.

But she had quite forgotten! In all the excitement of the morning Posie had forgotten to keep Lady Violet updated, as she had promised, and payment or no payment, the girl was still officially employing her.

Not wanting to move from her comfortable position at her desk, or to move Mr Minks, who was snoring gently, Posie decided to write to the girl rather than telephone. She would get Prudence to post the letter later on:

Lady Violet,

I believe I may know where Alaric has gone. It's just a hunch, and I'm not sure why exactly he is there, but I believe he's in Sicily, Italy. I think he chose to go, so please don't keep thinking the worst. I'm hopefully going to track him down, starting in Ortigia.

If you need me, get in touch with Prudence, my secretary. But I will telegram you as soon as I have more news.

Best wishes,

Posie

She wrote a brief note to Inspector Lovelace too, along the same lines, informing him that she would update him when she had reached her destination.

Posie was still munching her way through the plate of biscuits when Mr Minks woke up and silently shimmied away to a sunnier spot. Able to move freely again, and quite unconsciously, Posie found herself slipping her hand into the carpet bag and pulling out Alaric's bee coin.

Opening one of her desk drawers, she pulled out a small sewing kit and within it she pulled free a skein of dark blue embroidery silk. She looped it through the tiny hole which Alaric had cut into the top of the coin and pulled it taught: in one swift movement she had tied it around her own neck and pulled the silk tight. The coin nestled like a pendant in the hollow of her collar-bone. A perfect, snug fit. It felt right there, almost warm, as if Posie had worn it every day of her life. Posie tried not to think of how much the coin might be worth in monetary terms, but she smiled to remember Binkie's reverence for it and wished he could see her wearing it so casually.

Earlier in the year she had had the chance to hold a rare diamond which had been worth Seven Hundred Thousand Pounds, and every second of the physical contact had felt excruciating. This was the direct opposite: the story, the history, the strange and complicated symbolism behind the bee coin itself felt welcoming, intriguing. Posie vowed she would only take the coin off her neck when and if she met Alaric Boynton-Dale for real.

Posie crossed to the window. She looked out at the pigeons. This had been one of Len's favourite spots and he always came and leant nonchalantly against the wall, staring out, sharing a cup of tea or coffee with her. There was *still* no news.

Posie sighed. She was horribly aware that the train which would take her to Nice would be stopping off on the way at the nearby Cap d'Antibes, where Inspector Leferb had confirmed that Len was still residing in a boarding-house.

In fact, it was only a distance of some fourteen miles between the two seaside resorts. Should she get off the train at Antibes? Should she check for herself that all was okay with Len? Or was there no fool like an old fool, as Ianthe had once joked. Should she just leave well alone and stay on the train?

For once Posie simply didn't have a clue.

* * * *

PART TWO
France and Italy
(June, 1921)

Nine

It was eleven o'clock in the morning and Posie was sitting under a fresh pastel-coloured umbrella at a street café, anonymous beneath her broad straw-brimmed hat and her new sunglasses.

She sipped at a coffee and munched on a croissant, although really she would have preferred a nice shortcake biscuit. She watched the Saturday-morning locals walking their dogs along the promenade, and the tourists in their exotic sunbathing outfits tripping along between the potted palm trees towards the ridiculously blue sea, which sparkled and glittered like a promise out on the horizon.

She had been here an hour now, and she was amused to watch the Cap d'Antibes coming slowly to life around her: it obviously wasn't a place for early birds, and she guessed that many of the tourists and revellers would not emerge out onto the sun-drenched streets until well after lunch; that they were still now sleeping off the effects of the notoriously glamourous late-night parties which drew the same sort of people back here, year after year. She heard American women's voices all around her at the other small café tables, and took a good long appreciative look at their impossibly chic attire. Had Len perhaps joined such a crowd?

But such speculation was useless. Better still to wonder at her *own* motivation, which had seen her swear for the entire journey that she would stay on the train until Nice, only to find herself unaccountably getting off at Antibes station, as if in a dream. She was now ensconced in the safety of one of the numerous cafés which lined the promenade, and she had absolutely no intention of going to the boarding-house where Len had been staying. Somehow it was enough to *be* here, where he was. She would order one more coffee and then leave.

She had the luxury of one more hour until she needed to be back on the station platform, boarding a local train to Nice, so that she could make her connection to Italy. Posie held the bee coin at her throat between her thumb and index finger, reminding herself *why* she was here after all. She felt disappointed that she had allowed herself this ridiculous foible.

And then she saw him.

It was unmistakeably Len, coming along the promenade in her direction. But rather than the Len of her memory, the man she had last seen disappearing off into a snowy London evening in February, four months ago, the man walking towards her was sun-tanned and wearing sunglasses; his usual London attire of tweeds and homburg hat had been replaced by light, bright sports clothes in foreign colours of pale lemon and lime. He looked very well, and his handsome face was fixed in its habitual laughing manner.

Before she knew what she was doing, Posie had slapped some money down on the table, picked up her bags and the manuscript of Ianthe's novel which she had been trying to read, and she found herself running as fast as she could. On she flew over the road with its stream of traffic, on past the ornamental palm trees and onto the promenade and into the direct line of Len.

He smacked right into her and Posie dropped the manuscript, its pages fluttering wildly in the wind.

'Co-ooee! I'm so sorry, madam. Here, let me help you.' Len bent to pick it up and return it to her.

Posie had started to laugh under her huge sun hat, thankful for the chance encounter. But then her laugh froze in her throat and she had an uneasy feeling, as if solid ground were slipping away beneath her feet, for as Len passed the manuscript back to her something shiny on his finger caught the sunlight. Posie recoiled in shock – a wide gold circle on his left-hand ring finger was clearly visible – was it a *wedding* band?

A cold hand seemed to clutch at her heart. She found herself taking her glasses and her hat off in a slow stupor, as if hypnotised. Posie was staring at his hand, and then staring up into his face, and then in the same split-second she realised that Len was not alone.

Next to him, very close by, and holding onto his arm, bobbed a small, stick-thin girl with black shingled hair and a deep walnut tan. She had a small, sharp, pretty face with a watchful, slightly suspicious look about her eyes. She looked typically French and she made Posie feel horribly like an ungainly giant, for she towered at least a head and shoulders above the petite girl.

'Posie?' cried Len in disbelief.

He stood as if frozen to the spot, all the sun-tanned colour seeming to have drained from his face. His gorgeous green eyes and his ready smile were transformed out of all recognition and he looked as if he were about to be sick. To make matters worse, the crowds of people who were thronging the promenade and trying to get onto the beach were bottle-necking all around them, nudging and elbowing them out of the way as if they were an accident on a busy road.

'*S'il vous plaît!* Please!' shouted an immaculate French woman with a bevy of small dogs on crystal-encrusted leads, looking far too elegant for this time of the morning. '*Vous etes sur mon chemin!* Get out of the way!'

'What on earth are *you* doing here, Po?' Len breathed quietly, somehow moving all three of them to the very edge of the promenade, next to a potted tropical plant.

'POSIE?' shouted the black-haired girl, and in that instant all of Posie's hopes and dreams came crashing down around her and she realised that this girl was not just some fly-by-night French fancy.

This girl spoke with the same cockney London twang as Posie's friend Dolly Price, although where Dolly managed to sound friendly and companionable, this girl sounded sharp and mawkish. This *must* be the long-term girlfriend Len had had for years back in Leytonstone: a girl Posie had never met before, and whom she had fervently hoped was well out of the picture. But obviously not.

'What? This is Posie? Posie Parker, your boss?' said the girl, turning to Len in a rage. 'The one who's always hasslin' you and writin' letters to you here? What the bleedin' 'ell is *she* doing here? You didn't tell me you was havin' a business meeting! This is meant to be our *honeymoon* for gawd's sake!'

Too late, and like an idiot, Posie saw the gold band on the girl's left hand – a perfect match to Len's – paired with a whopping great citrine of an engagement ring. How on earth had Len afforded it? Posie thought for just a second that she was about to cry, but she recovered herself and found herself holding onto the manuscript tightly, as if for reassurance, horribly aware that with her bags at her feet and in her sensible flat shoes she cut quite the unglamorous figure.

Posie laughed, a hollow sound which sounded unconvincing, even to her own ears.

'Oh, golly! Don't mind me!' she found herself saying to the girl at Len's side.

'I'm just here on business. Pure coincidence to run into you like this! Nothing to do with Len at all! Please don't worry, or let me disturb you in the slightest. I'm actually on my way to Nice. I just stopped off here for a coffee and to take in the sights.' She checked her red wristwatch in a convinced manner.

'Actually, I'd better hurry. I'm due on a train out of here, leaving in twenty-five minutes. It was lovely to meet you, er…'

'This is Aggie,' said Len, his face still deathly white beneath the hot sun.

'As I said, a pleasure. Len, and Aggie, I wish you both a very pleasant honeymoon.'

Posie bent to retrieve her bags, and was just about to turn on her heel and walk away as fast as her feet could carry her when the girl stepped up to her and thrust her small pointed chin upwards, her stance one of confrontation.

'Not so fast, Miss Parker. You listen to me.' Aggie came closer.

'Now, what my Len is too polite to mention here out in the open is the question of the *money*. But you don't scare me.'

Posie blinked in utter disbelief. 'I'm sorry? *What* money?'

The girl scowled and crossed her arms over her chest, her pretty charm gone in an instant. She reminded Posie of a Billingsgate fishwife.

'Now don't you play the innocent wiv me, Miss Parker. You can't take *me* in wiv your posh fancy ways, the way you've taken my Len in.'

Posie stared at Len, totally uncomprehending. He had turned bright red and was staring at the patterned tarmacked pavement, avoiding her gaze.

'Come on, Aggie, give it a rest,' Len whispered, half-pleading, trying to take the girl's arm. She shrugged him off angrily.

'It's nothing,' Len muttered.

'Don't you tell me it's nuffin'!' shouted the girl. 'It could change our lives!' She turned again to Posie.

'My Len told me that you had an arrangement together,'

she snapped. 'Whatever you earned at that blimmin' Detective Agency of yours was split half each. He always honoured the agreement, even when you had precious little work on of your own. Do you deny that?'

Posie was almost shaking, but she had no idea why. *What* was she being accused of here? What had Len been telling this horrible little wife of his?

'No, of course I don't deny it! Why would I? But it cuts both ways,' Posie added, looking squarely at Len, who looked away to the sea on the horizon.

'Since February I've been managing on my own, running the place entirely out of my own earnings, putting aside half of the profits for Len on his return. I've been waiting for Len to come back – and of course I totally understand about his father being sick – but am I given to understand he is now better?'

Aggie ignored Posie's question.

'But you was given a lot of money, weren't you? As part of that last fancy case you was workin' on? The one with the missin' diamond? My Len was workin' on it wiv you, wasn't he? Risked his neck on several occasions; he almost died in some underground club, he told me. And then you was given TEN THOUSAND POUNDS! And by rights, half of that belongs to Len. It's ours! It could change our lives! But you've not mentioned once givin' half the amount to us! Just spent time braggin' about it in your letters!'

Posie was struck dumb: she was horribly aware that her face must be as red as Len's. She felt horribly guilty, and angry too, and caught off-guard. She *had* written to Len in February about her reward from the Earl of Cardigeon, it was true: she had thought he would be glad for her, and she had been writing under the (obviously horribly misguided) impression that she and Len might have some sort of romantic future together themselves.

She felt terrible: she had never, not even for a second, thought about splitting the reward with Len. Should she have? And now she was almost being accused of theft, certainly of fraud, by this horrible little woman. Posie made up her mind on the spur of the moment, speaking clearly and calmly although she knew as soon as she turned her back on the couple that she would dissolve into floods of tears:

'You are quite mistaken, Mrs Irving,' she said, getting past those terrible, difficult words in a shambling gush.

'Our arrangement was that we would split *profits* from earnings. That means services to clients that were billed for. What *I* received from the Earl of Cardigeon and which your husband has no claim on, was a one-off personal reward. I am sorry if you have been harbouring under some misapprehension.'

Posie stared at the huge citrine which flashed for a second in front of her, almost blinding her, before she turned and walked quickly away.

She hated to admit it, but it was a ring she herself would have loved to own.

* * * *

Somehow, in the dry dusty heat of the first-class train carriage, Posie held herself together. Mercifully, she was alone apart from one young woman, who had nodded off in her own corner. It was too hot to cry. And Posie was too angry.

She stared unseeing out of the open window. A hazy glimmer of strong midday heat caused the lines of the tarmac platform and the red-brick station house to shimmy together in a blur. It was simply too hot to be outside, and sensible people had boarded the train early or were staying put inside the station house. Out of the corner of her eye

Posie saw a fat old lady wearing a red shawl coming along the length of the train, carrying a basket. In the basket were sticks of French bread and cheese, melting in the heat. She also carried a few bunches of the flower of the region, yellow mimosa. For a horrible heart-wrenching moment Posie remembered the bunch of dusky mimosa she had received in May from Len; a token of remembrance, or so she had thought.

What had Len been playing at, exactly? Had he been keeping his options open, perhaps? Had he been unsure until very recently whether to stay with Aggie, or whether to commit to Posie? Or had their romantic tryst in February all been some horrible mistake? And if so, why hadn't he just had the guts to tell her so?

Posie realised now what she had always known deep down: that for all his charm, his good looks and his gun-toting chivalry, Len Irving was a coward. He probably hadn't wanted to jeopardise the comfortable little business they ran together, and he had delayed and delayed his return to England, even after his father had made a good recovery, fearful of how Posie would receive him.

Posie shuddered now to remember the vitriol behind Aggie's words. She could only imagine what Len had been saying about her to make Aggie think so badly of her. She must have been portrayed as some awful, greedy monster, desperate for money and desperate for Len... Her face burned in shame, picturing Len's embarrassment at her unabashed joy in seeing him on the promenade.

Just then there was a flurry of action on the platform. Posie looked out of the window and saw that a man had crashed straight into the fat lady in the red shawl. He was searching for someone at the train windows and calling out...calling out *her* name.

It was Len, still in his sports clothes, but all alone and with sweat pouring down his face.

Suddenly he came level with her window and before

she could move away and hide he saw her. The Conductor was just getting on the train and the Station Master was arranging a complicated series of flags and whistles. The fat lady had obviously seen a chance for a quick sale and had come up behind Len, waving a bunch of the yellow flowers in the direction of the window, adding to the general commotion.

'Posie! Po!' Len breathed, out of breath. 'I'm so glad I caught you!'

'Really?' asked Posie flatly. 'Why? What is there to say? What am I supposed to say to you?'

'Get off the train, love,' Len panted. 'You don't need to go. We can sort this out.'

The Station Master blew his first whistle.

'You're wrong, Len,' Posie said. 'I *do* need to go. I wasn't lying; I'm on a case. I was just passing through. I can't get off this train, even if I *wanted* to. Which I don't.'

'I'm sorry. I'm so sorry,' Len was looking at Posie with his lovely green eyes full of contrition. 'We can sort this out, I promise!'

'Len! How can we sort this out? You're *married*! And you couldn't even tell me!'

Len cast his eyes downwards.

'I didn't know what to say to you,' he muttered apologetically. 'I couldn't find the words. I'm so sorry. I don't want to hurt you. And we've only *just* got married! Last week, in fact. I was going to tell you. I swear!'

At her silence, Len continued:

'Please, Po. Get off the train, we'll sort this all out.'

A flash of understanding hit her: he meant the business, the Detective Agency, their nice little arrangement at Grape Street which seemed so far away now in grey dusty Bloomsbury. He meant that they could work *that* out, the business side of things. Had it been Aggie who had sent Len after her, desperate to 'fix' things, so he at least had a job to come back to when this glamorous little escapade in France was all over?

Posie laughed in disbelief. She was angry but she was practical too, and in the long-run she needed Len in the business as much as he needed her.

'Of course we'll sort it out. I'm not going to hold a grudge against you, am I? I'm glad one of us has found happiness, at least. Come back when you want to. Everything is still the same…'

Except everything would not be the same. Not for a while, anyway.

Len looked relieved. The final whistle blew and a lot of hot steam almost shielded him from her view. The fat woman came closer, pressing the mimosa through the window. Posie found herself handing over some change and taking a small bunch.

'Safe journey, then,' said Len, a half-worried smile lingering on his face.

'But one thing I don't understand,' said Posie just as the train started to move off. 'Why did you go to the trouble of sending me mimosa from here if you didn't want to give me the wrong impression?'

Len looked gobsmacked. He started to run alongside the train to keep up.

'Mimosa?' he shouted incredulously, as Posie's heart seemed to fall in on itself.

'I sent you a couple of postcards. But *I* didn't send you flowers! It must have been someone else…'

As Len was left behind, veiled in a misty cloud of engine smoke on the platform, Posie had the sense that she had no idea any more if she had ever really known him. Was he lying to her now as he had been doing for the last few months?

And if not, who the blazes had been sending her flowers?

* * * *

Ten

It was just possible that in the tiny island of Ortigia, part of the Sicilian town of Siracusa, Posie had found her favourite place in all the world. It was a perfect, stony jewel. It also gave every appearance of being a good remedy for a broken heart.

Posie sighed with contentment as she sat on her balcony. It was her first evening at the *Locatelli*, a comfortable little guesthouse she had found by chance. It was near the harbour, and she had a room which looked eastwards out over the mysterious sparkling Levant. The sea had turned from a dark indigo to rose pink at dusk, and was now a glittering pitch-black, punctured by the lights of tiny fishing-boats and yachts.

She sipped gratefully at her third glass of the local Nero d'Avola wine and remembered the delightful sights she had observed that afternoon in the blistering Sunday heat: the faded baroque stone buildings which rose up majestically to frame the small harbour; the ruined Roman palaces which were to be found on every street; the lush, plant-filled courtyards and dark straggly lanes winding in impossible directions, all colluding together to hide a myriad of secrets.

This was very much a town of secrets, Posie thought to

herself: a town to lose things in, and to lose yourself in. A town it would be easy to remain anonymous in. But would it be a town to *find* things in, too?

She needed to move forwards. The sheer stupidity of her feelings for Len and the fact that it was just possible that she had been made to look a complete fool by Len and his wife (and that Inspector Lovelace could well have known all of this all along and been too gentlemanly to tell her) had proved to be a lethal cocktail of thought-material on the long and lonely sea journey over to Sicily. So much so that Posie had not managed to read a single page of Ianthe's novel.

But now she had had enough of moping.

She was grateful for the magic of the new place, and this, coupled with the very real task at hand of finding Alaric Boynton-Dale, gave her an energy she knew she would not have managed to seize on anywhere else. Although the shops had been closed since her arrival in the afternoon, it was comforting to find that the twisty-turny streets below the *Locatelli* guesthouse were far from quiet. Throngs of people walked along the narrow streets, most eating ice-creams. Posie leant over the balcony edge and watched as a man wearing an eerie white Venetian carnival mask and a flamboyant black cloak came along the street wielding a lit taper on the end of a long wooden pole. He stopped every couple of paces along the street and lit one of the ancient street lamps which hung from metal brackets on the walls. Close behind him came a procession of other masked people, all dressed in gaudy carnival clothes. They were banging at drums, many wielding brightly-coloured puppets in their hands; hundreds of little knights and wooden horses bobbing along on strings.

One of the men in the procession caught sight of Posie staring and shouted up at her, gesturing at the puppets.

'I'm sorry, I don't understand!' Posie shouted back, feeling very stupid, wishing she had inherited her clever father's seemingly effortless knack of picking up languages. The entire group of puppeteers had now stopped in the alleyway below her balcony, half in shadow, and were peering up at her with interest.

'You American?' a girl with a wild and curly mop of hair in the group called up, pulling off her mask.

'English,' Posie shouted down.

'Come along with us! We have a Puppet Theatre at the end of the street. We are very famous for our shows! We will be starting in ten minutes. We wait for you here, no? Come now!'

Normally more cautious, Posie found herself nodding along in delight; after all, she had no other plans. She downed the rest of her glass of wine in one go and grabbed up her bag, heading off for an evening's entertainment with this mysterious masked group of strangers, desperate to banish all thoughts of Len from her mind.

* * * *

Frustratingly, the next day being Monday, everywhere that sold anything was closed, including the shop which sold the Hyblaean honey, whose details Mr Redmayne had given her. Posie would need to wait until Tuesday to move forwards with her investigation, but she decided to locate the shop anyhow.

Feeling refreshed after a good night's sleep, she set out armed with her map from Stanford's and a Thermos flask of English tea which she had made herself.

The shop (whose name, when translated, meant 'The Amber Jewel') was one of a muddle of tiny tobacconists and apothecaries in *La Giudecca*, the crowded medieval part of Ortigia, where lemon trees and palm trees fought each other for space among the cobbled yellow houses, and linen hung in zig-zags of ropes between the flats and apartments above. Most of the shops and restaurants were boarded up with unfriendly-looking metal shutters but Posie found '*Il Gioiello Ambra*' easily enough. Bright golden letters proclaimed its name across a wide glass window, and, to her surprise, while the place was obviously closed up for business, the metal shutters were not pulled down.

Posie pressed her nose right up against the glass door, spying into its dark recesses.

The shop was tiny, with a curving, low ceiling. It looked like a strange sort of cave. Posie had been expecting something which was all about bees, or honey at least, or with some obvious reference to the Hyblaean honey which was so legendary, but she had been wrong. There was no advertising for anything of the sort: no pictures, no posters, no signs up indicating prices or giving a clue as to what the goods for sale in the shop might be. The owners of the shop were obviously very wealthy, and every visible surface glittered with gold, even the floor and ceiling. There was very little in the way of products on display, just one narrow shelf running behind the main counter and the till, and that carrying perhaps just twenty glass jars of what looked like dried herbs and flowers, all with golden screw-tops.

Her breath misted up the golden-stencilled glass door and as Posie rubbed it with a bit of her linen jacket she gave a sudden start: a young man with very dark olive-coloured eyes was staring at her from the back of the shop in the gloom inside. He was wearing what looked like a strange long white gown and he stared at Posie's throat in a searching, hostile manner. Instinctively, and without knowing quite why, she reached up and covered the bee coin at her collar-bone with her right hand, obscuring it from the young man's view. How long had he been there, standing motionless, watching her?

Posie smiled and waved at the man, feeling like a first-rate fool. He stared Posie out, his arms crossed over his chest protectively, his lips set in a thin, grim line. His whole posture was guarded. She couldn't feign touristy ignorance: everything in Siracusa, and certainly everything on the island of Ortigia, was well known to be closed today; she couldn't pretend surprise at finding the shop not open for business. Posie made stupid and probably unfathomable '*I'll come back tomorrow*' movements, all the while feeling like a fat-head.

Just then a bright, vicious, luminous light lit up the whole shop, bouncing off the golden, glittery surfaces and filling the glass door, blinding Posie and making her scrunch up her eyes in pain. Could the young man have actually been taking a *photograph* of her from the other side of the glass door?

Was he trying to scare her off?

* * * *

Her real quest thwarted, the rest of Monday was spent being a good tourist: Posie shuffled around the inside of Ortigia's dark but cool Cathedral; sipped on a frozen almond granita in the busy Piazza del Duomo; meandered by the romantic Roman fountain of Aretusa and then ate a tasty seafood lunch at a café near her guesthouse.

After a refreshing nap Posie decided to cross out of Ortigia and visit another part of Siracusa. She had heard much about the Archaeological Park made up of Roman and Greek ruins and she headed there by bus. She happily spent a couple of hours wandering in the dry, rough-hewn Roman Amphitheatre and the Greek Theatre and sat under the palm trees drinking her tea, fanning herself in the heat, watching the lizards sunbathing on the ancient rocks.

On her way out she quickly visited the lower part of the Archaeological Park, the old quarry, where the famous whispering cave could be found hidden amongst lush undergrowth and groves of orange trees. A long queue of people snaked in the heat to enter the huge cave. Nicknamed the 'Ear of Dionysius' due to its pointy shape, Posie was not keen to spend much time inside as it was embarrassingly full of amorous young couples trying out the famous acoustics, which ensured that you could whisper something at one end of the vast cavern and hear it perfectly well at the other end. Posie had no desire to be reminded of how very *alone* she was on this visit, and how she had no-one to whisper to.

She strolled through the Ear of Dionysius as quickly as possible. She had just reached the far end and was heading out into the brilliant sunshine again when she heard a sharp whisper beside her, coming from the depths of the rock:

'POSIE! POSIE PARKER!'

Gasping, Posie swung around, holding onto the cool stone wall for support.

But of course there was no-one there, and if someone *was* whispering her name at the cave entrance she wouldn't be able to see them anyway. But had she heard correctly? She frowned: probably too much sun and not enough water to drink were making her hallucinate. Almost laughing at herself, Posie recovered herself and was about to move off outside when the voice came again:

'POSIE! POSIE PARKER...'

Her heart pounding, Posie searched around frantically, and then started to run back the way she had come, through the many couples and tourists enjoying the shadowy cool. She was back at the entrance to the cave within a minute, coming out the wrong way, much to the chagrin of the museum guard who started shouting in a babble of angry Italian and making desperate hand gestures at her. Ignoring him and the stares of the other people in the queue, she looked around desperately, searching this way and that among the shrubbery and the lumpy old stone sculptures lurking in the undergrowth.

Something made her fearful, and it was with a distinct feeling of creeping unease that she made her way back to the ranks of tourist buses outside the Archaeological Park, checking all the way to make sure she was not being followed.

Getting out at one of the bridges to the island of Ortigia, Posie walked the rest of the way to the *Locatelli* guesthouse, turning at every street corner to make sure she was alone.

It was just as she had convinced herself of her mind's fabulous ability to play tricks on itself that she saw a strange figure out of the corner of her eye, a block behind her, seemingly matching her pace. It was a tall figure in a black cloak wearing a black broad-rimmed hat and a white Venetian-style carnival mask, just like the man she had seen lighting street lamps near the guesthouse the night before.

She felt a smidgen of relief at having recognised him as the lamp-lighter, but experience had told her to test her hunches before disregarding them completely. Coming off the wide square at the Cathedral and speeding up considerably, she forced herself to walk at a trot down the winding higgledy-piggeldy streets filled with cafés and eateries. For a second she thought she had lost him and that she had been imagining that the lamp-lighter was following her, but there he was again, coming faster now down the cobbled street behind her.

She took off her wide straw-brimmed hat to make herself more inconspicuous in amongst the crowds of tourists and she slowed right down. Likewise, so did her tracker. Her heart beating wildly and fluttering up into her throat, Posie realised that the maze of streets in the old

127

baroque town were indeed good for hiding things, but at the same time, and for someone who perhaps knew these streets better than she did, they were a gift: a trap.

What on earth was she being tailed for? Had this man been hired by someone she knew – someone to do with this case – or an older enemy altogether?

At a junction in the tight road just before the fountain of Aretusa, Posie spied an ice-cream shop which didn't have a queue outside it, and which promised a cool, dark interior with locals standing at a counter sipping their coffees and reading their newspapers. She ducked inside and peered out.

Sure enough, her mysterious tracker had come to a standstill at the junction, and was now moving his head left and right, and turning around, as if checking he hadn't somehow outpaced Posie and left her behind him.

Unseen, just a couple of feet away, Posie almost gasped in sick horror at what happened next: she had somehow assumed that the man dressed up in a carnival mask was a local, that he knew the streets like the back of his hand. But she had been wrong: the man took a map from the folds of his black cloak and shook it out in frustration. Posie recognised it at once, for it bore the unmistakeable red and gold cover of Stanford's Map Shop in Covent Garden, and Posie had the very same map in her bag! It was an English map, and the Venetian-clad stalker must therefore be English!

No-one in the street gave the strange carnival figure a second glance, and it was with a feeling of real relief that Posie saw him fold back the map into its neat squares and seemingly make up his mind. He turned down a dark alleyway to the left, away from her.

She ordered a granita and stood drinking it through a paper straw, declining the café owner's kind and persistent attempts to draw out a chair and cloth-covered table for her outside on the street. She preferred instead to stand in the cover of the dark shop, fathoming out how she could get back to her guesthouse, and just who on earth the strange figure might be…

* * * *

Later, she placed a call with the International Operator, having paid the owner of the *Locatelli* an exorbitant amount for the privilege of talking on the telephone just for three minutes. She got through to Inspector Lovelace at Scotland Yard just as he was leaving for the day.

She gave him her exact location and the name and telephone number of her guesthouse as fast as she could. She could hear him sighing and a scribbling noise of pen on paper.

'I wasn't at all pleased to get your note to say you'd just upped and left like that, all alone. For one thing it would have been good to have you at Ianthe Flowers' Inquest – now I'll have to rely on your Witness Statement. I take it you actually have some good leads on the evasive Mr Alaric Boynton-Dale? Hard evidence that he *is* actually out there in Sicily?'

Posie didn't have anything of the sort, but she wasn't about to admit that. She had a hunch, at best. She ignored the question and skilfully changed the subject:

'How is the investigation into Ianthe Flowers' death going?'

'The formal Inquest is set for Wednesday.'

'Any clue who did it yet?'

The Inspector harrumphed down the line. 'No. I was there again at Boynton Hall on Friday afternoon, going over statements and re-questioning witnesses. They were all complaining of course, going stir-crazy all locked up together in one place, under house arrest. But to be honest, if one of them did it, they've been ruddy clever about it. There's not a single rogue fingerprint or bit of evidence to incriminate any of them! Not even Lord Roderick, who I'd hoped to nab for this murder pretty quickly…'

'So you've let them all go?' asked Posie sharply. Sharper than she had intended.

The Inspector caught the edge in her voice. 'No. No, we haven't. I've still got round-the-clock surveillance on the house. The local police force are standing guard, but no-one has left the place, I guarantee it. On Wednesday the whole household will be taken by police escort to the Inquest. I want to see their reactions in Court. After that, unless I get some concrete evidence on one or some of them, I'm going to have to let them all go. Why do you ask, Posie?'

'No reason!'

'WHY?'

She crumbled, and told him about the person whispering at her in the Ear of Dionysius, and the person following her in the street earlier. Just then the International Operator cut in, asking if they wanted three minutes of extra time. Posie accepted readily, regardless of the cost. It was a comfort to hear the Inspector's voice, so calm and reassuring. He seemed very close by.

'I had this stupid feeling that somehow the person following me today was connected to Boynton Hall. That it could have been Ianthe's murderer, come here for Alaric. Perhaps warning me off?'

'Not possible,' said the Inspector firmly, assuring her, and she could visualise him shaking his russet-red head in the failing light of his office, grabbing his homburg from the hatstand. 'No way. Which makes me feel strangely comfortable with the fact you're over there all alone. Are you sure you're not imagining things?'

Posie tutted non-committally.

'Well, take care Posie. Don't go looking for trouble. And if I was you I'd try and find Mr Boynton-Dale as quickly as you can and then turn on your heel and get out of there, pronto. I can protect you from the little lot at Boynton Hall, but heaven only knows *who* else you might have twitching on your heels over there! Goodness me, you court danger like no-one else I've ever met before! I have to go, but if you need me, I'm here. I can always try and find someone in the Sicilian police force to lend a hand, I suppose…'

No puppet shows were on the agenda that evening for Posie. In fact, she didn't even venture out on the balcony to watch the sunset over the lagoon, scared in case the strange carnival-clad figure had somehow found her and was lurking in the shadowy street below.

Instead, Posie started to read Ianthe's book. She hadn't got far through it when she fell into a deep sleep on the counterpane of her four-poster bed. But her dreams were far from restful.

In them she was spinning around in a circle, chased by figures who were all wearing white carnival masks and black cloaks and hats. However, she knew who they all were: one was clearly discernible as Codlington, with those bright sparkling ruby-and-gold cufflinks flashing from underneath the dark folds of his cloak, the engraved initials 'B-D' clearly prominent; one was Lord Roderick, swigging from a silver hip-flask which he hid in the depths of the black outfit; another was Mr Burns, his gaudily-coloured tartan trousers sticking out conspicuously from under the Venetian outfit and one was Eve, Lady Boynton, a blush-coloured Sobranie cigarette dangling from her scarlet-painted mouth beneath the white mask. And then another figure appeared, dressed in the same way, leading Posie and the others through Ortigia's tiny, crowded streets to the strange *Il Gioiello Ambra* shop.

'Here we are!' said a familiar voice in her dream, and

the figure turned and took off her mask, grinning with impish pleasure, shaking out her fair curls. And it was with a mixture of horror and delight that Posie recognised poor, murdered Ianthe.

And as the door opened to the strange little shop, Len stepped out, beaming. He was holding his camera aloft and blinding the whole group with the strong white light.

* * * *

Eleven

Tuesday morning found Posie bright as a button at the *Il Gioiello Ambra* shop. She was their first customer of the day. It was very early and still a little fresh out, and Posie had studied her own red and gold map from Stanford's carefully before setting out, swearing to find a way through the jumble of streets of the *Giudecca* area which a non-local pursuer would be hard-pushed to follow her through. And sure enough, although she had been vigilant and prepared, no-one had been on her tail.

Dressed smartly in her cream linen suit, newly made up and with a firm resolve not to be thwarted in her quest to find out where Alaric might be, or at the very least to learn about the location of the Hyblaean honey-makers, she stepped into the cool interior of the shop.

The young man from yesterday was nowhere to be seen. Instead, an elderly bearded and heavily sun-tanned man wearing a white gown smiled quizzically at her over the top of a pair of small half-moon glasses. Posie saw with a flash of surprise that the old man was wearing a thick gold crucifix over his gown.

'*Parli Inglese*?' asked Posie hopefully. Actually, she had no idea what she was going to do if the man *didn't* speak any English…

The man nodded briefly and drew out a high stool for her to sit on, all the while gazing intently at her necklace. Posie introduced herself formally, passing across one of her smart little business cards.

'How can I help you, signorina?' asked the old man, reading her name on the card and raising his eyebrows. 'Are you after a particular remedy? You know this is an apothecary? And an *expensive* one, too…it does not suit every person's pocket.'

'So I have heard,' she retorted resentfully, climbing onto the seat and remembering Harry Redmayne's comments about the cost of one spoonful of Hyblaean honey. Did she really look so shabby that this old man needed to warn her of the cost of his wares?

'I'm not after a remedy. I am after some *information*. I travelled here especially from England. I was given your shop's address by an Egyptologist at the British Museum. His name is Harry Redmayne, and he spoke about your shop to me and what it is you sell here. The *honey*… See here.'

She passed across the scribbled address of the shop which Harry Redmayne had written down on the back of his business card. She untied the bee coin deftly, turning it around before placing it in the man's hands. She pointed:

'There,' she said resolutely. 'Those words. I know what the second word means, or at least I can guess. But I need to know what "Serafina" is, or *who* she is. Can you help me?'

The old man frowned and clutched tightly at the coin in the palm of his hand, the other hand gripping at his crucifix. He looked up at her directly, his hand shaking slightly.

'What is it that this Mr Redmayne wants to know *exactly*? Why has he sent you here as his messenger?'

'No, no,' Posie said impatiently. '*He* doesn't want to know anything. I told him I was looking for something, for *someone* actually. He was trying to help *me*. And he told me to start here. At your shop.'

'Just who are you looking for, signorina?'

Posie sighed. There was obviously no point in beating about this particular bush. She spoke Alaric's full name aloud and watched the old man's face: cool, composed, secretive. Giving nothing away.

However, at the very back of the shop there was a very small rustle of a gold-beaded curtain, and Posie caught a flash of dark olive eyes disappearing behind the moving glitter. She felt a stab of fear as she realised her whole exchange with the old man had probably been overheard. She continued, trying to sound unflustered:

'Can you help me? Or point me in the right direction? I believe the man I am looking for is here on this island. Have you heard of Alaric at all?'

The old man shook his head, still staring hypnotically at the coin in his gnarled hand. Posie felt irritated. She was certain the old man was lying to her and at the same time she was reminded of the annoying Binkie Dodds who had failed her so spectacularly. She reached across and grabbed the coin back. She got down from the uncomfortable high stool and tied the necklace around her neck again. The old man stared at her, his eyes wide behind the glasses.

'This coin which you seem so impressed by is the personal property of Alaric Boynton-Dale. It is my intention to return it to him. That is all. I want to see with my own eyes that he is alive and well. I think he has been in danger and is hiding from some very evil person. I will not harm him, or give his location away. I can give him my word of honour. If this Serafina is a person who is protecting him, you can tell her from me that I mean him no harm. Alaric might have other people to fear, but I am not one of them.'

Posie noticed that the man had pocketed both of the business cards she had given him, and so she searched inside her bag for a piece of paper and scribbled the address of the *Locatelli* guesthouse on the back of it. She

135

noticed as she passed it over to the old man that it was in fact Alaric's own typewritten sheet of the fairly worthless small coin collection he had inherited from his father, and which she had thrown in her bag whilst rootling around in the annexe at Boynton Hall.

'You can reach me here, if you think of anything. *If* you can help me…' she said, trying to keep the bitterness and sense of failure out of her voice.

But she wasn't holding out much hope.

* * * *

Posie spent a while reading in her room. She enjoyed Ianthe's light, almost comical style and she recognised several of the characters who were leaping out of the pages at her from *The Tomb of the Honey Bee*.

Here was Alaric, recognisable even though she had never met him before – dashing, brave, untameable – thinly disguised as a bee-loving character named Viscount Robert Rowse; here too was a character to all extents and purposes like Eve, Lady Boynton – rich, nasty, bejewelled – but with the key difference that she was madly in love with Viscount Robert Rowse, and would go to any lengths to ensnare him away from his lover… Posie put down the book. She found herself strangely frustrated: why on earth did the book have that odd title?

She yawned. She wasn't really in the mood for reading. Still less did she want to read a fictional account of a murder mystery set in a version of Boynton Hall, the memory of which, even out here on the beautiful island of Sicily, gave her the creeps. She looked across at a small blue puppet of a knight which she had bought in a market on her way home, and thought how apt it was: she couldn't shake off the feeling that some clever hand had been at work there, at Boynton Hall, puppeteering everything. She hoped Inspector Lovelace would be able to cut through it all.

Posie looked out of the window at the blue sky melding with the fantastic sparkling sea. Suddenly she felt like a prisoner trapped inside…just like the household at Boynton Hall, she supposed. They would be let out tomorrow, packed off in police cars to sit at the grim Coroner's Court in Victoria, their every twitch and gesture observed by the detectives as they listened to the grisly details of Ianthe's death at the Inquest. But Posie knew in her heart that the killer would be much too clever to give anything away in such an obvious fashion, and she couldn't help but feel the Inspector was clutching at straws.

She determined to go out and send Lady Violet a telegram, updating her, although in truth she had no real news. She was frustrated at the way her pursuit of Alaric was going, and cross at herself for her lack of progress. She *knew* he was here now; she had seen that glint of guilt, of knowledge, in the old man's eyes at the apothecary's shop.

She decided too to spend some time in a little touristy market she had seen nearby, to buy some postcards and gifts. If she had failed in her mission to make this an investigation, she would at least make it look and feel a bit like a holiday.

* * * *

Posie spent an enjoyable late morning wandering the streets near her guesthouse. She continued to look over her shoulder for anyone on her tail, but she had also taken the precaution of employing Enzo, the teenage son of the bellboy at the *Locatelli* to be her 'guide'. While they didn't share a common language, she had sketched out a diagram of a man dressed in the black Venetian costume with a white mask, and had managed to communicate enough to Enzo so that if and when he saw such a character appear, he was to tell Posie at once. If the boy thought her a little crazy, he didn't say so, and he proved himself both eager and conscientious in response to the tip Posie had given him at the start of the walk.

After sending her telegram, Posie loitered in the local harbour market. She bought triple-milled soaps, and a jet-black beaded purse for Prudence. She also found a beautiful framed watercolour of the lagoon which would make a perfect wedding present for her friends Rufus Cardigeon and Dolly Price, whose wedding in September she had been looking forwards to with great excitement.

After a while, she instructed Enzo to carry her purchases back to the guesthouse. Posie felt convinced that she was safe alone, and she wandered aimlessly among the postcard-stands.

She was focusing on a choice between two almost identical postcards of the Cathedral when she became aware that someone was watching her. Moving surreptitiously along the stands, as if she hadn't a care in the world, she picked up a few more postcards from the racks and then turned a quarter-circle, apparently fishing around in her purse for the correct change to give to the stall holder. From beneath her dark sunglasses but without moving her head at all she took a quick look at the stranger who was loitering on the other side of the pavement, observing her.

Posie almost gasped in shock as what she saw registered, and she dropped her postcards, her change, her carpet bag and her purse in one stupid, careless movement. Everyone turned to stare at her clumsiness and when she looked up from her crouching position on the ground, retrieving her belongings, the loitering person had disappeared. Were her eyes playing tricks on her?

That flash of a glance had left her with the impression of a tall willowy woman, all long limbs, her face obscured by an enormous sun-hat. But there had been no mistaking the red, red coils of hair which had been escaping in wild, curling tendrils from beneath the hat.

Could it be Cosima Catchpole, here on the island with her? It was certainly possible; she wasn't officially one of the suspects in Ianthe Flowers' death, and she was not being observed back at Stowe-on-the-Middle-Wold by the police surveillance team.

Had Cosima Catchpole known more about Hyblaean honey and where it came from than she had been letting on? Had she, under her cool and somewhat aloof exterior, still been harbouring feelings of love for Alaric, despite her insistence to the contrary? Had she been lying when she had said their love affair was all over?

Or was she here for more sinister reasons? Had it been Cosima dressed in the carnival outfit, following her and whispering her name at the cave? Posie remembered suddenly the conversation she had had with Major Marchpane about his wife: he had told her that Cosima loved to dress up and act.

So was she here on the island as friend, or foe?

* * * *

Twelve

Having trailed unsuccessfully through the market in pursuit of the woman who might have been Cosima Catchpole, Posie gave up at last, admitted defeat and retreated to a shady café in the precincts of her guesthouse.

Try as she might Posie couldn't see Cosima's motive for any of the dangerous events which had led to Alaric's disappearance, or to the murder of Ianthe Flowers. So what was she doing here on the island? Posie took a long unsatisfying slug of her strong coffee and scowled: none of this made any sense at all. She stuffed another soft pastry cake into her mouth, a Sicilian cream-filled fancy known as a cannoli, which she was developing quite a taste for.

Her thoughts were broken into by a bland, calm, non-descript Englishman's voice cutting through the busy sounds of the café:

'Excuse me, do you mind if I join you at your table?'

She had quite forgotten where she was, and without looking up she found herself nodding and making space at the wrought iron table, much as she would have done back home on a café terrace in Covent Garden.

'But of course…please do.'

When she looked up she got her second shock of the day: so much so that she dropped most of her hot coffee down the front of her lovely cream silk blouse.

'BINKIE?' she almost shouted, although the words seemed to get stuck in her throat somewhere. And it was indeed Binkie Dodds, dressed in tweeds as if for an English winter, unfetchingly red and sweaty in the face and peering at her through his bottle-bottom thick glasses.

'What-ho, old chum!' he smiled cheerfully, slapping a guidebook to the island down on the table.

'Don't suppose you can get a nice cup of English tea in this place, can you? It's always ruddy coffee on the continent, isn't it? I'll have one of those cakes, if you don't mind, too. You look like you've packed on a few pounds in recent years; you won't mind skipping on just one, will you?'

He swiped the last remaining cannoli, and scoffed it in one. Posie fumed, especially at the remark about her weight, which probably had a grain of truth to it, but was not at all what she wanted to hear. Binkie waved at a passing waiter and ordered coffee.

'Bit ruddy hot here, what?'

His manner was friendly and almost carefree, totally unlike when she had last met him in his horrible brown office. Posie stared at him in utter disbelief. This was all she needed to complicate matters! She couldn't help but notice that Binkie kept his beady eyes fixed on her necklace.

'Bet you're surprised to see me here, eh?'

'I would say "surprised" is an understatement,' she said slowly. She gave him one of her looks.

'How did you know I was here, in Ortigia of all places? And more specifically, Binkie, what is it you *want* from me?'

He was drumming his fingers on the snowy cloth of the table. He took his coffee and swigged at it, wincing at its strength.

'I was due some leave…thought I'd come out here for a holiday, check out some of the archaeology. The Ear of Dionysius alone is meant to be worth the trip.' He didn't meet her gaze but stared out at the harbour. He was lying.

'The TRUTH, Binkie.'

He sighed, flicking the pages of the guidebook absently. 'That obvious, is it?'

'I'm not a detective for nothing,' Posie said sourly.

'I'm here because I heard you talking to my colleague Harry Redmayne on Friday. I loitered outside my office for a while and heard him telling you to come to Ortigia. I panicked.'

Posie bit her lip on the anger she felt mounting up inside her.

'Why would you panic?'

'I thought you were coming out here to give the coin back to them. But I see I'm just in time, it's still in your possession. Although you really shouldn't be wearing it like that, you fat-head. It's a world-class museum piece! It should be in a cabinet, not around your ruddy neck!'

Posie stared at Binkie in horror. He had never been her, or her brother Richard's favourite person in the world, but now she was convinced that there was something mentally unhinged about him.

The echo of a sentence uttered by Harry Redmayne suddenly came back to her: '*He gets awfully excited about coins, he could even kill for one!*' She gasped aloud. Could this whole wretched pursuit on the island, the man dressed in the Venetian costume and the whispering at the Archaeology Park have simply been Binkie Dodds trying to intimidate her, desperate for the coin back?

But then reality kicked in: somehow she couldn't imagine Binkie being creative or ingenious enough to dress up in such an elaborate outfit, or to trail her around in the sweltering heat. He also looked as if he didn't have the puff, or the willpower.

Binkie stretched out his hand in Posie's direction, palm upturned. 'I need you to hand that coin over to me. Now, please.'

Posie laughed incredulously at him. 'It's not mine to give you, Binkie,' she said curtly, gathering up her bag and the postcards. 'You *know* that.'

And then something he had said replayed again in her mind:

'Just *who* exactly did you think I would be giving this back to anyway?'

'Why, the monks of course!' Binkie retorted as if she were stupid. One look at her confused face made him realise she didn't have a clue what he was talking about.

'At the Monastery of Serafina,' he sighed wearily. 'That was where the coin *came* from in the first place; it was found by an English explorer who infiltrated the Monastery in the 1600s. He took it for his own collection and then donated it to the British Museum later, where it stayed nicely until your pal Alaric got his hands on it. The monks of Serafina would probably give their eye-teeth to have it returned to them. It's an ancient coin, priceless. Their Monastery is cut off in the mountains and in a secret location, but I thought you might have sussed it out by now and got there before I'd found you! Anyhow, don't feel bad: the monks don't need it; they're known to be rich beyond belief. And *who* will ever see it stuck up there? Not like at the British Museum where thousands can visit it every year...'

Posie stared at Binkie, her mouth open. Serafina: not a person after all, and not a Goddess, but a Monastery!

Binkie drivelled on. But Posie wasn't in the least bit interested in his potted history lesson. Instead, she was putting pieces of the jigsaw together: a secluded Monastery, a perfect place to hide if you were in danger; a secret Monastery, high up in the Hyblaean mountains where in all probability the legendary honey was made; a flash of a gold crucifix swinging against the white robes of the old man at the *Il Gioiello Ambra* shop; the sumptuous interior of the shop, and the way the old man had stared at

143

the bee coin in a kind of haggard disbelief.

It all fitted nicely! The *Il Gioiello Ambra* shop must be run by the monks, selling their select wares from the Monastery!

'Do me a favour, Binkie. Do you happen to know if they make honey up there at this Monastery?'

Binkie scowled. '*Honey*? I haven't a clue. Now, that coin. Are you going to give it to me, or what?'

'No,' said Posie firmly, rising from her chair. 'Over my dead body. And if you keep hassling me like this I'm going to call the police. Now, go away and leave me be.'

* * * *

Back at the *Locatelli*, Posie stopped at the Welcome Desk to ask if there were any messages or telegrams for her. She stood in a queue of fellow guests with an ill grace; she was tired and fidgety, longing for a bath and to change out of her coffee-stained blouse. She was also planning on having another stab at reading Ianthe's book, and then she planned to focus all her energies on trying to locate the Serafina Monastery, using Inspector Lovelace's contacts in the Sicilian police force if she had to.

Tired though she was, she felt giddily happy at the thought of finding the Monastery, and, if she was right, finding Alaric safe within.

When Posie reached the front of the queue the Hotel Manager started up in a wild jabber of Italian. Posie shook her head in frustration:

'*Io non capisco*. I'm so sorry; I don't understand.'

Just then a man's voice cut through the echoey blue-and-white tiled entrance hall. Posie looked to her left and noticed a tall man standing in the shadows, near the birdcage lift, blocking the route up to her room. She couldn't see his face but something about his stance was vaguely familiar.

'The Hotel Manager is telling you that people have been here today, asking if you were staying here,' said the man in a halting but impeccable English.

'First, an English man visited. He had thick glasses. Then, later, a woman came here with long curling red hair. The Hotel Manager says both of these people were very strange; they didn't want to leave their details. The woman wanted to see your room upstairs, but the Manager sent her away. The red-haired woman also asked after Alaric Boynton-Dale. She asked if he was staying here with you...'

Posie's mind raced. Binkie had obviously been the first visitor, and then Cosima. So, she *hadn't* imagined Cosima's presence lurking in the market, after all. She felt a sense of light relief that she wasn't going totally crazy.

The man by the birdcage lift suddenly stepped out into the light, and Posie recognised him at once as the young man with the dark olive eyes from the *Il Gioiello Ambra*. She now saw he was wearing the same white cassock as the old man in the shop, and that a thick gold crucifix also hung about his neck.

'I, too, have been waiting for you,' the man said, motioning for her to follow him.

'My name is Brother Luca and I am sent to collect you. We need to leave right now. It is imperative that we are not followed. Where we are going is a closely-guarded secret, and it seems you have more strange people sniffing around you than can altogether be considered desirable. So we will leave by the back exit, here. Come!'

'*Who* sent you here for me?' asked Posie guardedly. She had been on the receiving end of tricks such as these before, most recently in February of that year, when she had been convinced to get inside a supposed police car which had turned out to be packed to the gunnels with world-class jewel thieves. They had then kidnapped her.

'I think you know *who* sent me for you. I don't think I need to repeat his name,' said Brother Luca infuriatingly. Posie's heart was hammering in her throat: *could it be this easy?* Was she being handed Alaric Boynton-Dale on a plate? It seemed so.

'Come!' Brother Luca started to walk towards the dim back quarters of the guesthouse.

'Wait!' Posie squealed indignantly, making up her mind on the spot that she should indeed follow the monk, but feeling that she was horribly unprepared. 'I need to change! Freshen up!'

'No time for that!' said the monk firmly. 'It's now or never! You choose if you want to stay behind to dress up nicely. But I'm not hanging around for you!'

Jeepers, Posie thought to herself at the monk's bluntness. *How very rude!*

But she puffed along behind Brother Luca as quickly as she could manage. He didn't bother to look around to see if she was keeping up.

* * * *

They travelled out of Ortigia together on foot, in silence, through a series of tiny back alleys and lanes, with Posie constantly turning her head to check she wasn't being tailed by what now amounted to quite a collection of possible stalkers.

Eventually, on one of the three bridges which joined Ortigia to the main part of Siracusa, Brother Luca indicated towards a green van parked up hard against the kerb, its canvas sides painted with gaudy pictures of fruit.

'Get in the back,' he whispered, and Posie clambered up into the dark, canvas-drawn interior, to find herself sitting amongst empty fruit crates on the hard metal floor. She was not altogether unsurprised to get a glimpse of the old monk from the apothecary shop sitting behind the steering wheel, his fingers drumming impatiently as Brother Luca swung in beside him, pulling the canvas partition firmly closed so that Posie was left without any view.

For the next hour they travelled uphill, bumping and jumping and feeling every little rock under the van's tyres. But Posie felt confident it would all soon be worth it: the Serafina Monastery was almost in reach.

* * * *

Thirteen

At last they arrived. Posie was aware of falling shadows, and the sun going down behind low, rocky mountains covered in verdant vegetation. Everywhere she looked she saw olive groves and orange orchards and trees with stars of jasmine on every branch. The scent was overpowering.

'This way, please,' said Brother Luca flatly, without any emotion.

Behind a curve of a grey mountain a glossy white marble stone building was suddenly revealed, complete with an ornate glittering golden-tiled roof. The sun was reflected in its many stained glass windows, flashing from the huge golden crucifix mounted on the top of a square bell tower. From a far-off chapel came the sound of chanting.

Posie found herself quickly ushered into a huge white-painted room with a grand curved roof. It smelt chalky and felt restful, and was low lit with a series of candles in sconces along the walls.

It was a moment before she realised that Brother Luca had gone, but as her eyes adjusted to the gloom she realised she was not alone: at one end of the room was a plain wooden table, and at it sat Alaric Boynton-Dale.

'Miss Parker?' he said, standing up with a half-smile, indicating she should join him at the table. His voice was pleasantly gravelly, totally unlike what she had been expecting. She marched across the tiled floor purposefully. She extended her hand and he gripped it firmly.

'Welcome to the Serafina Monastery.'

She studied Alaric quickly, and found herself surprised. Heaven knew she was not the kind of girl to go weak at the knees when she came across the rich or famous, but she realised with a start that the newspapers, which loved to print his image and details of his exploits again and again, had never done him justice: here was a man who was strikingly handsome; tall with very stark, lean features which were softened just slightly by laughter lines which creased around his eyes, and by his light brown hair which was worn slightly longer than it should have been. He looked older than she had thought he would, too. Definitely a man who had reached his mid-forties, rather than a man in his late thirties, as she knew he was.

His face was deeply sun-tanned and he had deep-set eyes which were the colour of old bronze coins: at once green, then golden, then brown. Alaric was also looking at her neck with an arched eyebrow. Posie sat down on the wooden chair which was offered to her and untied the silk thread around her neck.

'I can give this back to you now!' she declared. 'I told myself that as soon as I delivered this back to you, and located you, my job was done! Golly, I'm so pleased to find you here. And well. And alive!'

Alaric picked up the coin but did not look at it. Instead he looked directly at Posie, a mix of inquisitiveness and humour playing about his eyes. But what Posie read there most of all was sadness.

'*Who* asked you to find me?' he asked softly, in the low gravelly voice. 'How did you know I was here? How did you track me down? It says here you are a detective...'

She now saw that he had papers and various bits of information spread out before him on the table. He was holding onto her business card, and also that of Harry Redmayne. She saw with a start of surprise that there was also a blurry, smudgy photograph of her peering nosily through a window – the one Brother Luca must have taken yesterday at the *Il Gioiello Ambra* shop – and she also recognised Alaric's typewritten list of coins on which she had written her guesthouse address. The old monk must have given Alaric all of the information in one go, and he must have agreed to meet her off the back of it.

'I need to know *who* you are working for. I am sure you are aware I am hiding out here, lying low. Someone wants me dead, Miss Parker. I cannot be too careful.' Alaric indicated quickly to a small black pistol half-concealed under a thick wad of papers.

Never one to be shocked, Posie nodded. Besides, guns had never scared her – Len had carried one around with him on a daily basis – in fact, he probably still did, even in the Cap d'Antibes.

'I understand,' she said, more confidently than she felt. 'I'll start at the beginning.'

She told him about Lady Violet instructing her to find out what had happened to him, the way that Lady Violet feared he had been murdered. She described the main list of suspects Lady Violet had outlined and the brief, horrible visit she had made to Boynton Hall. She described her encounter with Major Marchpane and his entrusting the bee coin to her, as he had been flummoxed by its meaning. She described Ianthe Flowers' wish to tell her something important, and then she told him about Ianthe's death by poison, not forgetting to include the detail of the missing page of the manuscript of *The Tomb of the Honey Bee*.

She watched Alaric gasp in horror and grow pale beneath his sun-tan, and then look by turns sickened, then shocked. He was muttering under his breath:

'Murder? Oh, poor Cousin Ianthe, what a way to go… she didn't deserve *that*…'

Posie described in some detail Scotland Yard's involvement in Ianthe's murder inquiry. She then outlined her trip to the British Museum and her encounter with Harry Redmayne, the Egyptologist who had called Alaric to see if he wanted to accompany him out to Luxor. She described how Harry had provided her with clues as to the significance of Hyblaean honey, and Ortigia, and crucially, with the address of the little shop.

'It's not a very nice story, really, is it?' she said, sadly. 'But here I am anyway. I'm so glad I found you. I have to confess that at points I was worried about you myself, especially when I saw you had left everything at home: your tent, your clothes, your travelling kit. But I can tell your sister that you are alive and fit as a fiddle!'

To her surprise Alaric clutched his head in his hands and emitted a low groan. Had she said or done something wrong?

'Don't fret,' she reassured him. 'I won't tell a sausage *where* you are, if that's what's worrying you. I know this place is a secret; both the Serafina Monastery *and* the honey. I couldn't find it again if I tried, either! The fruit van they brought me up here in was as good as any blindfold I've ever come across!'

Alaric looked at Posie with scrunched up concentration in his eyes, not speaking.

'What is it?' she said softly.

'You're a very clever girl,' he said at last. 'Finding me like this. I take my hat off to you. But you're jolly well right, it's not a very nice story. Not one bit of it. And please don't tell anyone where I am. None of this has happened like it was meant to…I got a shock when the monks told me someone was looking for me. Well, that it was *you*, and not Cosima…'

'How do you mean? *Not* Cosima?'

Alaric sighed:

'All this beastly stuff kept happening to me, as you

know. The final straw was the destruction of my beehives: a heartless, terrible action. It upset me far less that it was *I* who was probably intended to die, than the knowledge that those thousand hives of hard-working bees had been murdered… I couldn't hang around at Boynton Hall any longer, staring at the destruction of those fields. I realised my life was in danger, but I needed peace and quiet, above all else. I left on the spur of the moment, just in the clothes I was wearing. I left everything behind. I just had time to send a message to Cosima. And then I came here, to get away, to reassess my life. To hide. I couldn't believe someone was trying to kill me, it was terrible. I *told* Violet this in a telegram I sent from the station: I told her not to jolly well worry.'

Posie thought it was not a good time to mention the fact that the scantily-worded telegram had posed as many questions as it had answered, and that she for one had originally thought it was a suicide note.

Posie nodded. 'How did you know about this place? The Monastery seems to be a secret. Even Harry Redmayne didn't know about it, or didn't know it was the place which makes the special honey…'

Alaric smiled and Posie caught a glimmer of amusement beneath the sadness.

'I've always known about it. As long as I can remember, anyway. I was a spoilt child, and my father always gave me what I wanted, which included this coin here. You know it's from here originally? That the monks kept it safe here for centuries before it ended up in the British Museum? I made it my business to know about the Serafina Monastery, and the Hyblaean honey which they produce. I told myself that one day I would track it down, and come out here. It was right that I came here *now*. I knew the monks would hide me.'

'How did you find it?'

Alaric laughed: 'I'm not an explorer for nothing, you know! Same as you're not a detective for nothing!'

'Fair enough,' said Posie nodding. 'But I'm surprised the monks just let you come up here and stay, even a famous explorer like yourself. They seem a pretty hostile bunch to me. Did you have to pay them?'

Alaric shook his head. 'Not as such.' He waved the bee coin on its piece of navy silk at Posie.

'*This* is the payment. I told the monks that it would be arriving here any day, and that in exchange for sheltering me in the safety of the Monastery and for letting me observe them at work making the Hyblaean honey, they could have their ancient coin back. That's why they were so excited to see you pitching up at their apothecary in town wearing it around your neck, and why they've surpassed themselves in getting you up here. You told them you wanted to see *me*, but all they were interested in was the coin!'

'Along with half the world, it seems,' said Posie with a raise of a not altogether approving eyebrow. She told Alaric briefly about Binkie Dodds and how he had followed her to Sicily in pursuit of it, like a man driven mad.

'I'm glad it's going back to where it belongs, anyway,' she said. 'But one thing puzzles me: how did you expect to *receive* the coin here? Forgive me for saying it, as I know he is a great friend of yours, but entrusting the coin to Major Marchpane without any proper instructions was a bit risky, wasn't it? He told me himself that he was never one for "clues". In fact, it turned out that Major Marchpane had never, in all the years you knew each other, noticed that you wore the coin around your neck! How on earth could he have brought it out here for you?'

Alaric sighed wearily. 'I didn't send the coin to Hugo Marchpane,' he said, his shoulders drooping. 'I told you just now. I sent it to *Cosima*, asking her to look after Bikram, my dog. And I sent her a message…a note…'

Realisation dawned on Posie. It was all a stupid mix-up, with incomprehension on every level, on *all* sides. It amazed her sometimes that the cleverest, brightest people in the world could be so obtuse.

'You said in the note something like "You know what *this* means", didn't you?'

Alaric nodded quickly.

'The bee coin was a double sign, wasn't it? First, it was a sign that you were okay, and that you had chosen to leave of your own accord, rather than been murdered, and second, you thought you had given Cosima enough information in that brief note for her to get the coin back to you here…'

And Posie tailed off. She had suddenly realised something: Alaric must still have been in love with Cosima when he sent that note to her a week ago. Which meant he loved her still. He had wanted Cosima to come out here too, to join him. For some reason Posie felt a pang at this. Perhaps the sting of her recently-thwarted romantic dreams with Len Irving had made her more sensitive to the feelings of others in similar situations?

'Yes,' said Alaric resolutely. 'That's exactly right. Spot on. When we were together, before she broke up with me, that is, I would talk on and on about Hyblaean honey, the mountains here, the Monastery where this coin came from. She knew it was my dream to come out here… I can't understand how she didn't realise what I meant in the note; it must have been obvious that this is where I would have chosen to hide. What happened?'

Posie cleared her throat tellingly. She was going to have to be cruel to be kind, but *gently*.

'Two things happened. Forgive me, Mr Boynton-Dale, but you overlooked one important detail: your dog Bikram and Lady Cosima do not get on. At all. I don't know why, but Bikram prefers Major Marchpane, and Lady Cosima is afraid of Bikram. Clever though he is, and even if you instructed him clearly to find Cosima, the unfortunate fact is that he went and found Major Marchpane instead, thus delivering the message to the wrong person. And Major Marchpane thought it best to keep it a secret. BUT, even if Bikram *had* delivered the message to Lady Cosima, I am very much afraid that she would *not* have made it out here either.'

Posie toughed it out, gritting her teeth as she spoke:

'I questioned her about the coin, and it meant very little to her. She seemed to recall the word "Hyblaean" as being linked to honey, but very little else. Certainly nothing as concrete as was required to find you out here. Perhaps, after all, the Major and Lady Cosima are more suited to each other than you think. Neither of them are very details-oriented, and perhaps neither of them are very good at listening to people, or observing people either.'

Posie vowed she would not mention Cosima's stinging words which came back to her in a horrible flurry: '*My love for Alaric was not strong enough to make it work in the long-term*', coupled with the revelation that '*in truth, I probably wasn't listening…sometimes I just drifted off…*' She would not mention the steely way Cosima had implied Alaric had loved her far more than she had ever loved him, or the resolve she had heard in Lady Cosima's voice when she had spoken of her newly-mended marriage. Or of how Major Marchpane, obviously not the brightest when it came to emotions, well and truly believed that Alaric had given Cosima up for good.

Alaric hung his head for what seemed like an age, and Posie was just beginning to feel like a dreadful fat-head when she saw that he had recovered himself a little and was even attempting a half-smile.

'It seems, Miss Parker, that you alone seem to have had the sense that all three of us were lacking. I, in particular, feel a first-rate fool. Fancy not realising that Cosima was not enamoured of Bikram, and then sending him to her anyway! I suppose love must really be blind… It seems I could do with some of your clear-headedness in sorting this nasty mess out once and for all.'

He stood up. 'Would you care to walk in the orchards and see the legendary beehives? Many, Harry Redmayne included, would give their eye-teeth for such a pleasure! We may just catch the last of the light. And afterwards, you must stay for tea, and try some of the honey. You can stay here in one of the guestrooms tonight: it's too late, and too dangerous to start back again for Ortigia tonight.'

Posie followed Alaric out, watching him as he passed the bee coin solemnly over to an unsmiling Brother Luca, who had been standing like a sentry outside the door to the room they had been cloistered inside.

What a mess, Posie thought to herself as they passed down ornate tiled corridors of brightest gold, lit by candles, on their way out. They passed a monk in the process of lighting some of the sconces, and Posie remembered with a horrid little jolt the Venetian-masked tallow-lighter in Ortigia, and the similar costume worn by the person who had been following her around in such a sinister fashion. As yet, and she didn't know why, she hadn't got around to mentioning it to Alaric.

And with a guilty tug at her conscience, she realised that she also hadn't told him about having seen Lady Cosima in the market earlier; that as vague and uncaring as Cosima had proved or pretended herself to be with regard to her feelings for Alaric, she *had* managed to get herself out here to Ortigia, after all.

* * * *

Fourteen

'The bees have all gone to Bedfordshire for the night,' joked Alaric, as they walked in the twilight beneath the linden trees.

Alaric showed Posie an entire side of a stony, nubby mountain filled with fico d'India plants, dispersed among which were hundreds upon hundreds of wicker beehives. A white-robed monk was moving among the hives in the far distance carrying a low-burning torch.

The light was failing as they walked, and if she were being very honest, Posie could smell more than she could see, but the delicious evening perfume coupled with Alaric's almost touching enthusiasm for the rare concoction of flora which made the Hyblaean honey so very special raised her spirits. It was a paradise here, even if it was a paradise which Alaric had obviously been hoping to show to Lady Cosima, not her.

As they walked back towards the Serafina Monastery it seemed almost in bad taste to mention the 'nasty mess' which had led the explorer to seek sanctuary here. But time was pressing and Posie was interested in hearing the explorer's thoughts on *who* exactly wanted him out of the way.

'I was tasked to find you, and I have,' she said. 'But it's all got so complicated now, and I feel I have to see this thing through to the end, even if I'm no longer "officially" instructed.'

They had reached a low stone bench set on a terrace outside the main entrance to the Monastery. Posie sat down wearily, Alaric following suit. It was still very hot, and she batted midges away from her face.

'I was given a list of suspects at the very start of this case. But now one of those very suspects, Ianthe, has herself been murdered. I think she had found something out about the person who wanted to harm you, and she wanted to tell me, and she was killed because of it. I therefore have a personal connection to her murder, and this case. But I feel no nearer to pinpointing anyone on that original list! The trouble is, everyone seems to have a motive for wanting you dead. Even my friend, Inspector Lovelace at Scotland Yard, doesn't seem to have a firm lead. You must tread carefully, Mr Boynton-Dale. Even hiding out here, if this is where you intend to stay.'

'Call me Alaric, please,' he insisted.

'Fine. But somebody very dangerous was among those gathered at Boynton Hall, Alaric. I could feel the evil there.'

Alaric smiled in the almost-darkness. He was miles away, back at the home of his childhood, before the time of the Great War, before the loss of his parents, before he gave up his title.

'Ah! Dear, dear Boynton Hall,' he reminisced fondly. A grave, dreamy look stole over his face.

'You talk of evil, but that evil is a very new thing, you know. A very new atmosphere pervades the place now. Time was when I couldn't wait to get back there. I dreamt of it when I was needing comfort in the Great War; I thought of it when I was up in my little Sopwith Camel, tearing through the machine gun fire. Boynton Hall has weathered the ages and it will go on doing so. I kept remembering its permanence: wars, sieges, changes of government and religion. Why, did you know there is even a Priest's Hole and a secret chapel in the house, with loads of secret tunnels? They was built in the sixteenth century, when it was a crime for the Boynton-Dale family to be Catholic, and they had to hide their priest away somewhere. At my lowest points it comforted me to think that Boynton Hall would be there for a long, long time after me. It comforted me, even though I had given it up when I was much younger to my fool of a brother!'

'Do you regret that decision?'

Alaric shook his head firmly. 'No! None of that aristocratic title nonsense was important to me. It still isn't.'

'My friend the Inspector thinks that your brother Roderick is the prime suspect in both Ianthe's death and in plotting yours: the damaged aeroplane, the burnt beehives. Do you agree?'

Alaric made a noise somewhere between a choke and a laugh. 'No! Roderick hasn't got it in him! He might want my money but he wouldn't kill me for it!'

'But would he pay someone else to do his dirty work for him?'

Alaric shook his head.

'But you agree this *is* about your money?' Posie said casually. 'Your Will, more specifically. You did bring it out here, didn't you? The new one you signed in favour of your sister? Your lawyer, Mr Proudfoot, is apparently going out of his mind with worry, he wants it safely locked up in his strongroom. If your new Will is lost, everything stays the same way as in your old Will. Roderick gets the lot!'

Alaric turned in the semi-darkness and looked at Posie appreciatively. 'Cooe-ee! Not much gets by you, does it?'

He nodded and lit a cigarette, offering one to Posie from a cardboard packet, which she declined. He blew a perfect smoke ring which hung between them in the mosquitoey blue air.

'You're right. I think this *is* about my Will, wretched thing. These attacks only started up around the time I announced I was changing it! And yes, I do have the new Will here with me. Don't worry, I'm not going to lose it. It's safe here. I wish I could have given the Trust monies away when I signed away the house and title to Roderick, but I couldn't. No legal way out of it, apparently. So now I'm stuck with some lunatic on my heels trying to kill me for that money. Maybe poor Ianthe found out which particular lunatic it was, and she wrote about it in her new book. I wouldn't be surprised: she was awfully clever, a bit like you actually.'

Alaric stared for a second too long at Posie, making her feel uncomfortable. He blew another smoke ring.

'She made it her job to ferret out interesting stories about people. All of this would really have appealed to her. The perils of being a writer, eh? Poor soul, paying with her life like that.'

'You announced you were going to change the Will,' said Posie carefully, 'but did you actually tell anyone you *had* gone to the lawyers' office and changed it for definite?'

Alaric shrugged, shaking his head. 'I don't think so,' he said slowly. 'I can't remember really.'

Was it her imagination or had a cloud of darkness settled over Alaric's features? A fleeting frown of worry which hung there, caught. She changed tack:

'So then, which particular lunatic do *you* think is trying to kill you?' asked Posie in an even tone. She watched as Alaric drew another mouthful of smoke, exhaling it around him. He crossed his long legs and uncrossed them again.

'I haven't really got a clue,' he said quietly, after a time. 'I think if I were a betting man I would have put money on it being Roderick's wife, Eve. She's the recent evil I was speaking of at Boynton Hall; things haven't been the same in that house since Roderick brought her there. She wants the money in the Will but she wants something else, too.'

'Oh?'

Alaric sighed. 'I'm surprised you didn't find out sooner,

what with your nose for a story. Eve is in love with me, has thrown herself at me countless times over the years. She met me first, you know, at some party in London, and pursued me for months. She married Roderick when it was obvious I wasn't interested in her, and he only married her for her money. Unsurprisingly, she doesn't really love my brother, it's all a big face-saving act: those adoring looks, the way she won't leave his side. But in private she has continued to pursue me, even after their marriage. It's got past the point of being embarrassing now. Just ghastly! That was one of the reasons I set up home in the annexe a couple of years ago, to get away from the wretched woman. Talk about awkward!'

Posie stared at him, incredulous. It had never crossed her mind! Was Alaric, in common with many very good-looking men, capable of believing that every woman he met was madly in love with him? He didn't seem the type somehow, not vain enough. Too down-to-earth.

'Really? But your sister Violet told me Eve hates you with a passion! She even came across her in the Library once, cutting up newspaper photos of you, scoring through your face with a razor. Perhaps you didn't know?'

Alaric laughed bitterly:

'Oh, poor Cuckoo!' he said fondly.

'My sister Violet gets the wrong end of the stick sometimes, that's all. I know exactly what you are referring to. Lady Eve is a great lover of scrapbooks. She cuts out photos and articles all the time. Her favourite subject is *me*. She's obsessed. I've seen the books – she showed me. She's made at least twenty, just of me! What sort of skewed compliment is that? Please don't think I'm boasting, either. I find it very disturbing. I've never really spoken of it to anyone, and certainly not to Violet. Cuckoo probably never guessed: she was too young at the time to remember how Eve had come to meet Roderick in the first place. But I'd say the signs were all there, if you knew what to look for. And what Violet saw was probably Eve cutting out another picture, ready to glue into her scrapbook, but when Eve saw that she was cornered she probably thought she would play-act and pretend to deface it instead. Easier.'

He ground out his cigarette out under his heel. 'And perhaps Ianthe realised Eve was in love with me, and wrote about it. Who knows?'

Posie suddenly saw how all of this made sense. She remembered Eve's particularly venomous, over-the-top tones when she spoke about Alaric, which now made sense if you saw it as a weird form of self-preservation, defensiveness. She remembered the strange light which illuminated Eve's ugly face when she spoke of Alaric. She recalled talking to Eve's father on the lawn at Boynton Hall, and his words about Alaric came back to her now, but they had taken on an altogether different meaning: '*If you ask me, my girl Eve has taken his disappearance mighty badly...*'

And then she remembered what she had been reading earlier in Ianthe's novel; the characters who she now realised were all obviously based perilously closely on the real-life occupants of Boynton Hall! So Alaric was right! Ianthe *had* realised that Eve was in love with Alaric and had created a horrible character based on Eve, who was so bewitched by the explorer in the book that she spent all her time plotting how to get him away from his lover.

If Ianthe had understood people as well as Alaric implied, and wrote about them in her new book, it seemed probable that she had come across the person who had been aiming to harm Alaric, and had exposed him or her in the book, and hence it had proved crucial for the last page to be removed by the killer. Posie vowed to finish the novel as quickly as possible and come to her own conclusions. But was it really possible that the murderer was Eve, as Alaric seemed to think?

'But if she's in love with you, why would she try and harm you?' cried Posie incredulously.

'Search me,' said Alaric, sounding tired of the discussion. 'Maybe she thinks that if she can't have me, no-one can. I know she wants to cause trouble: I swear it was Eve who sent that telegram to Hugo Marchpane last month, informing him about my affair with Cosima.'

'Well, what about Codlington, the Valet?' Posie described his surly tone with her, the inexplicable bright ruby and gold engraved cufflinks which she had seen him displaying proudly, and which were much too fancy for a servant to wear.

'Did you discover him stealing from Roderick?'

Alaric shook his head.

'No. What makes you think that? He's a slippery character and no mistake but I've never accused him of stealing. I told him fairly recently to stop placing bets which Roderick can little afford, but that was it. But it's up to Roderick how he spends his money and runs his life. And the cufflinks sound like my father's. Perhaps Roderick has given them to him as a thank you for all the extra work Codlington does for him. Goodness knows he's the only one who can keep him in check, especially when he's been hitting the bottle hard!'

'So, Codlington is *not* a suspect in your mind?' Posie asked, confused. She drank this in: Codlington's own story seemed to be tallying up.

Alaric shrugged. 'Who knows? I wouldn't have said so. Perhaps I should come back with you to England, take part in this investigation. After all, I can't hide away here forever.'

'But I thought you wanted to stay up here? That this is a legendary place for you? You've only been here a week! It also has the advantage of being safe.'

'I don't really "do" safety,' Alaric said bitterly. 'Besides, I'm getting restless. I've learnt the bee-keeping tricks from the monks up here, now I want to move off. I'll accompany you back into Ortigia tomorrow, for starters. Then let's see what happens. Shall we go and have a bite to eat now?' he said, standing, offering his hand to her gallantly.

They walked back inside the Monastery together in a tense silence. Posie was thinking through everything Alaric had said to her. *Still* nothing made sense. Nothing at all.

At the end of a very long dim corridor, Alaric opened a door into a delicious smelling high-beamed refectory where monks were moving around bearing plates laden with food. The monks mainly ignored them and Posie and Alaric collected plates and helped themselves to a stew from silver platters on a sideboard.

Alaric poured red wine from a great golden jug and they sat down at a candlelit trestle table, some way away from the monks.

'I'm intrigued to know what Harry Redmayne is doing on this dig in Egypt. Did you say something about a Honey God or Goddess? He called me, did he?'

Posie was surprised that Alaric wanted to change the subject away from his likely attacker, and she told him so.

Alaric smiled a watery smile. 'I'm sorry. It's just that all that danger feels such a long way away. Please don't think I'm being dismissive of your attempts to work out who has it in for me: quite the opposite. But I fancy a nice evening now, and you seem terrific company, and I've been pretty much alone with my thoughts for over a week now. You understand?'

'Oh, quite.'

'Splendid. So tell me more about Egypt. And then you must try the Hyblaean honey, and the honey cake made by the monks. It's probably not as good as the one my sister Violet makes, but even so…'

Posie appreciated Alaric's light-heartedness and his efforts to entertain her as his guest. She did her best to fill him in on the sketchy details she remembered from Harry Redmayne's brief discussion. But Alaric was only half-listening to her. Something was worrying him, that much was obvious.

She tried to forget about the Venetian-masked stalker in the back streets of Ortigia, and Cosima lurking in the market. She thrust them to the back of her mind and concentrated on drinking her wine and eating a good deal of the honey cake.

It was only later, when she was lying in her starched white monastic bed, unable to sleep, that something tugged at Posie's mind: for all Alaric had spoken about danger being far away, he hadn't really sounded that convinced of it.

And neither was she.

* * * *

Fifteen

Ortigia lay spread out before them like a cloudy gemstone on Wednesday morning, set against the sparkling early morning sea. And for the first time since she had seen Len together with his wife on Saturday, Posie realised she had managed to go a full twelve hours without thinking of him. She congratulated herself and took in the beautiful scenery as she walked with Alaric along the old harbour wall.

'This is my guesthouse,' she said as they reached the *Locatelli*. He nodded, and entered the tiled blue entrance hall with her.

'I'll wait here for you,' he said, removing his panama hat and setting his small rucksack down on the floor.

'I'll be quick,' Posie promised, and she meant it: she was not one of those girls who took an age to get ready anyhow, but right now she was starving, and she was looking forwards to the hearty breakfast they had promised themselves as a well-deserved treat after the long, winding descent down from the Hyblaean mountains in the back of the fruit van at the crack of dawn with Brother Luca.

Brother Luca had been silent and surly the entire trip down, and Posie had almost fallen over in shock at the end of the journey when he had presented her with a small gold-and-white bag as she climbed out of the van and said goodbye through the window. Inside the bag was a very small jar of the dark brown, almost acidic-tasting legendary Hyblaean honey which she had tasted the night before, and which, to be honest, wasn't exactly to her liking, but which she realised was a very, very special present indeed.

In her room Posie quickly changed in a mad dash, relieved to be out of her soiled clothes at last. But then she noticed that something wasn't quite right; the room wasn't as she had left it. It had been ransacked.

Hurrying over she saw that her holdall had been emptied, and the few contents were spilled willy-nilly across the wooden floorboards. Her purchases from the market yesterday were scattered carelessly around the place, and the lovely painting she had bought as a wedding gift had been swept onto the floor, shattering the glass frame. The expensive soaps were broken and splintered. The bag for Prudence lay on the floor. Outraged, Posie spun around and checked through her possessions again. Odd! Although the place was a mess, nothing was missing. What had the intruder been after? How fortunate that she carried her most valuable things like her passport and tickets around with her at all times in her carpet bag!

She tried to make some order, and then she spotted something hidden way back under the little writing desk, discarded or dropped in a hurry. It was a single typewritten page.

Posie got onto her hands and knees and retrieved it. It was a random page which had obviously come adrift from Ianthe's novel, the staple hanging loosely at the corner. It was clearly the very end of a chapter, as there was only one short paragraph typed on it. It was unfamiliar to Posie as she had only read the very start of the novel, and it obviously belonged to a much later chapter. She scanned it briefly:

"So, she had done it after all! She walked in a calm sort of triumph, all the while unaware that she was being observed from up on high.

BLOOD WILL OUT, the observer thought to themselves!"

The rest of the page was blank. Posie smiled at Ianthe's dramatic turn of phrase. She searched around the room looking for the rest of the manuscript so she could place it together with it and cursed aloud, not finding it. Strange!

She remembered leaving the manuscript on the counterpane of the bed yesterday, before going out to the market, and she searched under the bed, through the bed covers and even under the pillows.

With a rising sense of panic she ran around the room looking for it. But it had gone. It was the only thing missing from all of her possessions, and with a feeling of creeping certainty she realised that this was the very reason her room had been searched.

The intruder had slipped up though, leaving a page behind. If it had not been for that, it might have been hours until Posie had realised the manuscript had been stolen.

But it made no sense! This was not the only copy of the book by any means – it was about to be published and printed in London by Bernie Sharp – soon anyone would be able to pick up a real copy at a news-stand, for reading in their coffee break or on their lunch hour.

Posie felt cross with herself for not having read the whole book, heaven knew she had had the time! And now she knew just how insightful Ianthe had been about the real-life characters involved, the book could have proved invaluable.

She shoved the page in her bag and sighed as she went down in the birdcage lift. It seemed likely that the person who stole the manuscript had done so deliberately, not wanting Posie to finish reading it while she was out here in Ortigia. And who had taken it? Cosima? The man in the mask? Binkie Dodds?

As she exited the lift she realised that all was not well in the entrance hall. Alaric was motioning for her to come quickly to the Hotel Manager's front desk. He passed her a telegram which she ripped open. It had been sent by Inspector Lovelace half an hour previously. It was the shortest telegram she had ever received. She read:

URGENT. CALL IMMEDIATELY.
    R. LOVELACE.

'I've been talking to the Hotel Manager. Apparently you've been getting phone calls every ten minutes or so for the last hour,' Alaric said, frowning with worry. 'All from Scotland Yard. It must be serious, eh?'

Posie nodded, taking the telephone, but refusing to panic. Today was the day of the Inquest into Ianthe's death at the Coroner's Court in Victoria. Perhaps Inspector Lovelace needed to confirm a point of detail with her about her discovery of the body? If she had been in London she would have been called to give evidence in person, but as she was away they were relying on her Witness Statement. Perhaps something was missing from it?

As the International Operator put through the call, Posie checked her wristwatch and realised it was only seven o'clock in the morning in London. Alaric hung back, arms crossed, pensive. Within a minute she heard Inspector Lovelace's brisk voice, more harried than usual:

'Posie? Oh thank goodness! Thank goodness! Are you all right?'

'Yes. What's happening?'

'Something terrible!' the Inspector said anxiously. 'I take full responsibility, of course.'

Her blood froze and she avoided Alaric's searching eyes, his head bent low beside her, listening in. Posie had a sudden horrible feeling that Lady Violet had come a cropper, that somehow the murderer had killed her, or attempted to, possibly for something she knew, or for her now rather considerably-enhanced inheritance prospects from Ianthe.

'Oh my gosh! What is it? Has something happened to Violet?' she stammered, a cold hand of fear clutching at her heart.

'No, no,' the Inspector continued. 'It's rather a case of police misconduct. You remember how I told you on Monday that I had last been to Boynton Hall on Friday?'

'Yes. Yes, I remember. You placed the household under house arrest. The local police force were standing by, making sure no-one came or went. You reassured me that there wasn't a chance anyone from the house could have left, and certainly not have followed me over here, tailing me around...'

She heard Alaric gasp beside her, and Inspector Lovelace groaned into the receiver.

'I know! I know! It seems I messed up by using the local bobbies. I should have placed Rainbird or Binny down there continuously. It seems that the local police thought it was adequate enough to remain *outside* of Boynton Hall, making sure no-one came or went. They haven't been inside the place since I left it on Friday! Can you believe it? Sergeant Binny went down at the crack of dawn today to collect the whole ruddy lot of them to bring them to London for the Inquest, and guess what?'

Posie's stomach lurched. 'I don't want to,' she answered in a small voice.

'I'll tell you! Binny called through in a blind panic about an hour ago. It turns out that the whole household have gone and bally well disappeared! At some point since Friday each and every one of the following have left: Lord Roderick Boynton, Lady Eve Boynton, Lady Violet Boynton-Dale, Mr Burns and Codlington the Valet!'

'WHAT?'

'I know,' the Inspector said in a small voice. 'The only ones who are left are the old Butler and the maids. We've had some important information come our way now about key access to and from the house. But it's a case of too little too late!'

'I don't understand!' Posie wailed. 'How did they all leave?' and then Posie's voice tailed away, for suddenly she knew. When she spoke again it was in unison with Inspector Lovelace in London and with Alaric at her side, ashen-faced, and they all said the same words in a bitter, resigned manner:

'The Priest's Hole!'

The Inspector continued: 'So *it is* entirely possible that someone from Boynton Hall has followed you to Ortigia and has been stalking you. I'm so sorry, Posie. I've been giving you false assurances about your safety. And you're there all alone, with goodness knows who on your tail…'

Posie calmed him down somewhat, explaining about having found Alaric safe and sound. Inspector Lovelace breathed a sigh of relief down the phone:

'Well, let's be grateful for small mercies. But *he* should be watching his back, too. I'd feel better if you both got out of there, pronto. Put me on to Boynton-Dale, please.'

Alaric took the phone and obviously had the same warning from the Inspector before he handed the receiver back to Posie.

'And there's something else you should know,' the Inspector continued, sounding more upset and harassed than Posie had never heard him before. 'Do you remember Bernie Sharp, the literary agent?'

'Of course!'

'It *could* be accidental, of course, but I very much doubt it. There's been a fire, this morning, at his office in Covent Garden. The whole place is gutted, a smoking wreck. The fire brigade are over there now. They seem to think petrol was involved, which means it was deliberate. Nothing has survived. Unfortunately for Bernie Sharp it seems that he was a total workaholic, and he was already in his office at the crack of dawn today. His body has been recovered. He died of smoke inhalation.'

Posie gasped in horror. Another death! She felt dreadful for asking, but ask she must:

'And the manuscripts of *The Tomb of the Honey Bee*? What about them? There were two left over: Bernie told me he was sending one copy to the printer, and that he was holding on to his own copy for safekeeping.'

'All gone, I'm afraid. The printer was due to receive the copy for typesetting today by courier, but it was never sent out. It's been burnt to a cinder and so has Bernie Sharp's own copy. Am I correct in thinking that you have another copy?'

Posie groaned, bracing herself, and told him how she had just realised there had been an intruder in her room and how her copy of Ianthe's manuscript had been stolen. She was met with yet more silence.

'Well, someone is obviously desperate to destroy the copies which existed,' the Inspector said at last. 'Ruddy good job we've got Ianthe's original copy sitting here locked in our evidence room at Scotland Yard. We'll keep it well protected. Oh! I almost forgot! Some good news on that score! You remember the final page went missing from the original manuscript at the crime scene?'

'Mnn?'

'Mr Maguire in Forensics seems to think he might be able to recover the last page from the typewriter ribbon which was left inside the machine. It was sloppy of the killer not to have cleared it out at the same time as he stole the final page. It's going to take a while and we'll need to call in a special expert but Maguire is hopeful for a good result. Maybe that reconstructed page will give us some key information?'

Posie agreed. 'Now I need to tell you something new,' Posie said into the mouth-piece quietly to Inspector Lovelace, trying to avoid Alaric's gaze.

She told the Inspector about her possible sighting of Cosima Catchpole in the harbour market and how there had been reports of a woman matching her description hanging around the *Locatelli* guesthouse. She didn't bother to mention her run-in with Binkie Dodds; she had decided it was entirely unimportant, that he couldn't possibly be dangerous to her.

The Inspector said nothing.

'Are you there, Inspector? Did you jolly well hear any of that?'

'Yes. Unfortunately.'

'And? What do you make of it?'

'I don't like it,' the Inspector said. 'Not one bit. I don't understand it. I'll obviously send Binny down now to their house and check on Lady Cosima – see if she really has disappeared, or whether you might just have seen someone else. That's not what worries me: it's rather the masked chappie you were telling me about on Monday, following you around. I'm guessing now that that might have been Codlington. He would have had enough time to get out there if he left Boynton Hall on Friday or even Saturday. Please take care, Posie.'

The Inspector sighed wearily.

'I must dash. I've got to prepare for this Inquest and then hold a Press Conference. The public interest in Ianthe Flowers' death is unbelievable! They can't get enough of it! She's more famous now she's dead than she ever was alive! But too late for poor old Bernie Sharp, eh? Her books are flying off the shelves and the journalists can't get information quickly enough for their liking! Anyway, I'm happy to hear you've got Boynton-Dale out there with you, at any rate. Now get the hell out, as I said. Come back home. And if you run into any trouble in the meantime, make sure you get in touch with my contact at the Police Station in Siracusa; name of Inspector Geraldino Gobbi. Here's his number. You got that?'

Posie took the details and hung up.

Alaric was giving her a strange, resigned look, but all he said as he picked his rucksack up off the floor and threw his hat on again was:

'Better get your stuff from your room and we'll clear out quickly. We'll talk about what to do next over breakfast. I know a little café nearby on a hidden square. It's jolly nice and quiet there. We'll be undisturbed.'

* * * *

Sixteen

However, it turned out that the whole of Ortigia was bound up in a crazy musical procession, with hundreds of revellers wearing carnival masks and bearing musical instruments and drums. The streets and cafés were anything *but* nice and quiet.

As they followed the street away from the *Locatelli* guesthouse, Posie and Alaric got caught up in the very thick of it, and it was with a sense of real relief that they found a free table in the shade at the small café in the hidden square Alaric had mentioned. The café was very busy and full of people who were also glad to have found a seat in among the chaos.

A masked waiter dressed in a harlequin's outfit brought them coffee and croissants, and another one dressed as a pirate served them with plates of local cheese, fish and meat. They ate ravenously and in a tense silence as they watched the little square filling up with throngs of carnival characters, several bands of musicians and even a mobile Puppet Theatre. Bunches of tourists were now trailing in too, curious to see what all the fuss was about. The sun baked down relentlessly on the crowds in the square, even though it was still early morning.

'I'm so sorry,' Posie said at last.

'I don't know why I didn't tell you about having seen Cosima yesterday. I think it was because I wasn't quite sure of what I had actually seen. I don't even know if it *was* her or not. I realise how much she means to you and it was wrong of me to hide that information from you,' she tailed off flatly.

'It's fine,' said Alaric in a resigned manner, like he meant it. He wiped the sweat away from his face with a linen napkin. He seemed preoccupied, but he also seemed to have come to a decision which had cost him much effort, and he looked out over the square with a new resolution in his strange-coloured eyes:

'I acted like a first-rate ass, hoping everything would come right between Cosima and myself. The signs were there for me to see: I just ignored them. Heavens! She even broke up with me and I still couldn't get it through my thick head that it was over! To be honest, even if she *has* come out here to find me, which I doubt, I think the scales have finally fallen from my eyes. And I have *you* to thank for that.'

Posie gulped at her strong coffee in some embarrassment: she was not used to men speaking so frankly with her about matters of the heart.

'I can't love her anymore,' Alaric continued in his gravelly voice.

'Oh?'

'Wasn't it Bernard of Clairvaux who said "Love me, love my dog"?'

'I don't know, I'm afraid,' said Posie, feeling stupid and uneducated for once. But then she remembered Lady Violet telling her that Alaric had always been 'the clever one' in the family, and Hugo Marchpane saying that a lot of what Alaric said went right over his head. And it turned out that even Lady Cosima hadn't bothered to listen!

'Well,' Alaric said, smiling, 'all I mean is that if someone is no friend of Bikram, they're no friend of mine. I can't believe I didn't see it sooner. Anyway, you're right to have doubted whether you actually saw Cosima here: she famously hates travelling; gets sick in planes, buses, cars. Moans non-stop if she has to travel anywhere further than London. She *just about* tolerates trains. See how misguided I was? A pretty poor companion for an explorer, eh?'

Posie nodded, not liking to add that Cosima was a *married* companion into the bargain, and that made her unsuitable, too, but she held her tongue. She was perplexed. If what Alaric was saying was right, there was no way Cosima could have made it down to Sicily by train alone.

Alaric smiled. 'Now, shall we order an almond granita to drink? It's so hot here, even in the shade.'

As they waited for someone to take their order they discussed what to do next.

'The next boat will leave tonight from Palermo,' said Posie, who had found that a strange calm had descended on her. 'We can get to Genoa on the ferry, then try and get a train home through France. We'll just have to lie low and make sure no-one is following us.'

Alaric was staring at her strangely. He started to laugh:

'Boats?' he uttered in disbelief. 'Trains? Home? Who said anything about any of *that*?'

Posie looked at him in surprise, tucking her hair behind her ear nervously. 'Well, I just thought…'

'That's complicated. And dull. And it takes a long time. I did that already on my way down here, too. What I need is an aeroplane and an air field. Do you have a map on you by any chance? I did have one but I left it behind at the Monastery. I didn't realise I would be leaving Sicily quite so soon.'

'Oh my gosh!' Posie was scrabbling in her bag, searching for the red and gold Stanford's map. She was pulling out other random bits of paper too and heaping them up carelessly on the table. 'Did you leave anything else important up at the Monastery?'

Alaric shook his head, then spied the single remaining page of Ianthe's manuscript sitting on the table. He picked it up idly.

'That's the only bit of Ianthe's *The Tomb of the Honey Bee* that I have left!' Posie said quickly, focused on shaking out her map and pressing it down carefully, looking for the symbol for an airfield in the key at the bottom.

'The intruder into my room must have dropped it in his hurry to get out carrying the rest of the book. That page was lying under my desk, unnoticed.'

Alaric read the text casually, with a lopsided grin of amusement on his face and then suddenly he drew in his breath sharply and sat up very straight in his chair. Posie noticed the change of body language and looked at him quickly. He was reading and re-reading the text, and he looked ashen in the face, his eyes like dead black holes.

'I say, is everything okay? Jeepers, you look like you've seen, or read about a ghost!'

He didn't answer, but folded the page carefully into quarters and put it in his breast pocket.

'Everything is fine,' he said, nodding, still pale.

'Does that mean something to you?' asked Posie, not believing him for a moment. 'Do you think it was a message from the intruder? That they left that page for me *on purpose?*'

'No,' said Alaric firmly. 'I don't believe for one moment that you were meant to see this. Absolutely not, in fact. You told me you hadn't yet read the whole of Ianthe's novel, didn't you?'

Posie nodded. 'Unfortunately, I had only read the very start. A nice country house murder mystery by the look of things…'

'I wonder what else Ianthe managed to put into it,' Alaric whispered, crossing his arms, miles away. 'Never mind. What's done is done.'

He seemed to snap back to earth and he looked at the

map with her, tracing his finger across possible airfields and aerodromes which were marked there. They were focusing intently, heads down, when a voice horribly familiar to Posie suddenly broke into their study:

'What-ho, Posie!'

Posie looked up to find Binkie Dodds looming alongside their table, fanning himself in the heat with a menu. He looked searchingly at Posie and then at Alaric, who was now observing Binkie with polite surprise. Binkie's face was the colour of beetroot, and his thick glasses were fogged up with the heat. He was still wearing his unsuitable English tweeds and he looked like a steamed plum pudding.

'You look like you need a granita, old chum,' said Alaric, cordially. 'I'm Alaric, by the way. Sit down, why don't you? Any pal of Posie's is a pal of mine.'

And before Posie could protest and explain, he had managed to call over another waiter and had ordered three almond granitas.

Binkie sat down heavily on a third seat, eyeing them both suspiciously.

'Terrible noise,' he moaned, indicating with a backwards hand gesture at the ever-swelling crowd behind him in the square. Posie noticed however that his eyes were moving quickly behind the bottle-bottom glasses from her to Alaric, and he was looking at both of their necks. She sighed, and introduced him formally to Alaric, who had only just noticed that something was amiss in Binkie's manner and in Posie's reception of him.

'Where is it then?' Binkie suddenly snapped at Posie, all decorum gone. 'Where the blazes have you taken it?'

'Sorry, old chap. What are you on about?' said Alaric, a beat behind. The waiter hovered at their table briefly, placing a cold glass of frozen granita in front of each of them, lingering to place long paper straws in each glass. Posie caught a glimpse of black-gloved hands and saw that a handwritten bill was being placed on Alaric's plate with solemn courtesy.

She sighed. 'It's gone, Binkie,' she said guardedly. 'It's been given back to the monks of the Serafina Monastery, where it *belongs*.'

Binkie's mouth dropped open and he stuttered in outraged disbelief. He turned to Alaric:

'You worm! You spineless worm! You could have consulted *me* first!' He grew redder and redder in the face and then burst into tears. By now people at other tables had started to turn to him and point and laugh.

'I say!' Alaric muttered. 'I'm sorry, old bean. Drink some of your granita and then we'll speak about it all, what? You look very hot. In fact, you're overheating.' He looked down at his own drink and then back at Binkie's with a frown on his face.

'On second thoughts,' he said, switching his glass for Binkie's, 'let's swap. You take mine. Look at this! Mine is nearly frozen solid and crystally – how it's supposed to be, in fact – and will be much more refreshing in this heat. Yours is almost fully melted! Dratted waiter! Drink it up, old chump. That's right!'

Surprisingly, Binkie obeyed Alaric, much like a child, and was slurping up his granita through the paper straw. He didn't stop until he had finished every last drop, never once taking his eyes off Posie and Alaric, who drank down their own iced drinks in an awkward silence, averting their eyes. Posie was just wondering how they could politely get rid of Binkie and make their excuses and leave when she noticed that the people at the next table were pointing over in their direction again and laughing hysterically. She looked up at Binkie and gasped.

He was puffing and blowing and frothing at the mouth. He started to thrash around and his eyes bulged horribly.

'Get some water!' said Alaric sharply in Italian as another waiter swung past. 'Golly, I've never seen heatstroke like that before!'

But Posie's blood froze, an icy grip at her throat. Binkie suddenly lost his balance and hit the table head first, his glasses smashing to the floor. He was as dead as a dodo.

'He's dead,' Posie whispered under her breath. She sat rooted to her seat, a horrible calm certainty stealing over her. 'And that wasn't heat-stroke! Sure as bread is bread, that was poison!'

She ignored Alaric's horror-stricken face and grabbed a napkin; with it she picked up Binkie's granita glass and sniffed. She picked up her own glass and did the same. She remembered Inspector Lovelace's words about the almondy smell of veronal being similar to cyanide.

'See here? Binkie's glass smells overpoweringly of almonds. But it's a strange smell – like *bitter* almonds – it smells synthetic. Our glasses, even though they held almond granita too, smell only faintly nutty, like real almonds. Like Christmas marzipan.'

'So?'

'I'd say that Binkie's drink was spiked with veronal. Probably the same drug as was used to kill Ianthe. But a huge dose of the stuff! Oh Alaric! It means we're not safe. Not even here!'

Alaric was staring in horror at the dead face of Binkie Dodds.

'But that's not all,' he whispered as crowds and waiters and carnival-masked locals started to flock over in unhelpful droves.

'That drink was intended for me! I swapped it with Binkie and made him drink it! It's my fault he's dead now! That wretched poison was intended for me!'

* * * *

About one hour later Alaric and Posie finally left the café, having called in the specialist services of Inspector Lovelace's contact in the Siracusa police force, Inspector

Gobbi, who handled the scene and the ensuing chaos like the professional that he was.

The Inspector had, fortunately, already been briefed by Inspector Lovelace and knew of their urgent need to leave the island, and of the danger they were facing, which had unfortunately proved to be all too real.

When asked about the best possible airfield to use, Inspector Gobbi had come up trumps, nominating the Water Aerodrome in Siracusa itself, the '*De Filippis*', and providing directions on how to get there. Inspector Gobbi assured Alaric that he would be able to hire a Sea-Plane without much trouble, and he had signed an important-looking warrant enabling them to side-step the usual formalities.

Having given their Witness Statements and left Inspector Gobbi and his officers taking away Binkie's body, they managed to gather up their luggage and slip away from the crowds relatively unnoticed.

Posie and Alaric walked in a shocked silence down a hot and dusty shaded alleyway, their thoughts still with the unfortunate Binkie Dodds. As they turned at the end of the street and trotted past a big pile of mouldering rubbish, Posie's eye caught sight of a family of black-and-white cats playing in the rubbish, frisking in the sun, and as she watched them she saw something else there which grabbed her attention.

Posie dashed over furiously, sending the cats scarpering off in all directions. She dragged a dusty black cloak, black gloves and a wide black hat off the top of the rubbish pile. Underneath the black clothes she found a cheap white Venetian mask, its plaster nose and eyeholes now broken and crumbled, as if someone had thrown it off in a sudden rage and stamped on it in a fury, disfiguring it.

'This was worn by the person pretending to be the waiter back there,' she said to Alaric. 'The person who served us the granita drinks! This is the very same disguise that the person wore who was following me about two days ago. They must have realised their plan was foiled! That they had poisoned the wrong person! Binkie instead of you! They've escaped down here! Down this alley! We should go back and tell Inspector Gobbi to start a search in this direction. That the killer came along here!'

She turned as if to head back towards the café, the soiled and broken costume heavy in her hands, but Alaric looked at her like she was crazy.

'No,' he said, grabbing her hand and forcing her to discard the clothes. 'We're getting out of here. Now.'

* * * *

At the *De Filippis* Water Aerodrome half an hour later, Posie found herself sitting in the back of a Sea-Plane on the water, with Alaric at the front behind the controls, studying a map given to him by the man he had hired the plane from. Alaric folded the map up quickly, and then indicated suddenly to the man, who was lingering nearby on the tarmacked jetty. The man came over and they spoke together in quick Italian. The noise from the other Sea-Planes buzzing in and out and revving their engines was very loud.

The man dug in his pocket and produced yet another map, which he passed to Alaric, who produced some coins in exchange. He then studied it intently.

'What's happening?' Posie shouted above the noise. She felt suddenly nervous. Goodness only knew, she was keen on trying most things but she had never flown in a plane before, let alone a Sea-Plane. She tried to forget the butterflies rising in horrible waves in her stomach.

'Change of plan, old girl,' Alaric replied, gently starting

up the motor of their Sea-Plane. 'We're not going home. We're flying to Benghazi.'

'Sorry?'

'And then I'll pick up another plane there and then we'll fly on to Alexandria.'

'Alexandria? In *Egypt*?' Posie gasped.

'Yep. That's right. And then we'll stop and either fly or sail down the Nile to Luxor. We'll go to this tomb which good old Harry Redmayne was telling you about. Sounds fascinating.'

Posie was speechless and goggled at him. She busied herself by tying up her hair. With a sweep of his white silk scarf, and pulling on his flying-glasses Alaric turned around quickly:

'After all, the killer is expecting us back home now. What are the chances they'll think to look for us out on an archaeological dig? And more importantly, what are the chances they'll follow us out there?'

* * * *

PART THREE
Egypt
(July, 1921)

Seventeen

'More tea, madam?' the handsome Egyptian serving-boy in his immaculate white outfit asked, bowing low to Posie, brandishing a teapot on a silver tray and offering some little nutty baked goods, too. She nodded and smiled, extending her empty cup, and passed him his daily tip:

'Please, Hammad. Thank you. And just a couple of those delicious biscuits, if you don't mind…'

From the shadow of her tent and the comfort of her deckchair Posie looked out over the huge archaeological dig at Luxor, which had been the ancient Egyptian city of Thebes in the far-distant past.

As far as the eye could see there were men in white turbans and tunics running about in all directions, local men who had been drafted in in big teams to help cut and lug away the vast quantities of dusty rubble. The men loaded the pale yellow stone onto their donkeys which were saddled up to low wooden carts, waiting patiently in lines under the blistering, unforgiving sun. A cloudless blue sky arched overhead.

Busloads of tourists from Luxor, mainly English and Americans, visited the site on a daily basis. There was a special tea-tent set up for them and some enterprising locals were even trying to sell roughly-carved souvenirs of Pharaohs' heads from the cast-off stone.

It was funny, but at first the vast site had seemed more like a building site than an archaeological dig to Posie. But now the lines of neat, white, ordered tents which housed the many archaeologists from the universities and museums of Europe felt like a second home.

There were several women out here, too, including a female photographer called Lenny from the British Museum, and a group of middle-aged volunteers from Guildford in Surrey who liked to stay at base camp in the shade and sieve the small finds which were brought back every day. All of them wore linen trouser suits like Posie's and she felt smugly satisfied that she had got every last penny's worth out of it, despite the fact that it was now turning orange from the hot desert dust and it would never be fit for wearing on the streets of London again. Prudence would be pleased.

Alaric and Posie had been in the Valley of the Kings at Luxor for three weeks now.

It had taken them nearly all of that time to get used to the soaring daytime temperatures and the strange pattern of the working days: early starts, long midday siestas, and the long productive afternoons which turned into gin-fuelled, raucous evenings when the archaeologists ate together at trestle tables in the one big dining marquee. Often they gave after-dinner talks on their most recent discoveries, or slide-shows on their pet subjects. Posie found herself looking forwards with great excitement to these lectures, which were advertised on a big blackboard outside the main tent. Sometimes these were planned way in advance and sometimes they were given at a moment's notice.

Alaric's arrival in Luxor had proved timely and he had been seized upon in a frenzy of great excitement by the archaeologists on the dig, some of whom had been stationed out there for months and were keen for fresh news and tales of daring exploits from someone famous.

Alaric had already given a couple of impromptu evening talks, one about his flying antics in general, and another about favourite places he had visited in Africa. Posie had been secretly impressed at his easy and humorous speaking style, but she figured it was hardly surprising given all the practice he had had. It was obvious that he relished public speaking, and it seemed that the archaeologists couldn't get enough of the celebrity in their midst.

'Golly, you must keep a low profile!' Posie begged him constantly, feeling like an awful nag and a spoil-sport to boot. 'You can't go and spoil it all now. Just decline politely! These fellows have international contacts, you know. The last thing we need is a newspaper article appearing in London advertising to the whole world your exact whereabouts, reporting on some wonderful talk you've just given! So far we've been lucky, Alaric. Let's hope our luck holds out. Besides, I *promised* Inspector Lovelace!'

When they had reached Alexandria, before travelling down to Luxor in an old Avro training plane which Alaric had managed to hire, Posie had insisted on calling the Inspector to let him know they were safe. She had also telegrammed to Prudence at the Grape Street Bureau, telling her not to expect an early return.

The Inspector had greeted the news of their location with thinly-disguised ill humour.

'Have you told anyone else where you are?' he groaned.

'No, of course not! I *would* call or send a telegram to Lady Violet and let her know our whereabouts, but there's no point – I have no idea where she is! Do you?'

'No,' the Inspector snapped, uncharacteristically. 'I haven't the foggiest! It seems we've lost the whole bally lot of them! I've got men on watch in London and at all the ports and airports but so far there have been no sightings of anyone. Which reminds me…You know you told me about Lady Cosima possibly being in Sicily?'

'Yes?'

'Seems you *might* have seen her there, after all. She left Stowe-on-the-Middle-Wold at much the same time as you did last week. She could be anywhere by now. Major Marchpane has been going off his head with worry.'

'I see,' said Posie, coolly.

'So stay safe and below the radar. Let as few people know you are there as possible. Promise me? And call me once a week from now on, Posie. I'd be happier if you were both back here, but I doubt our killer is going to follow you out *there*. It seems an awfully big leap of the imagination.'

She had reported the conversation to Alaric and while at first they had been incredibly careful, with Alaric even sporting a white turban and tunic on the dig, like the other archaeologists, and Posie always under cover of her sunhat and glasses, it had been difficult to stay vigilant.

In truth, they kept having to remind themselves *why* they were out in Luxor in the first place; they were almost having fun! Boynton Hall and London and even Ortigia and all the horror of the stalking and the deaths of Ianthe Flowers and Binkie Dodds seemed a long, long way away from the magic and the bustle and the easy excitement of the archaeological dig.

Harry Redmayne had been as excited as the next man about Alaric's arrival, and he had basked in the reflected glory of his having invited Alaric out on the excavation site. They had filled Harry in on all the details of the case on the first night of their arrival, including telling him about the death of Binkie Dodds, and Harry had listened, wide-eyed but unfazed by the whole sorry tale. Harry had promised to keep an eye on them both, and had insisted on hiring an extra local man, Didi, to act as a watchman around the clock, covering Alaric's back.

'Seems to me you have more to fear from the living than the dead, and that's not often the case out here!' Harry had laughed at the end of the revelations.

'People tend to get paranoid about things such as

Pharaohs' curses out here. Even in my own team of sensible, highly-trained experts superstition is rife. Funny, really. The tomb of Tutankhamun sure has a lot to answer for!'

The weeks at Luxor had given Posie ample chance to get to know Harry Redmayne, and she was impressed with what she had seen: loyal, friendly, hard-working and above all deeply excited by what he had been asked to excavate by the British Museum, his general demeanour was like a child on the night before Christmas, and it took a lot to repress his spirits. Even at five o'clock in the morning, when coffee and sweet sugary cakes were served as breakfast and the stars were still visible in the dark sky above the Valley of the Kings, his humour was irrepressible. He was always looking forwards to the long day of work ahead.

Posie felt slightly sad for Harry at points, remembering his comment back in London about 'stepping out' with Lady Violet and how he hadn't been rich enough for the relationship to continue.

It was such a great shame, Posie thought to herself, that when you reached the highest ranks of the aristocracy, money seemed to count for such a great deal, and she presumed that it had been Roderick who had forbidden the match. What a good job that there were *some* more forward-thinking aristocrats! Her friend Rufus for example, who was marrying Dolly, a lowly Wardrobe Mistress, and even Alaric, she would bet, would forgo the old habits and requirements of his class if he met a woman of a lower class who took his fancy. *If*.

No mention had been made in the weeks since leaving Sicily about Lady Cosima, and Posie didn't push the point: it was none of her business. Similarly, Alaric hadn't asked Posie anything at all about her private life, and she had skirted around the subject of the loss of her fiancé in the Great War, and touched briefly on her activities as an ambulance driver back then. But anything more recent was left unsaid, and therefore the painful subject of Len had never cropped up.

Anyway, they were crazily busy.

Every day after breakfast Harry Redmayne marshalled together his little team of five underlings from the British Museum, including Lenny the female photographer. Together with Alaric, herself, and their watchman Didi, the group left the base camp in the half-light. They drove in a big open-backed safari wagon through the main thoroughfare of tombs, pillars and monuments which made up the centre of the ancient city of Thebes. Teams of international archaeologists started work at the crack of dawn in and among the main tombs on the thoroughfare, and Harry would shout out cheerful greetings to them as they passed.

Their drive took them ten or fifteen minutes each day, up into the *Dra Abu Naga* necropolis, a city of the dead, where small teams of experts were working on newly-discovered treasures. Harry's pet project was up here; an Ancient Egyptian tomb set in amongst a vast catacomb of other tombs, and it was special in that although it didn't contain a Pharaoh, it obviously contained someone who in both life and death had been treated as something of a God by the Pharaohs of the Eleventh Dynasty: he had come to be known as 'Ammotep, the God of Bees and Honey'.

An underground hallway had been discovered, packed with grave goods. It was about sixty-five feet long, leading down to a huge burial chamber in which Ammotep slept his eternal sleep, which he had been doing now for over four thousand years. The underground hallway was simply stunning: covered in rich and glittering gold-leaf and painted in yellow-coloured murals and hieroglyphs. Rows and rows of bees were painted in fantastic detail, as well as paintings of ancient Egyptian workers scurrying around beehives at all points of the bee-keeping year.

The mummy of Ammotep himself was encased within several special amber-encrusted coffins which were each shaped like a bee, peeling back like a series of never-ending Russian dolls. As Harry and his team unwrapped Ammotep, layer by layer, they found all sorts of precious objects to do with bees and honey within, most made of purest gold.

Alaric was in his element. He was helping the small team to interpret what the objects might have been used for, or what they symbolised. Harry, who also kept bees back at home in the Cambridgeshire fenlands, would argue good-naturedly with Alaric about much of the bee-keeping paraphernalia which they found, but Posie noticed how he would usually bow to Alaric's greater experience in the end. Harry had also turned out to be a remarkably good draftsman and painter, and he spent a couple of hours every day copying the hieroglyphics and murals which he uncovered.

At first Posie had been scared to enter the tomb of Ammotep, but now it seemed entirely normal, and she came to the tomb every day, wandering in and out at she fancied, but mainly sitting outside under a parasol, carefully sorting and labelling the small finds.

When there were no new finds she helped Harry to prepare his notes for a big talk on Ammotep which he was giving to all the archaeologists on the dig at the end of the week, on the Friday. It had been planned for a while, and a sign announcing Harry's name and professional rank and declaring 'Ammotep, the God of Bees and Honey! First Insights from the British Museum!' had been chalked up by the dining marquee for ages. The talk was timely, as Friday marked the day that the mummy of Ammotep and all of his coffins were to be transported out of the tomb. The dig was coming to an end, the tomb was being closed up and it had been agreed with the Egyptian authorities that Ammotep and some of his treasures would be spending the rest of eternity sleeping in the British Museum in London.

'I think that's everything now, Harry,' Posie said on the

Thursday afternoon at lunchtime, the day before Harry's talk. She passed Harry the small buff-coloured folder she had been working on, complete with Lenny's immaculate photographs and several of Harry's beautiful paintings.

Harry took the folder nervously, flicking through the pages absently with a worried look in his eyes.

'Would you like to practice on me tonight?' Posie asked. She could tell that Harry was very nervous about both the upcoming talk and the transportation of Ammotep back to England.

'I can pretend to be your audience if you like?'

Harry nodded and then made light of his nerves, offering cheerfully to drive his team into modern-day Luxor for a spot of shopping or to make telephone calls, or simply to enjoy a drink on the terrace of the Old Winter Palace Hotel for an hour or so.

Thursday afternoon was usually a time for recreation for the archaeologists and workers, but Alaric, excited by the quantity and quality of finds at Ammotep's tomb, had decided to stay behind, working on, with Didi the watchman alongside him for protection. The rest of the team piled into the back of Harry's safari wagon and made the short ten minute journey down the road to Luxor town, passing truckloads of tourists going in the opposite direction.

In Luxor Posie put through two telephone calls from the Post Office. The first call to Prudence proved unexciting, save for the news that Len had reappeared at the Grape Street Bureau and had taken over his office and resumed his workload with diligence and enthusiasm. Posie didn't know whether to be delighted or downhearted, but at least someone would be getting paid for *something* back at the London office, she supposed.

'When do you think you'll be back, Miss, from wherever you are?' asked Prudence, not unreasonably. Posie was surprised at how little she was looking forwards to going home.

'Not sure, sorry. But soon. It could be two days, but it could equally be two weeks. Ask Len to pay your salary and whatever invoices come in. I'll settle up with him when I'm back. Are we very busy?'

'We're *always* busy these days,' Prudence had said darkly, before ringing off.

The second call to Inspector Lovelace had proved more satisfactory. He still hadn't managed to track down the various inhabitants of Boynton Hall, but there was real excitement in his voice.

'News!' he had begun. 'Do you remember me telling you about the fire at Bernie Sharp's literary agency in Covent Garden?'

'How could I forget?'

'Well, we have a witness here who has now come forwards and described seeing a man who exactly matches Codlington's description, acting suspiciously on the day in question. Apparently the witness saw Codlington emerge from Covent Garden Tube with cans of petrol. Thinking it was mighty suspicious, the witness followed him and saw him enter Bernie Sharp's building! The witness has been on holiday for the last three weeks and has only just got back and read about the fire! He came straight to us today to tell us!'

'But have you found Codlington? I thought he'd gone into hiding?'

'Yes, we're still looking for him, that much is true,' the Inspector sounded a little more flat. 'But we've upped the search. We're looking all through the East End and I'm interviewing several of his old buddies there, and his chum the bookmaker, too. Chances are one of them has seen Codlington recently, and one of them will blab.'

'Good,' said Posie certainly. 'But you know what this means? It means Codlington *wasn't* the man following me around Ortigia in the mask and carnival outfit.'

'Mnn. I realise that. Perhaps it's time to simply

revert to our original suspect, Lord Roderick. He's still unaccountable. And missing.'

'Any news on Lady Cosima?' Posie asked hopefully.

'Not a dicky bird. Gone to ground. Same as the others. Oh, some more exciting news!'

'Yes?'

'You remember Mr Maguire thought Ianthe's typewriter ribbon might yield some clues, recreate the missing last page? Well, the expert has been on bally holiday too! But he's back now, in fact I just saw him enter the building. We should have something within the day. I'll telegram you, shall I?'

'Yes please!'

There was just time to join Harry for a quick pink gin on the terrace of the Old Winter Palace Hotel before meeting the rest of the team in the car park to head back to the dig. Everyone was sitting waiting patiently in the back as Harry turned the key in the ignition of the safari wagon, but it failed to spring to life. He tried again. And again.

'Bother!' he exclaimed at last and got out. He flung the bonnet up and looked in quiet desperation at the engine, rubbing streaks of grease onto his face and his white tunic. Posie got out and came and stood next to him.

'Know anything about engines?' Harry asked pleadingly, his eyes full of hope. 'I'm terrible at stuff like this! I think Alaric said you had been in the Ambulance Brigade in the Great War?'

Posie shook her head uselessly. 'I only drove the things, I'm afraid. I never had to fix them. They should make it part of the compulsory training.'

Harry smiled a regretful, mournful smile. 'Oh how I wish Alaric had come out today!' he said. 'He could have fixed this in the blink of an eye. And so could Cuckoo. Handy talent that, runs in the family…'

Posie remembered Violet and her knack of breathing life back into the engine of her two-seater on the day

Ianthe had died. She saw suddenly how Violet and her accomplishments had reached almost mythical proportions in poor Harry's mind. He tinkered nervously with the engine, but it was obvious to everyone he had no clue as to what he was doing.

'Let's get a taxi from the hotel back to the dig,' Posie suggested after what seemed like an age. 'I'm sure the Old Winter Palace Hotel will be only too obliging at getting this fixed up overnight. Their mechanic can bring it back in time for us to use again in the morning.'

So they did just that. In the softly-settling twilight Harry's team bundled into two open-topped taxis and headed back to the camp. Posie was feeling happy and looking forwards to going through Harry's talk with him later and it was just sheer chance that she happened to look up as their taxi swung around a curve in the road, narrowly avoiding a collision with an open-backed tourist bus which was travelling back to Luxor.

She gasped and tried to crane her head backwards to check on what she had just seen.

She was almost certain of it! A blurry figure dressed all in white had been sitting at the back of the tourist bus, her long flame-red hair blowing wildly in the wind like a beacon through the darkness.

Cosima! Again.

* * * *

Eighteen

Friday morning dawned clear and starry, and Posie wandered over to the marquee feeling shattered and unrefreshed after a bad night's sleep. Even the comfort of her nice little sleeping-bag had not managed to insulate her from the chill she couldn't shake off during the night.

Harry seemed quieter than usual at breakfast, his nerves betraying him as he spilled his coffee all over the white tablecloth and left his toast and marmalade untouched.

'It's only a talk!' Alaric said in a carefree manner, chomping on a madeleine cake, taking in Harry's woeful face. 'Is that what's wrong with you, old chum?'

Harry nodded. Alaric smiled sympathetically.

'Don't worry. If you *really* can't face it I'll step in and do the talk for you this evening. But you'll see, you'll be fine!'

The Old Winter Palace Hotel's mechanic had come up trumps, and, as expected, they travelled up to the tomb of Ammotep in the newly-repaired safari wagon without any further problems and the morning started as usual. The archaeologists were focused on removing the carefully-wrapped bee-shaped coffins piece by piece into a waiting van. The temperature had soared by lunchtime and the team had just finished loading up the van, with Ammotep's mummified body leaving last. All thoughts were on returning to base camp and a congratulatory lunch, followed by a well-deserved siesta.

The team were all sitting in the safari wagon, just waiting for Alaric, who along with Didi was the last person in the tomb.

But just then a shout went up from the empty burial chamber. It was Alaric!

Harry jumped out of the driver's seat in a panic and grabbed up a torch. Everyone else followed, bearing torches, running through the dark entrance hallway.

'What is it?' called out Posie nervously, entering the burial chamber itself. Lenny was lurching alongside her, weighed down by her precious and heavy camera equipment. She was mumbling to herself, and Posie heard the words 'Tutankhamun' and 'curses' muttered fearfully.

'What *are* you talking about?' Posie snapped, sharper than she had intended.

'Danger!' hissed Lenny in a whisper. 'You'll see! We've removed the body of Ammotep, and now his spirit is angry. Something bad has happened, or will happen here! You mark my words!'

Posie felt a flicker of fear rise into her throat but then she saw that everyone had stopped up ahead, at the very back of the burial chamber. All heads were bowed, all torches were raised, and Posie saw that Harry and Alaric were on their hands and knees, scrabbling at what looked like a small black hole in the far wall. It was a hidden door, only about three feet high and cleverly concealed among the murals. Inside the black hole all was dark, but nevertheless, a strange golden flickering seemed to be emanating outwards from the gloom.

'What is it?' someone yelled.

Harry turned in great excitement. 'The discovery of a lifetime!' he whispered in a rapture. 'Alaric found it! A hidden room!'

* * * *

While the rest of the team returned to lunch at the base camp amid great excitement, Harry and Alaric worked on, aided by torchlight in the hidden room, guarded by Didi.

It turned out that the hidden room was a low barrel-roofed chamber, and it contained the best grave goods so far. There were chests filled with precious coins and nuggets of gold, and as far as the eye could see, large urns stood three foot tall, fashioned out of pure gold and as high as a man's waist, each and every one of them shaped like a bee. There must have been at least two hundred of the things, placed in rows like a small army.

When one of the bee urns was carried out into the light of day in the late afternoon, the whole team stood around holding their breath, watching as Harry unscrewed the pure gold disc of the lid with his Swiss army knife. Lenny stood poised, ready with her camera.

At last the lid was off. Harry stared anxiously down into the depths of the urn.

'Gold coins?' shouted one of the junior archaeologists hopefully. 'What is it? Money?'

But Harry seemed lost in a trance and dipped his finger into the urn, and stared at it in disbelief. He shook his head, before laughing aloud.

'No! It's better than that!' he declared. 'It's honey! Four-thousand-year-old honey! Intact! As fresh as the day it was placed here!'

* * * *

It was with a start of surprise that the team realised long shadows were drawing in and that it was high time for dinner back at base camp.

Harry suddenly looked mortified at the thought of heading back. 'I *can't* do that talk tonight!' he practically wailed. 'I want to stay on here! How can I possibly return to base camp when there is so much to document here! The dig is finished! I leave tomorrow! I simply don't have time to record all these new finds!'

'But you can't pull out of the talk now!' said Lenny, rather unfeelingly in Posie's opinion, and with an obvious eye to her own self-interest. 'The talk has been advertised for weeks! Think of everyone you'll be letting down, Harry! Think of all the work which went into preparing that talk! *My* photographic slides!'

Harry looked at Alaric pleadingly. 'You said you'd do it for me! Swap with me, Alaric! Be a sport! You're a natural when it comes to public speaking. You often do it! I'm just terrible. Awful! I'm a field archaeologist through and through, not an orator! Do it! All you'll need to do is read out my notes! They're here, in my satchel. Take them! Say you'll do it? Please? I need to stay up here and work on…'

'All right,' Alaric said with a shrug, unfazed. 'But keep Didi up here with you, he can keep a look-out. It could be dangerous working on alone up here in the dark!'

'When will you be finished?' asked Posie worriedly to Harry as the team piled into the back of the safari wagon and Alaric swung up into the driver's seat. 'We'll need to collect you!'

'Oh, who knows!' Harry declared, breezily, lighting another torch and adjusting his white turban. 'Later! Come back when the bally talk is over!'

* * * *

Dinner passed without incident, and Alaric took to the podium afterwards as easily as he had done before. If anyone was disappointed at not hearing Harry Redmayne of the British Museum expound on the joys of 'Ammotep, the God of Bees and Honey!' they were certainly keeping quiet about it. The marquee was packed to the rafters and the beautiful slides and Alaric's gravelly, easy tones contributed to an evening of real enjoyment.

Posie sipped at a gin and tonic in the front row and nibbled on a chocolate mint. She was half-listening to Alaric and half-worrying that what he was doing tonight was not exactly staying hidden, when she became aware of a slight disturbance behind her at the back of the tent. Hammad, the serving-boy, was moving up through the centre aisle of wooden seats, looking to and fro. Hammad suddenly darted forwards in relief when he spied Posie and placed a sealed envelope in her hands.

It was marked 'URGENT' and on ripping it open Posie saw that it was a telegram from London. It contained an exact transcript of the missing last page of Ianthe's novel, *The Tomb of the Honey Bee*.

She read it through and almost fell off her chair. Posie grabbed at her drink and her carpet bag and made a dash for outside, desperate to be away from the talk. She stood outside the tent.

Taking a great breath, she read the telegram from Inspector Lovelace over once again. Facts went spinning around her head, loose threads coming together. And suddenly, out of the crazy kaleidoscope of thoughts Posie knew with a deep certainty the person who was behind it all: the stalking, the pursuing of Alaric, the deaths which had taken place so far.

She heard for a single second Alaric's voice carrying out on the clear night air, and then the sound of rapturous clapping. The talk was over. And then she became aware of another sound: raspy shouting coming from across the camp in waves, coming from the direction of the thoroughfare to the ancient city of Thebes, from the road they drove along every day to get to the tomb.

Local guards were running in the direction of the main tent, and a very fat French archaeologist who Posie had only seen once or twice before was running behind them. He stopped suddenly, wheezing. He indicated towards the guards:

'They say they've seen a fire!' he called to Posie breathlessly, doubled over, panting.

One of the local guards started to speak in a very fast stream of Arabic. The French archaeologist listened, nodded, then translated hurriedly.

'He says the fire is very strong, it's coming from the necropolis. He thinks it's coming from the tomb of the Honey God, Ammotep! Isn't that one of the British Museum's projects? It's on fire! Like a beacon, apparently! Thank goodness no-one is up there! Was the talk good? I'm sorry I missed it!'

But Posie wasn't listening. Heart in mouth, she was running and screaming at the guards and demanding someone get the safari wagon. She was barely conscious of Alaric's voice going on and on again in the main tent, and the telegram in her pocket went unheeded for now.

She grabbed hold of Hammad.

'When Alaric has finished speaking get him into his tent quickly! Don't let him speak to anyone! Tell him to pack his things and be ready to leave.'

All she could think about was Harry Redmayne and how his nerves at public speaking had led him to swap places with Alaric and thus into a danger which none of them had thought possible.

She hoped against hope that Harry had survived by some miracle, but in her heart she knew that the killer was too thorough, and too much of an expert to have been cheated out of the death and destruction they had wanted to bring about.

And for now it was important to keep her head, to make the killer think that they had won.

＊＊＊＊

The sky around the tomb was very bright, and it reminded Posie of Guy Fawkes night on Clapham Common in London. Yellow and orange streaks filled the air and crispy black embers were rising and blowing in the wind.

As Posie and the fat French archaeologist drew up alongside the tomb of Ammotep in the wagon she noticed that the air was filled with a horrible sickly sweet tar-like smell. She guessed the smell was the burning honey, combined with another, noxious smell which she realised must be petrol. Tongues of fire were blazing outwards from the tomb. Other cars packed with guards screeched to a halt behind them.

'Be careful! Be careful!' shouted the French man as Posie jumped out of the wagon and approached the cave-like entrance to the tomb. The local men had brought jugs and vessels of water and they threw them at the entrance uselessly. Posie could see that they had arrived too late to save anything: the murals and the gold-leaf were blistered and blackened and she could see that the fire's quick path had burned everything inside to a cinder.

She knew that Harry would have been working in the back room, the hidden room, among the ancient urns of honey, cataloguing everything in a joyful, desperate hurry. She could well imagine the killer entering the camp earlier in the day, knowing that Harry Redmayne was giving a well-advertised talk in the marquee in the evening. Posie could imagine the killer easily learning about Alaric's discovery of the hidden room at the tomb of Ammotep, and hearing how Alaric had stayed behind to work on it for many hours during the hot afternoon.

The killer had obviously been lurking around for days, and had seen Didi stationed at all times with Alaric. The killer must have hung around tonight, too, and believing that Alaric was working on in the tomb during the evening, protected by Didi, he had seized his chance. He had trapped Harry and Didi inside the tomb somehow, sealed it up and set fire to it, in much the same way he had set fire to Alaric's hives at Boynton Hall. But tonight the killer had succeeded. Or they *thought* they had succeeded.

Posie got down on her knees in front of the tomb, trying not to choke. She realised with a shudder that she was probably being watched by the eagle eyes of the killer, somewhere nearby in the darkness.

'Oh Alaric!' she wailed into the flames. She sat there for a while, weeping, and then noticed some paperwork blowing around in the dusty undergrowth.

It was one of Harry's beautiful hieroglyphic paintings, strangely intact and barely charred at all. Posie held onto it, tears for Harry running down her face, and then she retreated to the safari wagon. As she did so she was aware of movement up ahead in the bushes and she caught sight of a pale figure dashing away through the smoke. So the killer *had* been watching, after all!

And as she stepped up into the open-back of the vehicle she was aware of a flash of colour in among the charred bracken and blackened stones. She bent down to retrieve it, and recoiled in horror.

It was a long, curling, Cosima Catchpole-like red wig.

* * * *

Nineteen

Heart racing, hiding in the shadows of the tent, Posie explained to Alaric what had happened and what they must do. Wide-eyed, he nodded in agreement and they left the archaeological dig in the safari wagon, driving with the lights switched off. The other archaeologists were still drinking gin in the big marquee and milling around joyously, oblivious to everything that had happened.

It was too late to use the Post Office in Luxor so they drove instead to the Old Winter Palace Hotel. Leaving Alaric hiding in the back of the wagon in the car park, Posie ran into the reception, enswathed in a silk headscarf and her big sunglasses, hoping that her disguise would be adequate.

The concierge ushered her into a small private room and she placed a call with the International Operator to the news-desk at the *Associated Press* in London. It was seven o'clock in the evening in England, but that was just the start of the day for the newshounds, and she was confident of getting what she needed. She could imagine her contact, Sam Stubbs, standing at his desk in the art-deco building on Fleet Street and looking out over the room of busy beetling journalists, all hungry for the next big story. Well, this one would blow everything else off the front page!

'Sam? It's Posie,' she said briskly.

He sounded very far-away and he started to ask pleasantly after her health in unhurried, tinny, tiny tones.

'No time for all that!' trilled Posie, expecting to hear the International Operator cut in any minute with the pips to finish the call.

'I have a HUGE story for you! It must go out tomorrow. I need you to keep leaking it over the next few days, too. Ready for the headline?'

She heard him scrabble for a pen and paper. He knew that Posie meant business.

'Shoot!'

'ALARIC BOYNTON-DALE, THE FAMOUS EXPLORER, IS DEAD!'

'*What?*' Sam Stubbs gasped. She heard him drop his pen. Then, less convinced:

'What's your source? Who told you? Where did he die? Where are you, anyway? You sound miles away.'

'I am. I'm in Egypt, the Valley of the Kings. For now. And *I'm* the source. I saw the body myself tonight. He died in an accidental fire in a tomb he was helping to excavate out here. Terrible! It will be a terrible shock for his family. It seems they've been blighted by bad luck recently. Feel free to share the story with any of your other journalist pals at other papers. I'm sure they will want to run with it too…'

She heard the pips go and rang off. She checked her wristwatch and called Inspector Lovelace at Scotland Yard. He groaned on hearing her voice.

'You and your timing! I was just leaving. I've even got my hat and coat on! Is this about my telegram to you, about the last page of the manuscript? Did it make any sense to you? I have to confess I'm baffled!'

'It made perfect sense,' Posie said. 'Everything makes perfect sense. Now.'

She explained quickly about Harry Redmayne's death, the fire, the way that Alaric had swapped places with him to do the talk, the fact that the killer thought they had actually managed to murder Alaric at last.

'So the killer has been out there all this time? Watching you?' asked the Inspector, his words chilled with fear.

'Yes,' said Posie certainly. 'There are so many tourists in and out of the camp all day long that it must have been easy. The killer waited for his chance, and he got it tonight, although they got the wrong man! I'm confident they haven't realised that yet; they've just scarpered away thinking everything has gone to plan. We need to keep up the make-believe, let them think they've got away with it, let them get comfortable. I've already fed the story that Alaric is dead to the newspapers!'

'But you've got a marquee full of clever people out there who all *saw* Alaric tonight giving a lecture in front of their very eyes! *They'll* know he's not dead and spoil the whole charade!'

'No,' said Posie confidently. 'The story about Alaric's death will break tomorrow across London. Our killer will return to England in the next few days and see those stories. They're clever, they'll get home fast. No-one from here will be going back to England as quickly as that. We just need a few days grace to let this sink in; a few days of confusion. A week, maximum. No-one from out here will see those English newspaper stories in that time and try and disprove them. News travels slowly out here. We're a week behind with the English papers out here!'

'How are you getting home?' asked the Inspector, worry in his voice.

'Alaric found an old training jet, an Avro, for the journey down here. I think it's still stationed in Luxor. We'll use that part of the way, then probably swap to another plane. We should be back by the middle of next week, latest.'

'Fine. What do you want me to do in the meantime?'

'Get hold of a *Who's Who*. I need you to look up something for me and confirm my suspicions on one point. And I need your men to keep a watch on the house, Boynton Hall. If I'm right, the breaking news about Alaric's death will ensure everyone who has been "missing" over the last few weeks will return, feeling they're safe at last. Once they're all together, let me know.'

'Anything else?'

'Yes! Get Mr Proudfoot the solicitor on board as part of the charade. When everyone is together in the house again, and we are just about to have our show-down, I need him to be there too. To formally read out the Will.'

The pips were rattling.

'Three more minutes, modom?' cut in the International Operator courteously, aware of the importance of the Scotland Yard connection.

'I only need one more minute!' Posie said quickly.

'I have news too,' said the Inspector. 'Good *and* bad. Just tonight we managed to rumble Codlington. That's the good news! We've got him! He's sitting here in our cells.'

'And the bad news?'

'The reason we tracked him down was that he had bribed a crooked policeman. One of our lot, I'm afraid to say. The policeman was bribed to go to our evidence room and locate the original copy of *The Tomb of the Honey Bee*. He found it and shredded it before we realised. So now there are no longer any copies of the wretched book in existence!'

Posie blew out her cheeks in exasperation. It was annoying, but fortunately not entirely necessary now for their purposes. At least they had a reconstruction of the final, most important page. Thank goodness for that printer ribbon in the typewriter! The pips ran again.

'Posie, take care,' the Inspector said pleadingly. 'Tell me. Do you actually know at this stage *who* the killer is, or do you need to wait for the show-down at Boynton Hall to come to a conclusion?'

Posie laughed. 'Oh, no. I know,' she said, bitterly.

She named the killer aloud, but couldn't hear the Inspector's reaction as the call was cut and the line died.

* * * *

PART FOUR
Oxfordshire and London
(July–September, 1921)

Twenty

Almost a week later, on a boiling hot Thursday afternoon in the last week of July, Posie found herself back at Boynton Hall.

Inspector Lovelace had tipped her off that all the inhabitants of the house had returned, and he had set up a formal tea-time meeting there, the reason for which was ostensibly for Mr Proudfoot to read aloud Alaric's last Will and Testament to all of the household, and also to Major Marchpane and Lady Cosima Catchpole.

The Inspector had hidden his men at strategic points all around the house and grounds, on the lookout for trouble.

Posie had sent a note to Lady Violet on her return to England expressing her sadness at the death of Alaric, and she had invited herself down for the meeting, declaring that it was the least she could do in the circumstances. She was greeted by Lady Violet at the station in the two-seater like last time, and she noticed how the girl had huge dark shadows under her eyes, and that she had lost weight since the last time they had met, which she could ill afford to do. Violet drove with an air of weary resignation, as if the news of her brother's death had sapped all of her energy.

'I'm so sorry I couldn't prevent his death,' Posie said guiltily. Even with Lady Violet it was necessary to keep up the pretence of Alaric's death, so that the whole plan wasn't ruined. Violet had nodded and wiped away a quick tear on the back of her hand.

'I'm so grateful for you coming here, Posie,' she said as they entered the house. 'It's good to know I have a real friend in amongst this nest of vipers. I'm getting out of here as soon as possible, you know. Today, I hope.'

'Oh?'

'Yes. Some of Ianthe's money has already been paid over to me. It's not much, but it's enough to rent a small flat in a nice part of London. That's where I've been these last weeks, you know; in London, flat-hunting. I couldn't stay locked up inside Boynton Hall like a prisoner. I know it was wrong of me to leave, but I felt like I couldn't breathe! Thank goodness for Ianthe's money! It will come in very useful. Although, sadly, it could have been more, *much more...*'

'Do you mean the extra money you would have got if *The Tomb of the Honey Bee* hadn't been destroyed?'

Lady Violet sighed and nodded:

'Exactly. Its income would have been very handy indeed. Still... I suppose you heard about Codlington the Valet? They say he'll hang for that literary agent's death. Serves him right! A shame they can't get Codlington for Alaric's death, either, but there we go. Apparently Codlington couldn't have been in Egypt at the same time as he was here in London, the dates don't work out. Goodness only knows *what* Alaric was doing in Egypt anyway, but I dare say you'll tell me later. Do you want to freshen up before this meeting kicks off? I've put you in the same room as last time. I'll get a maid to bring you up a cup of tea. No honey cake this time I'm afraid...'

* * * *

Over in Alaric's annexe Posie watched him as he moved around, systematically tidying the desk under its weight of messy papers, opening and closing drawers, straightening things out. His face gave nothing away and he didn't look tired – despite the long journey back to England.

Inspector Lovelace and his two Sergeants sat on the single bed rather awkwardly.

'Are we ready?' asked the Inspector, checking his wristwatch. 'Proudfoot should be here any moment now. Alaric, have you got the Will?'

Alaric passed it over, the new version of the Will which had accompanied him all around Europe and to Egypt.

'Let's make a start over at the house,' continued the Inspector.

'So far, everything's running to plan. You hide here, Alaric, and in fifteen minutes time make your way over to the house, listen at the door of the Library. When you hear two loud raps from inside you can make your grand entrance! Understand?'

'Yes,' he said certainly. 'I understand.'

But rather than looking jubilant, he was ashen-faced and shivering, despite the heat.

****

In the Library, it was as if none of them had ever been away, and the same hostile atmosphere persisted. Posie looked around her and saw the household all assembled. Here was Codlington, in police handcuffs, unshaven and grimy, sandwiched between Sergeants Binny and Rainbird, throwing dark looks around the place. And Mr Burns was sitting smoking a cigar, comfortable on the sofa, the only person to nod kindly at Posie as she sat down opposite him.

Lady Violet, tired-looking but at least dressed and made-up carefully for once, sat perched on a small stool near the fireplace. Lady Eve stood propped at the fireplace, her face thickly-powdered, as if for winter, absently toying with the silver framed photo of Alaric. Eve studiously ignored Posie and refused to meet her eyes. By her side and nervously fidgeting with his hip-flask was her husband Lord Roderick, eyeing the door and constantly checking his watch. The servants were grouped nervously in a far corner, almost hidden behind the drinks-trolley, flashing anxious glances at each other and dabbing at their faces with handkerchiefs.

Major Marchpane arrived late, breathless and alone, through the French windows, accompanied by Bikram. He looked terrible, grey and worn, as if all the fight had gone out of him. He sat down heavily at the free end of Mr Burns' sofa.

Inspector Lovelace opened the door, and the solicitor entered and took to the floor in the centre. Mr Proudfoot looked out over the top of his half-moon glasses, Alaric's Will clutched tightly in his hand:

'But this won't do at all! We can't start!' Proudfoot objected querulously, looking all around him. 'Where is Lady Cosima Catchpole? She benefits under this Will!'

There was a collective gasp from around the room and Mr Proudfoot looked beadily at the Major, who had turned bright red and was patting the dog vigorously.

'It's important that *everyone* who is mentioned in the Will is here now,' Mr Proudfoot said, a trifle pompously.

'Major?' whispered Posie. 'Where is your wife?' To her horror she saw the big man wipe away a tear from his good eye.

'She's gone!' he mumbled. 'She upped and left me a few weeks ago! Said she was bored of living down here, cut off from the rest of the world. She said she was bored of me, too! She left me a note saying she wanted a new adventure.

I wondered if she had gone off after Alaric, after all. But now I know he's dead…well, it puts rather a different spin on it, doesn't it? I don't know where she is, I'm afraid.'

Posie stared at the Major, feeling tremendously sorry for him. For a tiny second she wondered if she had got all of her conclusions wrong, after all. But Inspector Lovelace cut in, coughing dramatically to make everyone turn in his direction.

'My men have tracked Lady Cosima down, Major. She is safe and sound and living in a squalid bedsit in London. She's taken up with a small, very bohemian little theatre group in Soho. I'm sorry to say that she's taken up with one of their leading actors too. My scouts tell me that she will be playing the role of Lady Macbeth next week, starting on Monday, at a very seedy little venue in the West End. I believe she paid the theatre group a considerable amount to let her act with them. Perhaps that was the new adventure she was craving. Why not go down there for the Opening Night, sir? Surprise her. Work things out? My scouts tell me that after a month of this bohemian lifestyle she is running very low on funds. I'm sure she'd be only too pleased to come home to her previously boring life here in the Cotswolds. *If* you'll have her back, that is…'

The Major nodded stupidly, rendered speechless, while the whole room stared at him.

'So, then!' said Proudfoot quickly. 'Let's press on! First, the bequests!'

He consulted the Will in front of him. 'The possessions of Alaric Boynton-Dale pass to his brother, Lord Roderick.'

'NO!' breathed Lady Eve, almost dropping her cocktail cigarette and staring in wonder at the lawyer. 'But I thought he'd changed his Will? Gee, it seems he came good after all! See Roddy darlin'? All that worryin' for nothing!'

But the lawyer cut her off quickly:

'I am afraid, Lady Boynton, that I am referring to *possessions* only. Alaric's personal possessions were worth only a couple of hundred pounds, and consist of his coin collection in the annexe, his clothing, some personal effects and some family papers. Sorry!'

Lady Eve goggled, turning purple in the face. The lawyer continued:

'Alaric left any plane in his possession at the date of his death to his good friend, Major Marchpane.'

'But he didn't own a plane at the date of his death! It was sabotaged!' exclaimed the Major quickly, confused.

'Exactly!' said the lawyer. 'So you get nothing! Sorry!'

Proudfoot continued reading down the list. 'And now I come to Lady Cosima Catchpole. She is to receive a priceless ancient bee coin which Alaric wore as a necklace.'

He looked over at Posie, who shook her head. 'However, I am given to understand that the coin has been given away, so Cosima too gets nothing. Please offer her my condolences, Major. This is all highly irregular...'

He shook out the Will dramatically and stared around the room.

'Now we come to the rest of Alaric's estate, which essentially means the Family Trust, the exciting part! It is worth around Two Hundred Thousand Pounds! And can be distributed out almost immediately. And that goes to...'

The whole room waited.

'Lady Violet!'

The atmosphere in the room could have been cut with a knife. Lady Violet looked at the lawyer with a brief bright stare of incredulous wonder and then promptly burst into tears. Posie moved over to comfort her, squatting on the floor. A strange noise sounded up, and Posie realised that Codlington was emitting a strange growling noise, fighting off the policemen on either side of him with his elbows.

'I've been set up!' he was shouting. 'My Lord...' he turned to Roderick, who was looking as sick as a dog and was emitting low, strange, groaning noises.

'Help me! My Lord...?'

Just then Bikram started to bark frantically and threw himself at the door of the Library, behind Inspector Lovelace. There was the sound of two loud raps, and then, at some carefully discreet sign given by Inspector Lovelace, the lawyer called for silence amongst the chaos. Proudfoot raised his arms and held the Will out in front of him.

He then made a big show of ripping the Will in half, and then ripped it again, and again and again, throwing the pieces up in the air around himself dramatically, like confetti falling at a particularly strange wedding.

'It seems however, that we will not be needing this, after all! I am reliably informed that Alaric Boynton-Dale is, in fact, alive and well. And with us this very afternoon!'

Everyone stared at Proudfoot as if he had gone stark raving mad, but just then the door to the Library opened and Alaric stepped through. Bikram threw himself against his legs in a frenzy of barking.

Eve Boynton, clutching the silver photo frame of Alaric, fainted at the fireplace. No-one paid her the slightest bit of attention.

'It seems you can't get rid of me that quickly!' Alaric smiled calmly.

* * * *

Twenty-One

'Please forgive me, Lady Violet,' Posie said anxiously, 'but I couldn't tell you that Alaric was still alive. It might have foiled the plan, and put Alaric in even more danger than he was in already.'

Lady Violet flung herself at Alaric like a little girl lost and he put his arms around his sobbing sister, leading her to a couch where she curled into his side, burying her face in his shirt. Posie stood in the centre of the room, looking around at everyone assembled there. Inspector Lovelace gave her a barely perceptible nod, indicating that she had his blessing to move matters along.

'This has been a very strange case,' Posie said slowly. 'Very sad too. Due to the actions of one person in this room several innocent people have died.'

She listed off on her fingers their names: Ianthe Flowers, Binkie Dodds, Bernie Sharp, Harry Redmayne.

'And all because just one person wanted to get their hands on the Trust money in Alaric's Will. It had become an obsession. They needed Alaric to die!'

Posie continued, looking around. 'The trouble for me was that *three* of you in here had a really good motive. And of the three of you, it could have been any one of you.'

The whole room gaped at Posie expectantly. She turned to Codlington first:

'You, Codlington, are highly suspicious. You have been, by your own admission, covering for Lord Roderick, allowing him to fritter away his fortune. But *you* do pretty well out of your arrangement too: in fact, you wield far more power than any normal Valet usually does.'

Codlington stared at Posie, ashen-faced. 'Makes no sense. I told you already, why would *I* want to kill Mister Alaric?'

'Perhaps you knew of the money which was supposed to pass to Lord Roderick under Alaric's Will? And you also learnt that Alaric might be changing his Will. Perhaps you had an eye on self-preservation; that's what you do best, isn't it? If Alaric could be killed *before* he got around to changing the Will you would have been okay – the gravy trail of endless money from Lord Roderick wouldn't have dried up – you'd be safe. Perhaps you used your horrible contacts in the London underworld to try and kill Alaric and anyone else who just happened to get in your way? Why, you were even caught red-handed dousing Bernie Sharp's office in petrol and causing his death! If you are capable of *that* you are more than capable of arranging the threats to Alaric and organising all the other deaths, too. Even those which took place abroad…'

'*What?*' shouted Codlington, his surly face turning white. 'What are you on about? No! No! I'm already in enough trouble! I never left these shores! I never went abroad. I was hanging out in the East End the last few weeks, I swear it.'

Posie nodded:

'But you didn't *need* to leave these shores, did you? You have so many contacts it wouldn't have been a problem for you to have someone tail me to Sicily and follow me, and then locate Alaric… And then try and kill him.'

Codlington looked as if he were chewing a wasp and struggled in his cuffs between the policemen. Suddenly Posie swung around and pointed a finger at Lord Roderick:

'Or you, my Lord. You could have been *directing* Codlington to act in such a manner, rewarding him for his actions, giving him an expensive pair of cufflinks as part-payment and allowing him to take a cut in your race winnings for now. Perhaps you even promised him a slice of the Trust monies after Alaric's death? You could have been responsible for his every move. An indirect killer.'

'No!' wailed Lord Roderick. 'I swear I had nothing to do with any of this mess!'

'And *you*!' Posie pointed at Lady Eve, who was swigging brandy straight from the decanter.

'You were worried about the state of your husband's finances, and you were frantic at the thought that Alaric might leave his money to anyone other than Roderick.'

Posie spoke softly, but still everyone in the room could hear:

'And there was more to it, wasn't there, Lady Eve? I didn't realise until fairly recently that you were obsessed with Alaric. It was a twisted sort of love, a dangerous obsession. An obsession which led to your cutting out every single picture you could lay your hands on of him for your scrapbooks; an obsession which led to you deciding that if you couldn't have him, no-one else could, either. You realised that Alaric was still in love with Cosima, even after their affair had ended. And when you realised that he would never be yours, you became obsessed with hurting him instead. Perhaps you plotted that plane crash? The burnt beehives? Perhaps it was *you* out in Sicily following me around? Planting poison in drinks?'

'Of course it wasn't me!' flashed Lady Eve angrily. 'What a load of rot! Roderick and I never left England, either! The two of us were holed up in a suite at the Ritz Hotel in London, together with my father. We were trying to restore our relationship, and trying to keep cool in this dratted heatwave, too. It was the only place my father would agree to stay: it's the only place in England where they actually have air conditioning! It's not my fault if your idiot police force couldn't track us down there! And that they let us escape from Boynton Hall in the first place! Check the Ritz Hotel records if you must. And anyway, I've never done anything to *actually* hurt Alaric.'

Posie cocked her head to one side and then nodded, accepting Lady Eve's explanation.

'I believe you, as it happens. And of course, I *have* already checked the hotel register at the Ritz. But it's not quite true what you say, about not having done anything to hurt Alaric, is it? Your obsession led you to send that telegram to Major Marchpane informing him of Alaric's affair with Cosima, didn't it?'

'That was *you*?' shouted Lady Violet, incredulously, still burrowed in Alaric's shoulder. 'I thought it was Ianthe! More fool me!'

Lady Eve flushed darkly and stared at the floor. Roderick stared at her in total disbelief.

'Yes, it was Lady Eve!' declared Posie. 'It seems that Ianthe Flowers was a better judge of character than anyone gave her credit for, and her book, *The Tomb of the Honey Bee*, is key to this whole case. She describes Lady Eve and her obsessional love for Alaric perfectly in the book. In fact, *all of you* were in that book! It's a shame on so many levels that literally every single copy is now destroyed, but no matter. It did its job! It told me enough!'

'What do you mean, Missy?' asked Mr Burns, shuffling forwards on the sofa, his eyes wary.

'What I mean is that it told me who the true murderer was!'

All eyes swivelled onto Posie. She turned to Lady Eve. 'You, Lady Eve, are an obsessive when it comes to matters of the heart, but you don't have it in you to murder anyone. And neither do Lord Roderick or Mister Codlington.'

'So you're now ruling us out?' Eve gasped, incredulously.

'I was just running through the possibilities before,' Posie smiled. 'Hypotheticals.'

She turned to the room at large:

'From the very start of this case I thought that something here was strange, that perhaps one careful hand was at work, playing people off against each other. Things didn't stack up as they were supposed to, the clues were there and everybody had a motive, but nothing rang true. There was evil in this house, but I couldn't put my finger on it; it seemed to come from so many directions, with so many layers! Usually you find when a case is very complicated it means that the motive behind it all is very simple. Don't you agree, Inspector?'

Inspector Lovelace nodded from his place by the door. 'That's right, Miss Parker. And in this case *money* was the motive. Pure and simple.'

Posie continued:

'Our killer was well equipped for murder, and tried to kill Alaric in a number of ways, none of which worked. But then Alaric got suspicious and disappeared. And that is when our killer panicked, and needed to find him. And it was then that our killer found they were not so clever and not so well equipped, after all. They needed help!'

'I don't follow you,' said Mr Burns, angrily. 'What the blazes are you talking about, Missy?'

Posie smiled calmly. 'I mean to say that our killer was baffled. They had no idea where to look for Alaric. And so she came to me!'

Posie turned to Lady Violet. 'It was YOU, my Lady.'

Everyone gasped in unison. Lady Violet had sat up straight on the sofa.

'Yes, you, Lady Violet! You came to me with your clever story, full of woe and desperation for your missing brother! You came to me with your careful list of suspects, each one of whom you had given a motive to. And I admit, they were *good* motives, extremely convincing, most of them included a grain of truth, too – which was clever. But I began to think when I first came down here to Boynton

Hall that things were more complicated than how you had suggested, and I just put it down to your misunderstanding of people, to your preoccupation with your brother's disappearance. But you were arrogant. You assumed that I would take everything you told me about people at face-value, and just accept the twisted half-truths. You tried to stage-manage everything!'

Lady Violet was staring at Posie with narrowed eyes, a look of utter bemusement on her face. 'What on earth?' she cried out desperately, casting pleading looks around at Alaric and then at Roderick before looking back at Posie.

'Have you totally lost your mind? How *dare* you! It was *I* who employed you to come here and find Alaric. Don't forget that!'

Posie smiled and fished in her bag for a couple of items. 'Oh, I haven't forgotten that, Lady Violet. That is what I mean by your arrogance. You considered yourself a mastermind, much better than me, in fact. You considered my own detective skills too paltry to root out the truth. You thought that if you came to me and asked me to investigate Alaric's disappearance, it would seem as if you were utterly innocent. Unfortunately, it took me a good deal of time, several deaths and much travelling to realise the truth.'

Mr Burns was on his feet, his face red and angry.

'I say, Missy, you sure as hell have got this all wrong! You can't go accusing that little girl over there of murder! What do you think you're playing at? She's just a lovely little girl who makes the sweetest cakes in the whole darn world!'

'Oh, but there you are right. And there you are also wrong, Mr Burns.'

'Come again?'

'I always thought Lady Violet was complicated. And it seems I was right.'

Posie smiled, shaking out one of the items from her bag. It was *The Lady* magazine from June, with Lady Violet on the cover.

'You see, Lady Violet *is* just a sweet little girl who bakes cakes, but she is so much more than that. See this article? This is the key to it all! It sets out her motive. I wish I had realised it in the first place! In it she tells the world that she wants to open a chain of tea-shops to rival Lyons Corner Houses. And she *did* want that! Desperately! She still wants that! It was a long-held ambition. But she couldn't do that without money, a great deal of money. And there was precious little of that here at Boynton Hall. And there were few wealthy men left in the country to marry, not that she didn't have several admirers! I had the good fortune to meet one of them, Harry Redmayne, out in Egypt, and a nicer fellow you couldn't hope to meet! He told me that he had loved Violet, but that he wasn't rich enough for her. Now, at the time I thought that he meant the *family*, perhaps Lord Roderick, had declared that Harry wasn't rich enough for her and forbidden the match…'

'Of course I wouldn't have said such a thing!' shouted Lord Roderick. 'I just wanted Cuckoo to be happy! I never stipulated that a fellow had to have money! I don't know why people think I'm such a rotten sort of fella! You've got that all wrong!'

'EXACTLY!' said Posie, nodding sympathetically.

'But so has most of the country got it wrong! With good reason! I did a little digging, and I asked Alaric about it too, and it seems that the whole image of Lady Violet being kept here in penury without any money, and the reputation the family has of only allowing her to marry a rich man is totally wrong. It was *Lady Violet herself* who created that image, always wearing the same old clothes, getting people to feel sorry for her, bemoaning her lot in life to anyone who'd listen. And it was Lady Violet *herself* who turned down countless offers of marriage from men whom she deemed not rich enough for her. Men such as Harry…'

'What the devil are you talking about, you harpy!'

Lady Violet was on her feet now and looked at Posie in disbelief. Violet turned to Alaric, but he simply got up, avoiding her gaze and went and stood next to Inspector Lovelace over by the door.

The Inspector spoke to Violet directly, his face impassive:

'So when Alaric told you that he was going to change his Will, that the Trust money of Two Hundred Thousand Pounds would come to *you* on his death, he inadvertently set in place a murder scheme. Not content to wait years until his death, you saw that money as your right, a supply of ready cash to set up your tea-shops with. You just needed to ensure he died quickly! You assumed that the new Will naming you as heir was safely stored at the lawyers' office in London, and that your destiny as the heir to that money was certain.'

Posie smiled bitterly, continuing the horrible tale.

'And so you put into effect your horrid chain of events, Lady Violet. First you rigged the engine of Alaric's plane so that it would fail when he was flying. I didn't see how you could have done that at first, not without help, but then something dear old Harry Redmayne told me out in Egypt jolted me badly: he told me that *you were good with engines*, that you could fix things in the blink of an eye. And in fact I had seen this talent for myself! So then I thought to myself, a car engine isn't really so different from an aeroplane engine, is it? So you'd know what to do to disable one easily enough. That would be a piece of cake to a girl like you, if you'll forgive the pun.'

'My God!' shouted Major Marchpane from his sofa. 'Violet? Really? I don't believe it! Have you gone quite mad?'

'And then,' Posie continued, 'by the grace of God Alaric survived that crash. So you had to think again. And what better way to get at him than by killing off his precious hives of honey bees? You knew he would do his best to save them if there was any danger to them, and you made sure to use a really toxic poison, mixed with petrol, which if breathed in, would prove fatal for him. You tried it first as an experiment on the outer fields, and then you upped the dose a week later and made the chemical combination even more toxic. You used that to burn the hives nearest the annexe. And you nearly achieved your goal! Alaric would have died, but for Bikram raising the alert!'

'You have no proof! No proof for any of this!' Violet shouted hysterically.

'Oh, but I do!' said Posie infuriatingly. She waved the second document from her bag casually in the air.

'And so Alaric then disappeared, not telling you where he was going. And you got me up here to trawl through all the clever red herrings you had set up for me: the 'burnt' photo of Major Marchpane in the annexe, to illustrate the so-called hatred and jealousy between Alaric and him over Cosima; the pair of heirloom cufflinks which you gave to poor old Codlington as a gift which you swore him to secrecy about, therefore throwing suspicion on him as a thief; the story of Ianthe being in love with Alaric when in fact she was just doing some research for her book; the tales of Eve hating Alaric, when in fact she loved him. And lastly, and cleverest of all, the suspicion thrown onto your own brother Roderick: the mess you made in the annexe to make it look as if *he* was looking for Alaric's new Will in among the other papers, perhaps wanting to destroy it so that the old Will naming him as heir would remain in place? You were very clever. You stage-managed everything.'

Inspector Lovelace cut in. 'I must confess, Lady Violet, I did wonder if you had it in you to kill so maliciously, to frame all these innocent people. But then I realised that you had done it before. A long, long time ago. The key to your behaviour is in the past.'

The whole room stared at the Inspector, and then turned to look at Violet.

'What *do* you mean?' Lady Violet half-whispered, her eyes darting everywhere.

'Posie told me to look you up in the *Who's Who*. And so I did. And then I did a whole lot of other research. Your parents died in a car crash when you were a child. From which you were the only survivor.'

'And?' cut in Lord Roderick. 'Why is this relevant? Why dredge all this up again? It can only cause pain.'

The Inspector continued.

'The police reports from the time are very strange. They describe a brand new car with no reported problems taking a hair-pin bend in the road at considerable speed. Somehow the brakes seem to have failed, for no reason. There was suspicion at the time that the child, Lady Violet, knew more than she was letting on, that there was more to the accident than met the eye, but nothing was ever proven. The child didn't seem sufficiently upset at the death of her parents, for a start. But that's perhaps not so surprising… because the Boynton-Dales were not her real parents, after all.'

Posie nodded at Alaric and Roderick, who had both gone bright red in the face and stared at each other uncomfortably. She spoke as gently to the brothers as she could:

'That's why I got the Inspector to look up the entry for your family in *Who's Who*. It states that Lady Violet is adopted. I kept puzzling to myself why people kept referring to her as "Cuckoo". At first I thought it was just an affectionate nickname, but then I wondered if perhaps there might be a smidgen of truth behind it; that Lady Violet was the cuckoo in the Boynton-Dale nest. And I was right!'

Posie turned to Alaric. 'Your mother was a woman driven by compassion, by work for good causes. She worked on the Board of Women's Prisons, didn't she?'

Alaric nodded, his face troubled. Posie continued:

'She had two sons, you two boys. But she had always wanted a baby girl. And when a notorious mass murderer, Annie Sparks, was caught and placed before the Prison Board and found to have a new-born baby daughter in tow, your mother declared she would adopt the child on the spot. And so she did! Annie Sparks hung for her terrible crimes, and much was made of it in the newspapers at the time, but your mother swore you two boys to secrecy, told you never to tell anyone that Violet was not your own flesh and blood. That is correct, isn't it?'

Roderick nodded. 'It's a promise we've kept to,' he said wearily. 'We never told a soul. Not until now.'

Posie shook her head. 'You're wrong. I think Alaric told one person, and that was Ianthe Flowers, when she was following him around doing her research. Is that right?'

Alaric nodded. 'I only realised that Ianthe had written about it all when I saw that loose page from the novel at the café in Ortigia: it said "BLOOD WILL OUT"!'

Posie nodded. 'Exactly! It meant nothing to me at the time. But Ianthe had discovered something: the sins of the mother, Annie Sparks, were being continued by her daughter, Violet. Blood was proving much thicker than water! The capacity to murder had been inherited! And I am sure too that Violet had found out the identity of her real mother – my guess is that she found out on that fateful day of the car crash fifteen years ago. She decided that she had had enough of having the wool pulled over her eyes by the Boynton-Dales and she decided there and then that she would send their car off the road! As a punishment! She had little feeling for the people who had brought her up as their own child, so she didn't care if they died horribly. Isn't that right, Lady Violet?'

Sergeants Binny and Rainbird had left Codlington shackled on the sofa and were now standing over at the French windows. All exits to the room were blocked.

Lady Violet snarled, a horrible sound somewhere

between an animal caught in pain in a trap and a wild laugh: 'You have no proof of this, you lunatic! No proof at all!'

Posie smiled. 'Oh, but like I said before, I do! Ianthe was not a mean person, and she wouldn't have made a story out of your sad private family history if she hadn't known for a fact that you were responsible for the attacks on Alaric. You see, she SAW you! She was confused by what she had seen, but she had seen you nonetheless. She wrote about it too.'

Posie shook the "BLOOD WILL OUT" typewritten page.

'Unfortunately for you, Lady Violet, when you came to look for my copy of the manuscript in Ortigia, disguised as Cosima, you left a page behind. And it was a significant page! Let me read it out so everyone can hear:

"So, she had done it after all! She walked in a calm sort of triumph, all the while unaware that she was being observed from up on high."'

Posie continued.

'I think that Ianthe was looking out of her bedroom window, unable to sleep, when she saw you, Lady Violet, coming back from setting fire to the beehives. Perhaps you were carrying a can of petrol? Who knows? But apparently you looked happy. When the fire and the destruction of the hives became common knowledge, she put two and two together and wrote about it. She knew what you had done. And then she decided to tell me about it on the evening I arrived at Boynton Hall. You overheard her setting up a meeting with me and you got scared. You panicked. You realised she had to die.'

'But what about the manuscript?' asked Mr Burns. '*The*

Tomb of the Honey Bee? Why did Violet take the last page? Why not take the whole lot?'

Posie shrugged. 'I think Lady Violet looked quickly through the book and realised that her identity was only clearly given away on the last page. She flicked through the rest of the book and decided it was pretty mild stuff, which is why she left it all there. And also why she agreed to letting Bernie Sharp publish the book as soon as possible. He told her it would be a money-spinner, and Lady Violet was blinded by the prospect of yet more money coming her way.'

Posie turned to Violet. 'But you realised your mistake though, didn't you, when you started to read Bernie's copy, when you dropped by his office to sign some paperwork as Ianthe's heir. You realised what an accurate observer Ianthe had been, and how tiny, deadly clues ran through the whole novel. Clues that would lead right to your door. That was why every single copy, even the original at Scotland Yard, and the copy at Bernie Sharp's office, and the copy I had with me in Sicily had to be destroyed.'

Codlington had moved to the edge of his sofa:

'That's right! I told you I'd been set up! She called me from somewhere abroad and told me I had to get the copy back from Scotland Yard, by whatever means available to me. She told me to gut the office of Bernie Sharp, too. But I swear to God I had no idea he was in there at the time! I'm no murderer!'

'*Why*? Why did you do what she told you to, Codlington? Was it for money?' said Lord Roderick in quiet disbelief.

Codlington shook his head and looked at the floor. 'I'd have done anything for Violet,' he whispered, barely audibly. 'I love her. Always have done. Besides, she'd given me those ruddy cufflinks: she said she'd tell the police I'd stolen them from the family if I didn't obey her.'

'My God!' Roderick crumpled onto the sofa, head in his hands. 'How can we have all been so blind?'

'Don't beat yourself up about it, my Lord,' said Posie deftly, staring at Violet, who held her gaze defiantly.

'She pulled the wool over my eyes too, almost the whole way through. I even told her that I had discovered where Alaric was! I led her to him! I told her I had gone out to Sicily. So she escaped out of the Priest's Hole and made her own way to Ortigia. She followed me around the place, first dressed in a carnival costume and then as Lady Cosima, trying to scare me and convince me that there was a real element of danger to the case, but also trying to suss out where Alaric might be; she still had no idea. When she *did* eventually find us together, she tried to murder Alaric with a deadly cocktail of veronal, but unfortunately she got the wrong man, and an entirely innocent victim died instead.'

'And Egypt? How did she know to follow you out there?' asked Roderick, bemused.

'Your sister is a master of disguise, an expert at laying clues, and picking up on clues, too. It's a shame she didn't put her skills to a legitimate use and become a detective! I suspect she was lurking around at the Water Aerodrome in Siracusa and bribed the man in charge to tell her where we were going. She then hired her own plane and her own pilot and followed us down to Luxor. Time wasn't important; she was biding her time, seeing when best to strike. She played at being a tourist, entering the camp of the archaeological dig, again dressed as Cosima, sussing out how things worked there: *when* would be a good time to murder Alaric. She thought she'd found the perfect evening for it, too! Everyone was preoccupied with a big talk being given by good old Harry Redmayne, and Alaric had just made a fresh discovery to boot, and was likely to be working all alone and unprotected up in a remote spot. It was perfect! Except, yet again, but unbeknown to her, she got the wrong man. For such a clever girl, you're remarkably unlucky, aren't you, Lady Violet?'

Lady Violet sprung at Posie, fingers splayed. Just in time the police Sergeants crossed the room, restraining her, clipping her hands neatly together into glittering cufflinks. Lady Violet howled, a horrible noise, and Bikram joined in.

'You never will find out what that last page said, though, will you?' snarled Lady Violet as the Sergeants made ready to lead her out of the door.

'Ah, but that's where you're wrong!' said Inspector Lovelace, happily. 'We had an expert reconstruct it. In fact, it was the final jigsaw-piece which led Posie to realise that you were the killer! I sent it to her as a telegram!'

'What did it say?' asked Lady Eve, who sat puffing at a pink cigarette, looking like a shrivelled heap on the floor.

'I'll read it aloud, shall I?' said the Inspector. He searched in his briefcase and produced a crisp sheet of paper. He read clearly:

'"The murderer was the Queen Bee. But she had been caught! All the work she had forced the worker-bees to do, and all the trouble she had caused them was finally over. She had never really fitted into the hive; she had been brought in from outside, a changeling from somewhere else, but her greed had got the better of her. In the end, she had made herself a web of honey and trapped herself in it like a tomb."'

'Goodness!' said Major Marchpane from his couch. They all watched as Lady Violet was led out, snarling, and then Codlington was led out too.

'My God!' blathered Roderick. 'She'll hang for this!'

'Yes,' said Inspector Lovelace. 'More than likely. Unless she is declared insane, which I doubt will be the case.'

Posie crossed the room to Alaric, who was stroking Bikram's ears, both of them looking sorrowful.

'Are you okay?' she said softly. 'That was quite something to go through, wasn't it?'

He nodded.

'But,' continued Posie, 'I don't think it was a huge shock to you really.'

'What do you mean?' he whispered, looking up, fear showing in his green-bronze eyes.

'I think you started to suspect Violet even before you left England,' Posie said. 'Looking back there were points when I thought you suspected who the killer was, or at least knew more than you were telling me. I think you realised that it might be Violet. But I also think you didn't want to believe it yourself.'

Alaric grimaced.

'You *told* Violet, didn't you? You told her for certain that you *had* changed the Will in her favour. That it was all done and dusted. That was what gave her the confidence to act as she did.'

Alaric nodded dismally.

'And after you had signed your new Will,' Posie continued, 'you didn't take it with you because you thought it would be *safer* than leaving it with Mr Proudfoot. Far from it! You knew in your heart of hearts that in changing the Will you had made a terrible mistake: you took it with you because you thought of ripping it up every single day! You were always on the verge of destroying it. But you didn't, because you never truly wanted to believe that Violet was a cold-blooded killer.'

Alaric nodded. 'My baby sister,' he muttered. 'I always tried to look after her. I wanted to continue my mother's legacy. I loved Violet, for what it's worth. I still can't believe she's a full-blown murderer! But perhaps Ianthe was right? Perhaps the tendency to murder people is inherited? "Blood will out"…'

'Perhaps,' said Posie stoically.

'But I think we make our own luck. Now, I could do with a proper tea. Shall we get away from here? I know *you* have good memories of Boynton Hall, but quite frankly this place just depresses me.'

* * * *

Epilogue

The flat on the top floor of Museum Chambers on Bury Place was chock-full of fresh flowers, and yet more seemed to be arriving every minute. So much so that Posie simply left the front door open to her new home, and men from various florists across London were moving in a constant procession from the lift on the landing through to her bright, light-filled front room. Every possible surface was groaning under the weight of flowers and Posie busied herself by going around the room and pouring extra water into the vases. The day was incredibly hot for September, and she didn't want the flowers to wilt. They would be sent on later, after the wedding, to the bride and bridegroom's new London residence, a neat little Mews House on Pavilion Road in Chelsea, SW3.

A man in the smart turquoise green and gold livery of Fortnum & Mason placed a beautiful flash of white Calla lilies and a spray of silver leaves into Posie's arms and she sighed in contentment at the beauty of the arrangement.

'Dolly!' she trilled merrily to her friend who was still ensconced in a bedroom. 'Your bridal bouquet is here! It's wonderful. Just splendid!'

Prudence Smythe had been positioned on the front door downstairs, together with Inspector Lovelace's best

Constable, and together they were making sure that each florist who entered the building bore the necessary authority to do so. Prudence was enjoying being quietly officious, but there was a real need for the added security: the newspapers were keenly interested in the wedding of Lord Rufus Cardigeon and Dolly Price, which they were billing as 'the society wedding of the year', and hordes of journalists and photographers had crushed around the entrance to Museum Chambers, crowding onto the hot pavement, hoping to catch a first glimpse of Dolly as she left the building on her way to St Bride's Church in the City.

An apprentice who was lurking behind the man from Fortnum's suddenly darted forwards nervously, his arms filled with a bouquet of exotic purple roses, an exact match for the mauve-coloured long silk dress Posie was wearing.

'These are for you, Miss,' the boy muttered, checking a form in his hands.

'Oh no,' smiled Posie distractedly, 'there must be some mistake. I'm not a bridesmaid! There are no bridesmaids! So I'm sure we didn't order these.'

She checked her wristwatch and shifted Dolly's bouquet onto her hip, crossing to the door of the bedroom, knocking sharply, starting to panic somewhat. Dolly was an orphan, and had no sisters or brothers either, and Posie had somehow stepped into the role of making sure that everything ran smoothly at the wedding today.

'Dolly, are you ready yet?'

They really had to get a shuffle on: Rufus and all the guests would be taking their places in the wooden pews at St Bride's by now, fanning themselves with the Orders of Services to keep cool, admiring the banks of white roses and gypsophila which studded the dark interior like little stars. And it would take Dolly and Posie at least fifteen minutes to cross London to get there, even in a police car!

The senior florist from Fortnum's took the order form from the boy and studied it, frowning.

'No mistake, modom,' he said certainly, setting the bouquet of purple roses down on a coffee table. 'There's even a note with it for you. I'll just leave it here and we'll be off: I can see you've got your hands full.'

Suddenly Dolly emerged and all eyes in the room turned and stared at the future Lady Cardigeon.

Dolly, as befitted her former career as a Wardrobe Mistress, looked simply stunning in an ankle-length white silk dress. Swathes of silver veil and tulle cascaded down her back from a white skull-cap and tiny silver stars covered the outfit and caught the sunlight like winking eyes as she moved. Not many would have been able to pull off such an exotic, crazily off-beat gown, but for Dolly, who was tiny, like a little doll, and sported a racy peroxide-blonde bob, it was the perfect thing. Posie had no doubt that Dolly's bridal outfit would be splashed all over the London newspapers tomorrow, raising eyebrows and hemlines within days, and wedding-dress ateliers across the country would be taking orders for exact copies before the next week was out.

'How do I look, darling?' Dolly whispered hopefully from under silver-painted eyelids and thick eyelashes made black with lashings of Maybelline mascara.

Posie passed her the bouquet. 'Like an absolute dream,' she answered.

* * * *

Museum Chambers seemed awfully quiet when Posie returned home later from the Wedding Reception, stripped now as it was of friends and florists and flowery offerings.

She had stopped on the way back at her office on Grape Street, just around the corner from her new flat, and fed Mr Minks his usual prime piece of chicken for supper. Try as she might (and she had tried several times now over the month she had been living in her new home), she couldn't get the haughty Siamese to move in with her.

Mr Minks had clung in anger to his ripped-up shabby velvet curtains which Posie had installed specially for him to climb on in the kitchen at the Grape Street Bureau, and when she had had the bright idea of removing the curtains and placing them in her new flat and thus tempting him over in that way, he had simply sulked and starved himself for several days, refusing to look Posie in the eye and cowering in a corner of the new flat.

In the end she had had to admit defeat and had wearily traipsed back, carrying curtains and cat and all, and had re-installed Mr Minks at the office, which he obviously felt was his own private and sacrosanct domain. She knew enough about his personality to realise she would never try to move him again.

Posie sank into an armchair and kicked off her high-heeled shoes. She surveyed the apple-green living room and smiled with pleasure: buying the three-bedroomed flat in Bloomsbury on her return from Egypt had proved so much easier than she had ever thought possible – easier than choosing a hat when it came to it – because it had so ostensibly been the *right* place for her. And she was relieved to finally be in her own space and away from the old bedsit in Nightingale Mews. At last Posie felt she had a place to come home to; to *enjoy* coming home to.

She poured herself a small sherry and closed her eyes and thought about the day which had passed. It had been a wonderful wedding. The service had been impeccable, the church beautiful, the bridal pair radiantly happy. Even Rufus' father, the curmudgeonly Earl of Cardigeon, had been on his best behaviour and had joined in the singing and the throwing of silver-painted confetti with as much gusto as anyone.

The reception at the Savoy Hotel had been wonderful

too, and Posie felt relieved that it had all passed off without incident. She had enjoyed seeing Inspector Lovelace and Inspector Oats sitting proudly in the congregation dressed in their very best, their wives nervous and twitchy beside them, and she had smiled to see Sergeants Binny and Rainbird rendered almost unrecognisable, wearing top hats and tails. She had loved watching the outfits and antics of Dolly's many friends from the theatre, who made a wonderfully irreverent contrast to the legions of Rufus' straight-laced aristocratic cousins, whose disapproving stiff upper lip demeanour had given way to a more relaxed and approachable manner as the day wore on and the alcohol flowed in ever-increasing quantities.

But Posie had less enjoyed having to skirt diplomatically around Len and his wife Aggie, and it had been very awkward.

It turned out that Dolly and Rufus had issued invitations to their wedding back in May, as custom dictated, and unbeknownst to her, they had sent an invitation out to Len in his own right, assuming of course that he would accompany Posie. But things had changed, and how wrong they had all been!

The invitation had obviously sat unread in Len's in-tray during the months he had been away in France, and when he had returned to the Grape Street Bureau while Posie was in Egypt he had opened the Wedding Invitation and decided to accept, and bring his wife. Posie had no idea why Len had decided on such a strange and hurtful course of action, for Dolly and Rufus were *her* friends, after all. She had a horrible feeling that it was Len's wife who had pushed him to accept, snobbishly desperate for a chance to attend a society wedding.

Dolly and Rufus had been livid with Len when Posie returned and told them what had happened at the Cap d'Antibes, but they couldn't 'disinvite' him and his wife. Posie had found herself laughing and somehow convincing everyone that she was over it, that she was a grown-up, that she could manage one single day in the presence of Len and his wife.

But it had been hard watching the sharp-faced Aggie, limpet-like on Len's arm, giving off mock-haughty glances to all of Dolly's theatrical friends, no doubt thinking she was a cut above them. She had given Posie herself a withering and dismissive look, a curt nod and a screwing-up of the mouth being the only signs that she had actually deigned to notice her at all. Len had been embarrassed at Aggie's behaviour, Posie felt. But what on earth did he think he was playing at by inviting her along anyway?

Their working relationship at the Grape Street Bureau over the month that Posie had been back had proved workable; cool, calm, rational. They had slipped back into their work routines comfortably, with Len picking up his usual heavy workload of juicy divorce clients to shadow, and Posie taking whichever cases passed across her desk and took her fancy. They had even got back into the habit of sharing a cup of tea or coffee together at eleven o'clock in the morning, but now they took great care to sit together with Prudence in the waiting room, and neither disturbed the other in their private offices.

No mention was made again of the incident at the Cap d'Antibes, or of Aggie, or of the months which Len had spent in France and why he had not updated Posie on what was happening there. Similarly, no mention of Posie's reward from the Earl of Cardigeon for finding the stolen Maharajah diamond earlier in the year was made again, which was just as well, as Posie had sunk it all into buying her new bachelorette flat in Museum Chambers. On the whole, their working lives had been restored fairly easily, and Posie wished it were the same with her heart.

The wedding had also been interesting because Posie had seen Alaric again for the first time since the big meeting at Boynton Hall, and in the last month he had been trying desperately to sort out his family affairs; he had telephoned Posie when he could, but he had not had time for a social call. Not even to see her new flat.

Today he had been acting as a groomsman for Rufus and he had looked happy and smiling and in control, but Posie had known what an effort it must have been costing him. She noticed with fresh surprise how a great many people gravitated towards Alaric, anxious for a smidgen of his celebrity glitter to rub off on them. Indeed, spilling out of the church onto Fleet Street after the service she had been surprised anew at what a magnet he was for the press, almost in danger of eclipsing the bride and groom by being in such demand.

'OVER HERE! ALARIC!' shouted the photographers needily. Alaric had doffed his top hat and laughed and smiled, but Posie had seen him stiffen and his face become a sad mask when those same journalists shouted out comments about Violet.

'TELL US HOW YOU FEEL! WHAT IS IT LIKE WAITING FOR YOUR SISTER TO HANG?'

Goodness only knew how he could be feeling, Posie thought to herself. And the wedding had been so busy, and there had been so many things to do for Dolly, that she had not had much of a chance to ask Alaric how he was faring. She vowed to send a note to his club the next day, inviting him for a catch-up lunch; they both needed cheering up.

In the last month the Court had, as Inspector Lovelace had predicted, passed a speedy and certain sentence as to Lady Violet's guilt. She had been sentenced to death for the murders of Ianthe Flowers, Binkie Dodds and Harry Redmayne. Added to this was a charge of manslaughter for the killing of Bernie Sharp and a charge of attempted murder for trying to kill her own brother, Alaric Boynton-Dale.

While no doubt it was the right conviction and the Judge and Jury could not be faulted, there was no doubt that it was painful for Alaric. No-one knew when she would die, but it was surely any day now. Lady Violet was being kept as a maximum security prisoner in the new jail for women at Holloway. She had not received any visitors, and Alaric had told Posie that it was with a very hard heart and with much resolve that he ignored the begging letters which came to him daily from her.

A soft knocking noise came from the front door.

Surprised, Posie checked her wristwatch and roused herself from the comfort of her armchair. Midnight! Who on earth would call at this time of night?

She rustled across the small hallway and stood on the parquet floor in her violet ball gown and achy stockinged feet, checking the spy-hole.

It was Alaric.

'Oh!' she exclaimed in pleasure, unhooking the safety chain on the door. 'It's you! What a nice surprise! Come in!'

'Forgive the lateness of my call,' he muttered, hanging his top hat on her hat stand in the hall and peeling off his black tail-coat.

He followed Posie through the hallway and into the living room, throwing himself down in her just-vacated armchair. He barely looked around him, not even at the hieroglyphic painting by Harry Redmayne which Posie had rescued from the fire and had had framed and mounted in pride of place over her fireplace. Something was wrong.

Instinctively she moved to the drinks cabinet and poured a good two-fingers' worth from a bottle of single malt whisky which she kept as an emergency reserve. She passed the tumbler to Alaric.

'It's going to be tomorrow,' he said desperately and his coin-coloured eyes burnt with grief. Posie didn't need to ask *what* was going to be tomorrow: it must be the day for Violet's sentence to be carried out.

'Lovelace told me this evening just before I left the reception,' he continued. 'He didn't know whether I'd want to know or not, but he thought I probably *would*. I'm glad he told me.'

'Why on a Sunday?' Posie asked, stupefied.

'Less press interest outside of the prison. And fewer journalists hanging around. Sensible, really.'

'Oh Alaric, I'm so sorry.'

He shrugged and swigged the whisky. 'I hope you didn't mind my coming here. I couldn't bear to be alone tonight at my club, and I hardly got a chance to talk to you all day. I've missed you, you know. Don't you wish we could just jump in some old plane and fly off away from all of this?'

Posie, who didn't share Alaric's immensely itchy feet syndrome, half-laughed:

'No! Nice though our adventures were, I've just settled in here, thank you very much!'

Alaric looked around him deftly, as if only just realising where he was for the first time. 'Nice place,' he said. 'I'm sorry I didn't mention it before. Ass that I am!' His eye caught the bouquet of purple roses on the coffee table.

'You even have fresh flowers! Very nice! But isn't this place a bit big for you? You'll be rolling around in here alone like a marble in a glass jar! How many bedrooms are there?'

Posie smiled. Was that a hint that he wanted to stay over? She didn't mind: she was too old for having scruples about what the neighbours might say anyway.

'You're welcome to stay here tonight,' she said easily. 'The spare bedrooms are all made up and waiting. You even have a choice of room. Take your pick! You may be right, the place does feel a little bit too big; even my wretched cat doesn't want to live here with me. But I love it. It feels like home.'

Alaric finished the whisky and leaned over, replacing his glass on the table.

'I'm not sure if I've ever known what "home" feels like,' he said sadly.

He leant over and kissed Posie lightly on the cheek.

'But *you* always seem to make me feel at home, somehow,' he said, as if surprised at himself. Posie flushed at the unexpected compliment.

'Let's have a good lunch out somewhere tomorrow,' he said. 'Just the two of us. Mayfair, perhaps. My treat. I promise we won't speak about Violet. Or Cosima, or anything else which belongs in the past. We'll talk about the future.'

He reached for Posie's hand and gripped it tightly in his own. 'Do you ever wonder what Ianthe's lost book was about at all?' he asked, fixing her with his intense gaze. 'You only read the start, didn't you? I wonder why she called it *The Tomb of the Honey Bee*. Do you think she knew what was going to happen in Egypt? Do you think she had second sight?'

Posie stared up at Harry's bee hieroglyphs.

'I have no idea,' she said, shaking her head and letting Alaric continue to hold her hand. It felt quite nice, actually.

'I don't know why she called it that, or what happened in the book, but Ianthe *did* manage to give us the end of the story, didn't she? She knew how it would end. Whether that was at a tomb in Egypt or in a tomb of her own making, Violet was destined to trap herself in the end.'

****

When Alaric had gone to bed, Posie moved around the flat, shutting windows and tidying up and taking pleasure in putting things back where they needed to go. She was just about to go to bed herself and dim the light in the living room when she caught sight again of the purple roses on the low table, and she saw the edge of a note poking out from among the blooms. She cursed, having forgotten all about it before. Snatching up the note she read quickly:

Posie,

It's been a while now. A while too since I sent you mimosa from the South of France to remember me by.
I am very well, flourishing in fact.
I hope you enjoy the wedding today of your two dear, brave friends. My associates in London tell me that these roses should be an exact colour match to your outfit and I wish I were there with you to tell you how delightful you look. For now the flowers will have to suffice.

Yours, until we meet again (which I hope will be very soon),

Caspian della Rosa

Posie scrunched up the note, throwing it to the floor, staring at the strange-coloured flowers in horror.

Caspian della Rosa! Her old enemy! The man who had declared himself her nemesis! The man who had snatched the Maharajah diamond from the Earl of Cardigeon and left a trail of bloodshed in his wake when he had disappeared from under the noses of the police back in February. The man who had threatened to kill Dolly Price and who had begged Posie to come away with him and become a partner in his international crime ring! A man who had sent her flowers to tell her he was safe, and all the time she had mistakenly thought they had come from Len…

And here he was, if not in person, then with other people's eyes still following her every movement. He even knew her new home address. Posie shivered. Caspian della Rosa gave her the creeps.

Posie picked up the ruined note and pressed it flat, willing herself not to panic, breathing slowly. She had to be clear-headed about this. It was not a disaster.

She vowed that she would send the note across to Inspector Lovelace at Scotland Yard first thing on Monday morning, and see if he and his boys could somehow put a trace on the person who had bought the flowers. For now she would not let it spook her.

Besides, she was well protected with Alaric sleeping just down the hallway. Unconventional, perhaps, but handy nonetheless. And as she turned out the light, she remembered Alaric's comment about it being a remarkably big flat for her to live in alone.

Good job then that she was going to ask him to stay on. Indefinitely.

* * * *

Thanks for joining Posie Parker and the team.

Enjoyed *The Tomb of the Honey Bee* (A Posie Parker Mystery #2)? Here's what you can do next.

If you loved this book and have a tiny moment to spare I would really appreciate a short review on the page where you bought the book. Your help in spreading the word about the series is invaluable and really appreciated, and reviews make a big difference to helping new readers find the series.

Posie's previous cases are all available in e-book and paperback formats from Amazon, as well as in selected bookstores.

You can find all of the previous books, available for purchase, listed here in chronological order:

www.amazon.com/L.B.-Hathaway/e/
B00LDXGKE8 and

www.amazon.co.uk/L.B.-Hathaway/e/B00LDXGKE8

More Posie Parker books will be released in late 2016.

You can sign up to be notified of new releases, pre-release specials, free short stories and the chance to win Amazon gift-vouchers here:

www.lbhathaway.com/contact/newsletter/

Historical Note and 1920s Money

The characters in this book are all fictional (except for the brief mention in chapter eight of Sir Harry Omman, who was indeed President of the Royal Numismatic Society in London between 1919 and 1930).

The historical timings, dates, background and detail described in this book are accurate to the best of my knowledge (including the very real heatwave of 1921, the driest year in history since 1788). However, please see the following exceptions:

In England

1. Boynton Hall in the Cotswolds is entirely fictional. Likewise, so is the village of Stowe-on-the-Middle-Wold, although for somewhere similar, look no further than beautiful Burford, or Swinbrook village (home of the famous Mitford sisters) in Oxfordshire.

2. The solicitors' firm of Pring & Proudfoot on Bedford Row, London, is fictional. So too are the offices of

Bernie Sharp, the literary agent, in Covent Garden. The Army & Navy Store on Victoria Street (where Posie goes on a shopping spree in chapter seven) did exist but stopped trading under that name in 2005. Stanford's Map Shop is real and can be found on Long Acre, in Covent Garden (for more information see: http://www.stanfords.co.uk).

3.   The bee coin which is of significance in this book is fictional (it cannot be found in the British Museum). However, such coins bearing a bee-motif from the ancient world and from Sicily *do* exist, and for inspiration for my Sicilian bee coin in this story I looked to a good article by Andrew Gough, (see: http://andrewgough.co.uk/articles_bee2).

4.   Binkie Dodds, the numismatist, is a fictional character. However, the Royal Numismatic Society was based at the British Museum during the time of this story.

5.   Nightingale Mews, Posie's bedsit in SW7, does not exist. Museum Chambers, WC1, near the British Museum (Posie's new home in the epilogue) does exist in real-life.

6.   As ever, Grape Street in London, WC1, really does exist, although you might have to do a bit of imagining to find Posie's Detective Agency there.

In France and Italy

7.   The famous Blue Train, *Le Train Bleu*, (which Posie takes in chapter nine to the Cap d'Antibes) was already in service in 1921 (running from Calais to the fashionable hotspots of the South of France) but was not known by such a nickname until 1924.

8. The magical 'island' of Ortigia (a part of the town of Siracusa) in Sicily is indeed a gem. Siracusa itself is an absolute treat, especially the Archaeological Park. The sights described in Siracusa and Ortigia in this book all exist, save for Posie's guesthouse (the *Locatelli*) down by the harbour, and the apothecary run by monks (*Il Gioiello Ambra*) in the (real-life) area of the town known as *Giudecca*. For a similar location to Posie's guesthouse, see the *Des Etrangers Hotel*, Ortigia, Siracusa.

9. The Hyblaean honey which is referred to in this story does exist in real-life, and it *is* a unique honey due to the rare flora found in the Hyblaean mountains. However, it is not quite as rare or as legendary as I have described in this book, and I am not aware of it having any real-life magical or healing properties, nor is its production a secret. Likewise, it is not produced by just the one bee-keeping community. Bees and honey *do* however have a special significance on the island of Sicily and have always been of great interest to the ancient Greeks and Romans who settled there; both civilisations having Bee Goddesses at points in their histories. For the bee coin which is referred to in this book (and worn as a necklace by both Alaric Boynton-Dale and Posie Parker) see Historical Note 3.

10. The Serafina Monastery in the Hyblaean mountains of Sicily is fictional.

11. The Water Aerodrome (the *De Filippis* in Siracusa) referred to in chapter sixteen did exist and is historically accurate to the best of my knowledge. It closed in 2008. However, please note that it operated its *own* Sea-Planes to a variety of places (including Benghazi in Libya) and I am unsure whether or

not a seasoned explorer and aviator such as Alaric Boynton-Dale could simply have hired a private Sea-Plane for his own use, but I have assumed so for the sake of the story.

In Egypt

12. There were many international archaeological digs going on in the Valley of the Kings in Luxor, Egypt, during this time. Mine is made up.

   For Agatha Christie fans who are interested in the archaeological digs which are used as the settings for some of her novels (*Murder In Mesopotamia* is the most obvious), her autobiography *Come, Tell Me How You Live*, is excellent.

13. The Old Winter Palace Hotel in Luxor still exists, and for its current day incarnation, see: http://www.sofitel.com/gb/hotel-1661-sofitel-winter-palace-luxor/index.shtml.

14. The Tomb of Ammotep is fictional, but the *Dra Abu Naga* necropolis does exist. There are in fact very, very many Egyptian tombs and monuments which include references to bees and bee-keeping. Honey obviously had a huge significance (especially medicinally) in ancient Egypt. The real-life tomb of 'Pa-Ba-Sa' in Thebes provided me with some inspiration for the Tomb of Ammotep as described in this story.

15. I have played with dates in my references to the tomb and the curse of Tutankhamun in the Valley of the Kings. While the tomb *was* being excavated by Lord Carnavon in 1921 (the same time as this story is set) the later and legendary story about the curse of Tutankhamun did not start circulating until 1923.

A Short Note on Money

In England in 1921 there was decimalisation in place; a system involving the use of shillings, pence and pounds. I have tried to simplify things where possible to keep things light for the modern reader. However, the 1921 figures for money given in the book equate to:

1. Ten shillings and sixpence (chapter one, a jar of Alaric's honey) = an approximate 2014 value of £35 or $58.

2. Two Hundred Thousand Pounds (chapter one and chapter twenty-one, the Boynton-Dale Trust money which passes under Alaric's Will) = an approximate 2014 value of £8 million or $13,346,000. A vast, vast fortune.

3. Ten Thousand Pounds (mentioned in chapter seven, the reward given to Posie by the Earl of Cardigeon for finding the Maharajah diamond. Earmarked by Posie for purchasing a London flat and other living costs) = an approximate 2014 value of £414,375 or $693,495. But this would have been regarded as a huge amount in 1921, and would have seen Posie set up for life, exceedingly comfortably. As mentioned in chapter seven, a flat in the surrounding area of Bloomsbury would probably have cost Posie in the region of a few hundred pounds to buy.

4. Seven Hundred Thousand Pounds (mentioned in chapter eight, the value of the Maharajah diamond which appeared in *Murder Offstage: A Posie Parker Mystery #1*) = a 2014 value of £29 million or $48,531,923. A staggering, utterly breathtaking and almost fantastical amount.

****

Acknowledgements
and Author Note

Thank you to Red Gate Arts for producing my art-deco cover design, and to Jane Dixon-Smith for her formatting and design work.

Thank you to Kate Brolly of the Camden Local Studies and Archives Centre, Holborn Library, London, for her invaluable help in establishing the likely purchase value of a flat in Bloomsbury in the early 1920s. I am also grateful to my wonderful readers, whose support and comments are invaluable to me. Here I specifically thank Jules Davies who wrote concerning house prices in 1920s London, which proved very useful.

My continued thanks go to Marco, and also to Eden, who made this particular writing journey unforgettable. She raced this book into the world, and won.

* * * *

About the Author

Cambridge-educated, British-born L.B. Hathaway writes historical fiction and contributes to a number of popular history magazines and websites. She worked as a lawyer at Lincoln's Inn in London for almost a decade before becoming a full-time writer. She is a lifelong fan of detective novels set in the Golden Age of Crime, and is an ardent Agatha Christie devotee.

Her other interests, in no particular order, are: very fast downhill skiing, theatre-going, drinking strong tea, Tudor history, exploring castles and generally trying to cram as much into life as possible. She lives in London and Switzerland with her husband and young family.

The Posie Parker series of cosy crime novels span the 1920s. They each combine a core central mystery, an exploration of the reckless glamour of the age and a feisty protagonist who you would love to have as your best friend.

To find out more and for news of new releases and giveaways, go to:
   http://www.lbhathaway.com

Connect with L.B. Hathaway online:
   (e) author@lbhathaway.com
   (t) @LbHathaway
   (f) https://www.facebook.com/pages/L-B-Hathaway-books/1423516601228019
   (Goodreads) http://www.goodreads.com/author/show/8339051.L_B_Hathaway